...h Above the Line

D1636344

Praise for the Mysteries of Janet Dawson

"A nostalgic, wonderfully detailed look at an era when trains were still a major mode of transportation and life."

—*Kirkus Reviews* [on *The Ghost in Roomette Four*]

"Delightful... Dawson does a fine job of bringing World War II–era Los Angeles to life."

—*Publishers Weekly* [on *Bit Player*]

"Fascinating... Dawson writes so convincingly, she could have been a Zephyrette."

—*Mysterious Women* [on *Death Rides the Zephyr*]

"...interesting and enjoyable. So take a trip back to 1953...when riding the train was still considered romantic, in part because it was."

—*Reviewing the Evidence* [on *Death Deals a Hand*]

"This love letter to New Orleans has a great sense of place."

—*Publishers Weekly* [on *The Devil Close Behind*]

MYSTERY FICTION BY JANET DAWSON

CALIFORNIA ZEPHYR SERIES
Death Rides the Zephyr
Death Deals a Hand
The Ghost in Roomette Four
Death Above the Line

JERI HOWARD MYSTERY SERIES
Kindred Crimes
Till the Old Men Die
Take a Number
Don't Turn Your Back on the Ocean
Nobody's Child
A Credible Threat
Witness to Evil
Where the Bodies Are Buried
A Killing at the Track
Bit Player
Cold Trail
Water Signs
The Devil Close Behind

SUSPENSE FICTION
What You Wish For

SHORT STORIES
Scam and Eggs

Death Above the Line

A California Zephyr Mystery

JANET DAWSON

2020
PERSEVERANCE PRESS / JOHN DANIEL AND COMPANY
PALO ALTO / MCKINLEYVILLE, CALIFORNIA

A Perseverance Press Book
Published by John Daniel & Company
A division of Daniel & Daniel, Publishers, Inc.
Post Office Box 2790
McKinleyville, California 95519
www.danielpublishing.com/perseverance

Distributed by SCB Distributors (800) 729-6423

Book design by Eric Larson, Studio E Books, Santa Barbara, www.studio-e-books.com

Cover art © Roger Morris, IKAM Creative, Inc. All rights reserved.

10 9 8 7 6 5 4 3 2 1

LIBRARY OF CONGRESS CATALOGING-IN-PUBLICATION DATA
Names: Dawson, Janet, author.
Title: Death above the line : a California Zephyr mystery / by Janet M. Dawson.
Description: McKinleyville, California : John Daniel & Company, 2020. |
    Summary: "Zephyrette Jill McLeod meets a movie director on the train known as the California Zephyr. He insists he wants her to play a part in his upcoming film noir. Skeptical, Jill takes his business card and doesn't give the encounter much thought. Three months later, she finds herself before the cameras in a Niles warehouse that's been turned into a movie set. Her temporary job as an actress should be a lark, if it weren't for the black emotions and conflicts swirling around Jill. Some of the people around her have secrets they'd rather not share, and much antipathy toward a visiting studio executive who likes to wield his power. Someone winds up dead and once again, Jill finds herself investigating a murder"— Provided by publisher.
Identifiers: LCCN 2020015213 | ISBN 9781564746184 (trade paperback)
Subjects: GSAFD: Mystery fiction.
Classification: LCC PS3554.A949 D417 2020 | DDC 813/.54—dc23
LC record available at https://lccn.loc.gov/2020015213

*To my dear friend and
fellow mystery writer,
Sarah Andrews,
who is greatly missed*

Acknowledgments

Many thanks to fellow mystery writers Lee Goldberg and Eddie (Mr. Film Noir) Muller. Both write crime novels. Lee is also a screenwriter and publisher. Eddie has written nonfiction and hosts "Noir Alley" on Turner Classic Movies. I'm grateful to them for sharing their knowledge.

Thanks also to Kelsey Camello and Harry Avila, Museum of Local History in Fremont, California. And much appreciation to Roger Morris, my fellow Pullman pal, for his terrific covers for the California Zephyr mysteries.

Death Above the Line ⸺⸺⸺⸺

Chapter One

JILL MCLEOD WALKED into the railcar's lounge. In front of her, a man and a woman sat with their backs to the window. They leaned toward each other, heads almost close enough to touch. It looked as though they shared whispered secrets. The waiter at the bar poured a drink. At another table, a bulky, silver-haired man with a mustache watched the couple, a sneer on his face.

Then a middle-aged man wearing the cap and uniform of a Western Pacific Railroad conductor rounded the corner. He stumbled and fell. His cap went flying as he sprawled at Jill's feet.

"Cut!" the director called.

The man scrambled to his feet, muttering, "Damn, damn, damn."

Jill McLeod retrieved the cap and handed it to the man in the conductor's uniform. "Are you all right, Mr. Gallagher?"

"Nothing hurt but my dignity." He flashed a smile, laugh lines crinkling around his eyes. Then he set the cap on his head and brushed dust from his uniform.

"What happened?" the director asked, frowning.

Bert Gallagher shrugged. "Sorry, Drake. I took that corner too fast. I'll get it right on the next take."

"Okay." The director turned and conferred with the assistant director, the cinematographer and the cameraman. Outside the circle of light, the rest of the crew faded into shadows.

"We've had three takes already." The seated woman sounded annoyed. She leaned back and stretched her hands above her head, moving her back and shoulders in her figure-hugging jade-green dress. Her short platinum hair and pale porcelain complexion contrasted with her carmine lipstick and nail polish. The movie was being shot in black-and-white film, but the cameraman had told Jill that the fabric's texture and the makeup's sheen would come through on the screen.

The handsome, dark-haired man sitting beside the woman shrugged. "It's okay. We'll get the next one."

"I do hope it doesn't take us all afternoon." The silver-haired man reached up and stroked his mustache, as he often did.

The actor behind the bar, playing the waiter, didn't say anything, but his expression was equal parts annoyance and resignation.

Jill had never thought, not in a million years, that she would be working on a movie set. At first she figured it might be fun. But she had been here a week now and she had a new appreciation of what happened before the finished product finally appeared on the big screen. Making movies seemed to happen in fits and starts. The actors and crew did the same thing over and over again until the scene was polished to the director's satisfaction. And usually that involved multiple takes.

The set was supposed to be a *California Zephyr* dome-lounge car. It was as though one side had been peeled away to reveal the interior of the railcar—the enclosed vestibule at the front, then the café, then steps leading down to the lounge. The real appearance did not, however, extend to the Vista-Dome. In an actual car, that would have been above the lounge. Instead, the curved stairs ended at a platform.

The set looked authentic enough. But it wasn't quite the same. The car didn't move or have the right sound. Jill was accustomed to the sway of a moving train and the rhythmic clickety-clack of wheels on the rails. The sound and light effects would be added later. She herself was the one touch of authenticity on the make-believe railcar. Jill was a real Zephyrette, a hostess on the sleek silver streamliners that made daily runs between Oakland and Chicago. Now she was playing a Zephyrette in this movie. In addition to her lines in the script, she was learning a new language, one that included terms like gaffer, grip, call sheet, and best boy.

The blue uniform she wore had been created by a costume designer. Ordinarily, Jill would not have worn such a thick layer of makeup. It was hot under the relentlessly bright Klieg lights that illuminated the set. She felt a trickle of sweat in her short brown hair and hoped that she wasn't melting her makeup.

Drake Baldwin, the director, called, "Okay, one more time. Let's get it right."

The actors took their places. The stars—Leona Alexander and Neal Preston—leaned their heads together as though deep in conversation. Charles Bosworth, who played the villain, gave his mustache one last stroke and resumed his menacing expression. Jill and the ersatz conductor stood off-camera, waiting for the "Action" cue to walk into the lounge, as the boom operator adjusted the position of his microphone. The clapperboard, with its chalked production and take numbers, slammed down as the camera began to roll.

Jill walked into the lounge. The actor playing the waiter looked up from the drink he was pouring and spoke his dialogue, calling her by her character's name. "Hello, Miss Casey."

She smiled in return as the blond actress, playing a character named Dolores Bain, beckoned to Jill. "Oh, miss. When do we get to the next station?"

Jill looked at her wristwatch, much as she would in a real situation, and glanced up at the actress. "We should be there in an hour, Miss Bain."

"Thanks." The actress leaned back. Then, with a sidelong glance, she addressed the dark-haired actor next to her. "We can send a wire there. If that's what you really want to do."

"Let me think about it," he said.

The actress laughed. "You don't trust me, do you?"

Before he could answer, Bert Gallagher rounded the corner, all brisk efficiency as the conductor. "Miss Casey, there you are. We need you and your first-aid kit in the first chair car."

"I'll be right there." Jill turned and left the lounge, taking a left turn as though heading for the Zephyrette's compartment, where the first-aid kit would be kept. Once she was out of the scene, she breathed a sigh of relief. Behind her, the dialogue continued, with the actress saying, "If you don't trust me, how will we ever strike a bargain?"

"I'm not sure you're the kind of woman I want to bargain with," he said.

"Cut! Great. That's good. Now, let's set up for the next shot." The director gathered the actors around him as he told them how he wanted it to go. "Leona, you're walking in the passageway, coming from the sleeper cars. You hear Neal and Charles arguing in the lounge, and then you walk in. Charles, you're standing over Neal. You're menacing him, trying to intimidate him and push him into a corner. But Neal, you've got his number. You're not giving an inch." Then the director turned. "Jill, for this shot, you've been up in the Vista-Dome. Then you come down the stairs. You stop and say hello to Billy in the bar."

Billy, who was playing the waiter, nodded. Jill climbed the curved steps that led to the platform and waited for her cue.

The assistant director, a woman named Eve Stillman who always dressed casually in slacks and shirts, touched Drake's arm to get his attention. "Before we get started, what do you think about doing an over-the-shoulder shot here—" Her voice trailed off as she gestured with both hands, illustrating what she had in mind.

A makeshift office had been set up in a corner of the sound-stage, near the back door. An old office chair with arms and wheels was pulled up to a rectangular table made of scarred and stained wood. The table held a black telephone, an unshaded metal lamp and a solid gray Remington typewriter, as well as an assortment of file folders and a pint jar full of pencils. This was where Eve Stillman performed one of her many assistant director duties, typing out the call sheets that governed the day's shooting. The call sheets told actors and crew members what time they were expected on the set and what scenes would be shot.

Half a dozen chairs were clustered around a small black-and-white television set on a metal stand. The TV had been turned off just a couple of hours ago. Today was October 1, and the second game of the World Series had ended with a New York Yankees victory, much to the chagrin of the Brooklyn Dodgers fans among the group. So far the Yankees were two for two.

Now the phone rang, pealing over and over. "Somebody get that," Drake snapped. "And then take it off the hook before we start shooting again."

The production assistant, a young man with a harried expression, loped toward the table. He picked up the jangling phone in mid-ring and held the receiver to his ear, speaking in a low voice to whoever was on the other end. Then he set the phone on the table and walked back to the set.

Drake was nodding, his hands up, framing a view of the lounge. "I like the idea, Eve. Let's do it from this angle. Okay, places, everyone. Let's get cracking on this."

The production assistant, who had been hovering near one of the movable lights, tapped him on the shoulder. "You're wanted on the phone. The studio."

The director's voice sharpened, irritated at the interruption. "Not now. I'm busy. Tell whoever it is that I'll call back."

"You'd better take the call," the production assistant said. "It's Mr. Felton."

Silence greeted his words, but the looks on the faces of the cast and crew spoke volumes. A shadow passed over Neal Preston's handsome face. Leona Alexander's full red mouth compressed into a tight-lipped frown. Eve Stillman sighed and stuck her hands in the pockets of her khaki slacks.

"Damn," Drake said finally. "Okay, take five, everyone, while I get this call." He left the group, threading his way through the equipment to the table where the phone sat.

Jill, perched on the platform at the top of the curved stairs, surveyed the faces below her.

Who was this Mr. Felton? And why did the mention of his name cause such alarm?

Chapter Two ─────────────

July 1953

JILL MCLEOD WAS IN THE Vista-Dome, looking out at the Oakland Mole, a large, two-story building where the *California Zephyr* stood, waiting for departure. Passengers from San Francisco and the East Bay had already boarded the train, finding their way to the coach cars or the Pullmans. Now the conductor made his last walk along the platform, calling, "All aboard."

A moment later, the train moved and began its slow progress through the busy rail yard and the Oakland waterfront. The 360-degree view provided by the elevated dome gave Jill a panoramic view of the middle harbor, with the Bay Bridge and San Francisco in the distance. A freight train stood on the next track. Turning, Jill saw the inner harbor, a narrow channel the locals called the estuary. Beyond that was the island city of Alameda, where she lived with her parents.

The train stopped briefly at the Western Pacific station, which was on Third Street between Broadway and Washington. After taking on more passengers, the CZ pulled out of the station. This part of Oakland was often called the produce district because of the many warehouses on Franklin Street, which paralleled Broadway and gave growers access to both the railroad and the waterfront. Moving slowly, the train passed a truck loaded with yellow onions, another full of lumpy brown potatoes, a third carrying a load of squash, a fourth piled high with red and green apples. Workers lingered in the doorway of a busy café, smoking and drinking mugs of coffee. Once the train moved past Oak Street it picked up speed. The next station stop—if there was someone there waiting to board the train—was nearly an hour away, in Niles, a small rural community nestled against the East Bay hills near the mouth of a twisting canyon.

The eastbound run to Chicago took fifty hours, about two and a half days. Once the CZ arrived, Jill would lay over in the Windy City, then catch a westbound train for the return to the Bay Area. She enjoyed her job as a Zephyrette. She was the only female member of the onboard crew, a train hostess of sorts, whose primary duty was to see to the needs of the passengers. She made announcements, pointing out the landmarks and the spectacular scenery along the train's 2,500-mile route. Each afternoon she made dinner reservations for passengers. Jill also provided first aid when needed, mailed postcards and sent telegrams, and answered questions, lots of questions. In fact, she had just fielded several queries from a group of kids who'd staked out seats at the front of the Vista-Dome, excited about their first trip aboard the sleek streamliner known as the Silver Lady.

She had been working aboard the train for over two years now. She liked the variety, the opportunity to meet people. One of her duties included walking through the train on a regular basis, so she turned and headed down the steps that led from the Vista-Dome to the railcar's lower level. The Silver Hostel was a dome-lounge car, with a café at the front. In the middle of the car, below the dome, was a lower-level lounge with tables, a bar and a small kitchen. Crew quarters were at the rear, with a dormitory for the cooks and waiters, and two small compartments for the dining car steward and the Zephyrette.

When Jill stepped off the stairs, her plan was to head for the first coach car, and start her walk-through there. But the man way-laid her in the doorway of the lounge.

He was about thirty, she guessed, tall and good-looking, with short sandy hair and large hazel eyes behind wire-rimmed glasses. He was dressed in a tailored, charcoal-gray suit that fit him well and looked expensive. She had seen him earlier, when he boarded the train at the Mole. He had a compartment in the Silver Crane, a six-five sleeper. That was railroad lingo for a Pullman car with six double bedrooms and five compartments.

Now he smiled at her and said, "You're perfect."

"Excuse me?"

The man leaned toward her and she sidestepped him, intending to walk toward the front of the car. She figured the guy was a wolf, one of those male passengers who thought the Zephyrette was fair game for his amorous attentions. There was usually one on every trip. Jill had become adept at avoiding such men, while still being polite, as her job required.

"I'm not making a pass. Really, I'm not." The man in the gray suit smiled again, a reassuring note in his voice. "Please, let me back up and introduce myself. My name is Drake Baldwin. I'm a director. Maybe you've seen one of my movies?"

Now I've heard everything, Jill thought. A director? What a yarn.

She gave Baldwin a polite smile. "I don't know if I have. What movies have you directed?"

"*Parker's Cove.* That was my most recent film."

Jill felt a flicker of surprise. She had seen it, a romantic-suspense picture that took place in a small town on the coast. It had come out last fall and it looked like some of the scenes had actually been filmed in Northern California.

"I did see that. And I liked it," Jill said with a nod.

He looked pleased, flashing an even wider smile. "I'm so glad."

"Well, I go to lots of movies." I guess he really is a director, she thought. Now she was really curious. "What did you mean when you said I was perfect?"

Two passengers were walking toward them from the front of the car. He reached for her arm and steered her out of their way. As the man and woman passed them, Baldwin asked, "What is your name?"

"Miss McLeod. I'm the Zephyrette."

He laughed. "Yes, I know you're the Zephyrette. That's why I want to talk with you. I think you're perfect."

Jill was mystified. The man wasn't making any sense. "I'm sorry, I don't understand. Why do you think I'm perfect?"

"You're perfect for the part." At her mystified look, he added. "I'm not explaining myself very well. Let me give you my card." He drew a leather case from the inner pocket of his suit and opened it, removing an engraved business card. With a flourish, he handed it to her.

She examined the card. Sure enough, it read DRAKE BALDWIN PRODUCTIONS. Underneath was an address in Los Angeles.

Baldwin was talking again. "I have a new project, a film noir, a thriller. It's very dark and exciting, with a wonderful script."

"Film noir," Jill repeated. "A thriller. I see. Like *The Narrow Margin*." That picture had come out last year as well, starring Charles McGraw and Marie Windsor in a suspenseful drama that had taken place on a train.

"Well, it's similar," Baldwin said. "Both films feature a train. Mine will take place on the *California Zephyr*. That's why I'm up here, in the Bay Area. I'm scouting locations. The train, of course. I'm going to shoot in San Francisco, at the Ferry Building. And on the ferry, and at the Oakland Mole. And then the climax, up in Feather River Canyon." As he talked about his plans, his face became more animated, his hands moving. "I'm really excited about the movie, as you can see. The script is great. And I'm hoping to put together a terrific cast."

"That's very nice, Mr. Baldwin. I wish you the best."

"But I need you," he insisted. "I need a Zephyrette for my *California Zephyr* movie, and I think you're perfect for the role. You have the right look."

Jill smiled, amused. "The uniform helps. This all sounds very interesting, but I really must attend to my duties right now." She backed away and took a step.

Baldwin put his hand on her wrist. "Please, give me your phone number, so I can contact you."

Well, that's not going to happen, Jill thought. It was still possible that, business card or no, Baldwin was a wolf and this was an elaborate ruse to get her phone number. "If you need to get in touch with me, you can contact the Western Pacific office in San Francisco. Now, if you'll excuse me."

She removed his hand from her arm and walked briskly

forward, in the direction of the coffee shop. When she reached it, she glanced back. Baldwin had disappeared from view. She didn't know what to think, but she examined the business card again. It seemed real enough.

The waiter from the lounge, a man named Marcus Loomer, caught up with her a few minutes later. He was delivering a piece of pie and a cup of coffee to a passenger in the coffee shop. Jill stood by a nearby table, talking with another passenger. The waiter caught her eye and stepped over to speak with her.

"Was that man bothering you, Miss McLeod?" the waiter asked.

"Not really. But thank you for your concern, Mr. Loomer." Jill still had the business card in her hand. Now she showed it to him. "He says he's a director. And he wants me to play the Zephyrette in a movie he's planning to make."

"No kidding." The waiter leaned closer, a skeptical look on his face as he read the card. "I guess anybody can have one of those cards printed up. You'd better take his spiel with a big grain of salt."

"True enough. But he says he directed a movie called *Parker's Cove*, and I've seen it."

"Not familiar with that picture." Loomer shook his head.

"It was a romantic-suspense story. I liked it. Mr. Baldwin says he's going to make a thriller, what they call a film noir. And it takes place on the *California Zephyr*. So he needs someone to play the Zephyrette." She smiled. "He thinks I'd be perfect for the part."

"Well, of course you would, being as you are a Zephyrette." The waiter shrugged. "I'm not much on those romantic stories, but my wife sure likes them. Thrillers are fine. But me, I like Westerns. Those are my favorites. I sure did like that picture with Alan Ladd."

Jill nodded. "*Shane*." She had gone to see the film when it opened last month, with Ladd as the gunfighter helping a family of homesteaders, played by Van Heflin and Jean Arthur. "Yes, that was excellent. I really enjoyed it."

Loomer rubbed his chin thoughtfully. "You know, one of the other Zephyrettes was in a movie. Last year, it was."

"That was Rodna Walls," Jill said. "The movie was called *Sudden Fear*. She went down to Hollywood and had one scene with Joan Crawford. That was a thriller, too, come to think of it."

"I better get back to the lounge," he said. Then he laughed. "If you're gonna be a famous movie star, let me know. I'll be sure to see that picture."

"I certainly will." Jill glanced at the card again, then she tucked it into her skirt pocket. She turned and went through the vestibule into the dining car, saying hello to the steward and the waiters, and made her way forward, heading for the chair cars.

She saw Baldwin several times that day, as the train headed through California's Central Valley. He got off the train and stretched his legs, smoking, at the Sacramento station. Then the train sped north to Oroville and began climbing up the Feather River Canyon. Baldwin was up in the Vista-Dome most of the time, staring at the spectacular scenery and taking notes. Sometimes he would use his hands, as though framing a scene. Scouting locations, Jill thought. That's what he'd told her.

Baldwin got off the train in the small railroad town of Portola, in Plumas County. There wasn't much there. But it was one of his locations. She guessed that he would spend the night and catch the westbound *California Zephyr* in the morning. The train pulled out of the station, heading for Nevada. Her last sight of Drake Baldwin on that trip was the tall man with glasses standing on the platform, gazing at the departing train.

She didn't give Baldwin or his movie much thought during the rest of the run to Chicago. After a layover there, she caught the westbound train, number 17, back to the Bay Area. It was good to get home and sleep in her own bed, relaxing with her family. Though there wasn't much relaxing, since her mother and sister, Lucy, were occupied with plans for Lucy's September wedding.

Jill was helping her mother put oilcloth shelf liners in the linen closet next to the second-floor bathroom. "I have to tell you something funny, that happened on the train. I met a movie director. At least he says he's a director."

She cut another piece of oilcloth as she told her mother the story. Lora McLeod had a good laugh. "Goodness, I never heard of such a thing. He was just giving you a line."

"Maybe. But maybe he really is serious, and he does want me to be in his movie." Jill chuckled. "I still have his card. If you get a call from a director named Baldwin, he wants to make me a star."

As it turned out, Drake Baldwin was indeed serious.

Chapter Three

IN AUGUST, JILL got a phone call from Drake Baldwin. Later that day, she received another phone call, this one from a Western Pacific Railroad supervisor.

When the railroad asked Zephyrettes to take on additional duties related to public relations, the young women usually agreed. That might include representing the railroad at a banquet or a gathering of some sort, perhaps one evening or one day. Making a movie was an unusual commitment, one that would last longer. Jill was told her participation might last as long as two weeks, maybe more.

It might be fun, Jill thought. She said yes.

As it turned out, making movies involved a lot of hard work. And it was sometimes tedious and time-consuming.

After the director and the railroad contacted Jill, the movie had been delayed. Filming should have started late in August, but the schedule was pushed back to September. Jill didn't know why. At least not for sure. One of the talkative makeup artists had said original plans were to film in Oakland, near the rail yard and the Mole. But for some reason that fell through. Now they were in Niles, the small East Bay town that butted up against the hills at the mouth of the canyon. That was because one of the movie's producers, a San Francisco businessman named Dewitt Collier, owned a big empty warehouse that could be turned into a soundstage. And he had some pull with the executives at the Western Pacific Railroad. For that reason, the railroad had given the production access to a number of railroad sites and cars.

Despite the fact that it had been turned into a soundstage full of movie sets, everyone, Jill included, called it the warehouse. In a previous life, it had been both a furniture factory and warehouse. The large, cavernous building stretched a hundred feet or more along Front Street, Niles' main thoroughfare, on the east side of the train depot.

The lot was deep, extending about fifty yards from front to back, where it bordered on the train tracks. At the rear, a back door and two loading bays with ramps faced the railyard. The building was close to the tracks and the depot, but it had been sound-proofed so well that when all the doors were closed, Jill couldn't hear the trains going by. Where once equipment and storerooms had occupied the interior, now there were sets, like the one Jill had been on, tucked into the corners and arranged along the walls, as well as the middle of the huge space. In addition to the lounge, there was a set that looked like an observation car. There were two sets built to resemble Pullman cars, one a six-five sleeper with six bedrooms and five compartments, and another that looked like the inside of a ten-six sleeper, with its ten roomettes and six bed-rooms. There was also a mockup of a baggage car and the cab of a diesel engine, and a set that looked like a Vista-Dome and one like a vestibule. And of course, a dining car set, complete with silver serving pieces and the violets-and-daisies china used on the real *California Zephyr*.

Another section of the warehouse had been turned into a screening room where the director and his assistant looked at what they called the dailies, or the rushes. Each evening Drake Baldwin would drive the film canisters to the Oakland airport. He didn't trust the job to anyone else. The film was flown to Los Angeles for processing in the Global Studios lab, and the resulting footage returned to Oakland several days later. Dewitt Collier owned an interest in a small aviation firm, so he had arranged for the air transport. When he was notified that the film was on its way, Drake picked up the canisters and took them to Niles, where he and Eve watched the footage and determined whether the scenes were good, conveying what they intended, or whether retakes would be necessary. So far they hadn't done that many retakes, and Jill figured that was good.

The movie's plot involved the search for a stolen painting. The working title was *The Heist*. Those two words were chalked onto the clapperboard, along with the director's name and the scene number. Despite the unwelcome interruption of the phone call from the mysterious Mr. Felton, the clapperboard operator snapped it down as the cameras rolled, and the next scene went off without a hitch.

Jill wouldn't be needed for another hour or so. She left the set, taking care not to trip on the cables that snaked across the floor, and went to the dressing room she shared with several other female cast members. It was actually a trailer, one of several that had been parked on the east side of the building. Two of the trailers, lined up from the back of the lot forward, were for the two stars, Neal Preston and Leona Alexander. The next two were shared dressing rooms for male and female cast. Next to this was a trailer where the two makeup artists plied their trade, putting on the thick makeup that the cameras required. The trailer that was closest to the street was operated by a catering firm, providing food and drink for cast and crew members, who took their meals at a number of tables that had been set up near the trailer. At other times, they crossed Front Street and went to one of the cafés located in the Niles business district.

In the dressing room, Jill took off the shoes she'd been wearing and slipped into a pair of comfortable low-heeled shoes suitable for walking. Then she left the trailer, relishing the warmth and sunshine after the enclosed darkness and artificial light inside the movie soundstage. She liked to walk whenever possible. She was used to it. On the *California Zephyr*, she walked all day long, even though it was on a moving train. Part of her daily routine was to walk through all the cars several times a day, seeing to the needs of the passengers. And when she was off-duty, at home in Alameda, she walked every day.

In the warehouse, enclosed and dark except for the lights, she felt cooped up. When she traveled aboard the train, she was inside all the time, but it was different, somehow. The train was moving and she could see the changing panorama of scenery. She could also get off the train when it stopped at various stations along the way.

Glad for a break, Jill walked away from the lot where the trailers were located, past another loading bay and the front door leading into the building. On the other side of the building, a narrow brick sidewalk ran alongside the warehouse, bordering a gravel lot where cast and crew parked their cars. Beyond this, a huge valley oak separated the warehouse from the Niles depot. There was a rough wooden picnic table under the tree. A nearby park bench had once been painted green, but the color was now worn and weathered to a silvery olive. This spot near the oak, with the table and bench, had become a gathering place. She often came here on breaks, and so did other members of the cast and crew.

The seasonal rains hadn't started yet, so the East Bay hills on the other side of the tracks were tan and sere, humped like mounds of gold velvet on either side of Alameda Creek, which rose somewhere in the eastern part of the county and wound its way west through the canyon to spill its waters into San Francisco Bay. The rugged canyon had tight curves and the banks of the creek were narrow, making construction of this section of the transcontinental railroad difficult back in the nineteenth century.

Niles itself was an old farming town, one of several communities ranged along the East Bay hills, with Centerville, Irvington, Warm Springs and Mission San Jose clustered nearby. Back in the 1840s, when Alta California still belonged to Mexico, a *Californio* named Vallejo had built flour mills in the area. An aqueduct ran from the Water Temple in the small town of Sunol, some eleven miles through the canyon. In 1907, workers excavating for the new Western Pacific line found a large clay deposit on the south side of Alameda Creek. A group of businessmen bought the land, built a brick-making plant and formed the California Pressed Brick Company. Jill had seen some of the building bricks produced by the company, stamped with large letters that spelled NILES. The company had gone out of business, but Jill had learned that the bricks were used in building construction and as pavers. She'd seen a few of these bricks on the sidewalks of Front Street and the side streets as well. In fact, there were several Niles bricks in the sidewalk this side of the warehouse. Some of them were loose. Jill had stumbled over one of them a few days ago.

Across the street from the warehouse was downtown Niles.

Front Street was lined with shops and cafés, small-town businesses catering to residents of the community. The cast and crew were staying at a hotel near the corner of Front and H streets. On the first floor of the hostelry was a restaurant and bar where many of the movie folks could be found at the end of the day. A few doors down was a café that was popular with the locals for breakfast and lunch. Jill herself liked a small coffee shop on I Street, across from the Niles library.

She stood for a moment, enjoying the warmth of the sun, tempered by a slight breeze that stirred the air and rustled the oak leaves. She sat down on the old park bench. Then she heard someone call her name and looked up. Bert Gallagher was walking toward her, still wearing the conductor's costume, though he'd put aside the cap, showing his thinning brown hair.

"Hi, Mr. Gallagher."

He smiled. "Now, I've told you before. Call me Bert."

"All right, I will. And please, call me Jill. Although a Zephyrette would never call a conductor by his first name. The conductor is like the captain of the ship. He's in charge of everything. In fact, when we're on a run, with all the crew it's strictly a Mister-and-Miss basis."

"We can be formal when we're on the set," he said with a nod. "But out here, that's different." He took a cigarette pack from his pocket and offered it to her, but she shook her head.

"No, thanks. I never acquired a taste for it. Besides, my father is a doctor. He says it's bad for you."

"My doctor says that, too." Bert flashed a rueful smile. "But habits are hard to break, old or new. It's okay if I indulge?"

"Go ahead. I have friends who smoke." But she was certainly glad that Mike, the man she was dating, didn't smoke. Before Mike, she'd gone out with a fellow who smoked, and she didn't like the smell in close proximity.

He shook a cigarette from the pack and lighted it with a match. "Explain something to me. I've heard you use the term 'consist' in connection with trains. What does that mean?"

"It's a group of railcars that make up a train. On the *California Zephyr*, the consist is in a particular order. It starts with the loco-motive, then the baggage car. The chair cars come next, with the diner and lounge car in the middle, then the sleeper cars, with the dome-observation car on the end."

"The things you learn," he said with a smile. "How long have you been a Zephyrette?"

"Two and a half years," Jill said. "I was planning to teach school, but..." She hesitated. "Life intervened."

"Sounds like there's a story there." He didn't ask for details. She appreciated that. Her fiancé had been killed in the Korean War that had just ended with an armistice. Talking about it brought up memories.

Bert's face took on a rueful look. "I was going to be a star, with fame and fortune and my name in lights up on a movie marquee. But life intervened there as well. Turns out I'm a better character actor than I am a leading man."

"Now it's your turn to explain something. What exactly is a character actor? I've heard the term several times but I'm not sure what it means."

"A character actor has a bigger role than the bit parts," Bert said. "Those are the people who have a few lines, maybe just in one scene. Or the extras, the people in the background who don't speak at all. The character actor is what we call a supporting role. Not the star, or stars, but an essential part of the story. The name appears farther down the cast list in the credits. When a character actor works a lot, his face comes on the screen and you say, he looks familiar. That's because you've seen him in so many roles. Sometimes it's an odd character, you know, the eccentric. Or types, like a doctor or a banker."

Jill nodded. "I see. The grandfather type. Like Harry Davenport in *Meet Me in St. Louis*. He also played the doctor in *Gone with the Wind*."

"Exactly," he said. "Davenport was one of the best character actors in the business. He died a few years ago. You know, he came from a long line of stage actors, started when he was six years old. He directed, too, silent movies and shorts. He didn't come to Hollywood until the Thirties, and he was busy all the time. As a matter of fact, I was in several movies with him, including *Meet Me in St. Louis*. Just a small role, in that trolley car scene."

Jill chuckled. "I don't remember seeing you."

"Of course not. All your attention was on Judy Garland, and that's the way it's supposed to be."

"What other movies did you make with him?"

"Some well known, others not so much. *Juarez*, the one with Bette Davis. *You Can't Take It with You*, with Jimmy Stewart. Lots of movies over the years, silents and talkies, with big stars and the not-so-big. I've been in this acting game for nearly thirty years. The important thing to me is to work. I make a decent living and I work a lot. As a matter of fact, after we wrap up this movie, I'm heading to Arizona to make an oater with Randolph Scott."

"An oater?" She laughed. "Does that mean a Western? I guess it must, because horses eat oats. Movie people have the most interesting slang. Best boy, for example. Which I've discovered is like a foreman. You know, they used to make movies in Niles."

Bert nodded. "Oh, yes. Essanay Studios and Broncho Billy Anderson. I knew someone who worked here during those days. That was a long time ago." He paused, glancing across Front Street. Eve Stillman, the assistant director, had just come out of the local drugstore, carrying a bottle of Coca-Cola. She crossed the street, walking toward them.

"Miss Stillman seems young to be an assistant director," Jill said. "She can't be that much older than I am."

"She and Drake are about the same age," Bert said. "Late twenties, thirty at the most." He laughed. "I'm getting to be that age when it seems that everyone is younger than I am." He greeted Eve as she joined them. "You know, you can get a Coke from catering instead of walking over to the drugstore."

Eve took a sip from her bottle. "I know. But I like to support the local businesses."

Bert nodded. "It's a nice little town, I'll give you that. The cafés are decent and the hotel is comfortable. Once I was on location in the Monument Valley, shooting a Western. We slept in tents and took cold-water showers—outdoors. Brr!" He shivered at the memory.

Jill turned to Eve. "I'm curious. How did you get to be an assistant director?"

"I got my start as a cutter," Eve said.

"Now, that's a term I haven't heard before. What's a cutter?"

"A film editor. I take the footage that the camera crew shoots every day and assemble it into the finished product, the movie you see on the big screen when you go to the movies. I really want to be a director," Eve added. "Film editing is a good way to start. John Ford once told someone to start in the cutting room and work your way up. That's what I'm doing."

"I never gave the whole movie-making process much thought," Jill said. "Until now. I've seen you suggesting ways to shoot scenes."

Eve nodded. "That's my editing background, and part of being an AD. I have a good eye for framing a shot and putting scenes together. Fortunately Drake takes my input seriously. That's why he hired me. And someday I'll be directing movies on my own. Nice talking with you. I've got to get back to the set."

"Are there many women directors?" Jill asked as Eve walked away. "I know Ida Lupino directs. I like her as an actress."

"So do I. And I did a small part in one of the earlier movies she directed. These days, I see mostly men in the director's chair," he added. "But that wasn't always the case. There were plenty of women directing movies until a few years ago. Dorothy Arzner, she directed *Craig's Wife*. And Lois Weber, back in the silent era. Lillian Gish even directed a few silents."

Jill was about to ask Bert why the number of women directors had dwindled. But he was checking the pocket watch that went with his conductor costume. "I'd better get back." He put out his cigarette in the sand-filled coffee can near the bench that served as an ashtray.

After he'd gone, Jill heard a train whistle in the distance. She checked her watch. It was a few minutes after three on this sunny afternoon, and the westbound *California Zephyr*, train number 17, was coming out of Niles Canyon, blowing a warning whistle as it approached the depot. Niles was a flag stop. That meant the train didn't ordinarily stop here unless there were passengers boarding or departing the train. The train's next stop would be the end of the line in Oakland, some thirty miles to the north, where the passengers would get off the train, met by friends and family. Or they'd board the ferry and head across the bay to San Francisco.

She walked toward the Niles depot. On her first day of filming, she'd chatted with the station agent, who was knowledgeable about the depot's history as well as its architecture. The building dated to 1901, constructed of redwood by the Southern Pacific Railroad to replace an earlier structure. Colonnade-style architecture, he'd told her, pointing out the ornate carvings at the top of the columns, called capitals. He added that the horizontal bands atop the capitals were called entablatures, something common in classical architecture.

Now she stood near one of the columns and looked up at the carvings, then at the train that was coming into the station. The *CZ* slowed and then stopped. She checked her watch again. It was now 3:15 P.M. and the train was on time. The Pullman porter on the sleeper nearest her opened the vestibule door and set his step on the platform. Then he assisted two passengers, both women, as they left the train. As soon as they were on the platform, one of the women gave him a tip and he touched his cap in thanks. He climbed back into the vestibule and pulled up his step, then locked the doors. A few seconds later, the conductor called, "All aboard." The engineer blew the whistle and the train started moving again. It cleared the station, slow at first, then picking up momentum as it headed west. It would eventually angle north, terminating this run at the Oakland Mole.

It felt strange to be here at the station, instead of aboard the train.

Her regular job as a Zephyrette was straightforward. The train left the station on time and kept moving on its designated tracks until it arrived at its destination—on time. She had assigned duties and she performed them.

But now she was an actress. Well, that was stretching a point.

Jill stepped off the platform and walked to Front Street. When she reached the intersection of Front and H streets, she crossed to the corner and walked past the local movie theater, where posters advertised *Arrowhead*, a Western starring Charlton Heston and Jack Palance. At G Street, she saw an older woman walking toward her, preceded by a small black-and-white dog on a leash. The woman, dressed in khaki slacks and a green-and-white checked shirt, was a few inches shorter than Jill, with a slender, athletic frame. She had a pointed chin and large, wideset blue eyes. Her short hair had once been brown but now was streaked with silver. The dog, a female, was a terrier of some sort, with floppy ears and abundant whiskers surrounding a black button nose. She strained at the leash, eager to greet Jill.

"May I say hello to your dog?"

"Of course. Her name is Bella."

Jill held out her hand. Bella gave it a brisk once-over with her nose and wagged her tail with glee as Jill scratched her behind the ears. She straightened. "I'm Jill."

"My name's Rose. And you're in the movie."

"How did you know?"

Rose smiled. "The makeup. You wouldn't be wearing such heavy makeup unless you were in the picture. Besides, here you are in a Zephyrette uniform. I doubt that you got off the train that just stopped at the depot."

Jill touched her face, suddenly self-conscious about the thick layer of makeup that was applied each day she was on the set, so unlike the light cosmetics she usually wore.

"Yes, I'm in the movie. But I really am a Zephyrette. I met the director a few months ago on the train. He gave me his card and said I'd be perfect for the part. Well, I guess I would be, since I'm the real thing. Although I don't think I'm much of an actress."

"As long as you can learn lines and recite them on cue, I guess you'll do," Rose said.

"That's what the other actors tell me."

"The people here in town are very excited about the film."

"I know," Jill said. "When we first got here, we had plenty of onlookers, particularly the day we were filming exteriors at the depot. But the novelty wore off, I think. Everyone's inside the warehouse all day. Although they're staying at the hotel and eating at the local restaurants."

"The curious crowd may have thinned out," Rose said. "But I assure you the movie is a topic of discussion all over town. It's been a long time since a picture was shot in Niles. That's worth its weight in gold for publicity. We've already had a couple of reporters from the *Chronicle* and the *Tribune* down here, talking to people in the shops and cafés so they can do stories on it."

"Have you lived in Niles a long time?" Jill asked.

Rose nodded. "I was born and raised on a ranch near here." She pointed to the east, where cattle, tiny dots at this distance, grazed on the brown hills.

"Then you remember the movie days. Essanay Studios. And Broncho Billy Anderson."

The older woman smiled. "Oh, yes. I remember them very well. It was forty-one years ago, in 1912. That's when the movie people showed up in Niles to set up shop. The full name was the Essanay Film Manufacturing Company, but everyone just called it Essanay. It was a partnership between two men, George Spoor and Gilbert Anderson, otherwise known as Broncho Billy. They combined the initials of their last names. Spoor stayed in Chicago, but Broncho Billy came out to California. Essanay shot movies in Colorado as well as California. They were in Petaluma and Los Gatos before they settled on Niles as a more permanent location."

"My father is a big movie fan," Jill said. "He talks about the silent movies. Going to the picture show, as he calls it, to see Broncho Billy and Charlie Chaplin. I know they filmed *The Tramp* here in Niles Canyon."

Rose waved her hand, the one that wasn't holding the dog's leash, to encompass the scenery. "They used all sorts of locations around here, the hills, the canyon, even my family's ranch."

"Broncho Billy was one of the first movie cowboys," Jill said.

"He was an actor, certainly, and a good one. But more than that, he wrote scripts, scenarios, they called them in that day. And he directed movies, too." Rose's bright blue eyes took on a faraway look and she gestured at the intersection. "They built the studio right here, on this block of G Street, between Front and Second. And several other lots in town. This lot was a prune orchard back then. Broncho Billy had the trees cut down. He built six bungalows, housing for the cast and crew. They rented for twenty-five bucks a month. Someone started calling it 'the reservation.'" She smiled. "And the studio. Oh, that was something to see. It was huge, looked like a big barn. It had an open-air stage. That was temporary. Then they built a glass-enclosed stage. There was a working blacksmith shop, and the storage buildings between the studio and the bungalows had false fronts. The crew would make those double as a Western street set."

"It sounds like you saw the inside."

"I saw a lot. And yes, I was inside a time or two. Essanay was quite an operation. Strange that it lasted just four years. They shut down the studio in 1916 and people moved south. Los Angeles, Hollywood, that was where the movie business went. They tore the studio building down in 1933. Before that, they auctioned off everything that was inside. Wardrobe, furniture, wagons, even paint and brushes." Rose's face had that distant look again. There was something sad in her expression. Then she brightened. "The bungalows are still here, though. As a matter of fact I live in one, over on Second Street. I bought it a few years ago."

"Thanks for telling me about it," Jill said. "What an interesting history this town has." She glanced at her watch. "I really should get back to the warehouse. That's what we call it, though I guess it really is a soundstage now."

She gave Bella another ear scratch, said good-bye to Rose and walked back along Front Street.

Chapter Four

JILL CROSSED TO THE other side of Front Street. She heard another train whistle. Like a magnet, the sound drew her to the depot. The approaching train was a freight. She stood on the platform and watched as a diesel locomotive, bearing the markings of the Southern Pacific Railroad, slowly pulled a long line of boxcars past the station. The sound faded as the caboose got smaller in the distance.

She left the depot, heading for the warehouse, then stopped. Drake Baldwin, readily identified by his fair hair and wire-rimmed glasses, stood near the bench under the oak tree. He seemed to be waiting for someone. Then Eve Stillman rounded the front corner of the warehouse and walked toward the tree. She carried another Coke and joined Drake, leaning against the back of the bench.

Eve's voice carried on the late afternoon breeze. "What did Felton want? More changes to the script? If that's the case, Wade will be even more upset than he already is."

Drake sighed. "Worse than that. Felton is coming to town."

Eve stared at him. "Well, that's bad news. Really bad. Felton hates to travel, or so I hear. The man's got a reputation for never wanting to leave LA. Why would he leave the comfort of his ritzy office to trek to the wilds of Niles, California?"

Frustration colored Drake's voice. "I tried to get more information out of Felton. But that's all I got. He's flying up here tomorrow evening and he'll be on the set Monday morning."

"Maybe he wants a weekend in San Francisco." Despite her

words, Eve didn't sound convinced. "Hell, he must be up to something. It would be just like him. What does Felton want?" She pondered this, then shrugged. "Why are we worried? Peter Vesey's our studio executive. He's in charge of the production."

"But Felton's his assistant," Drake said. "You know he hated the idea of us filming on location."

Eve nodded. "Yeah. Not only does he want to stay in Hollywood, he doesn't want anyone else to leave town either."

"He tried like hell to talk Vesey out of letting us do location shooting," Drake said. "So Felton coming to town, for whatever reason, we know that can't be good. I don't like it at all."

"Same here. Did you talk with Vesey?"

Drake shook his head. "I tried calling him, but he's not in the office today. At least that's what his secretary told me. I'll keep trying."

"Good idea," Eve said. "In the meantime, I'll put out some feelers with my friends at the studio. You do the same. Someone's bound to know something." She took another sip from the bottle. "By the way, did you tell Wade that Felton is coming to town?"

"No. He'll have a fit. I'll have to choose my moment."

"I don't think you'll have a chance to. He's headed this way." Eve pointed.

Wade Ratliff, the man who'd written the script, had just come out of the hotel on Front Street. He was a wiry man with curly red hair. He moved constantly, full of kinetic energy. Now, he dodged several oncoming cars as he jogged across the street, heading for the bench where Drake and Eve stood. When he joined them, he pulled a pack of cigarettes from the pocket of his gray slacks. He offered the pack to his companions. Drake took a cigarette and reached into his pocket for a lighter.

"No, thanks. See you later." Eve shook her head and walked away.

I should get back inside, too, Jill thought. Instead of standing here eavesdropping. And feeling awkward about it. Even if, as they say, eavesdroppers learn interesting things.

She stepped between two parked cars, intending to head back

to the warehouse, as Drake said, "Things are going fairly well. It's early days yet, of course."

"Things are going as well as can be expected, you mean." The screenwriter's derisive tone made Jill turn and look at him. Wade was punctuating his remark with the hand that held his cigarette. "With the cast we've been saddled with. Is Global Studios trying to win an award for miscasting? You told me we could get Gloria Grahame and Robert Mitchum for the leads. They would have been perfect."

"I know that. But Mitchum wasn't available. He's up in Canada, shooting some Western for Otto Preminger."

"I heard about that." Wade took a drag on his cigarette. "Picture's called *River of No Return*. Marilyn Monroe's the female lead, if you can imagine her in a Western. What about Grahame?"

"She's in demand now," Drake said. "Ever since she won the Oscar for *The Bad and the Beautiful*, so I figured it would be hard to get her, As far as I can tell, she's not shooting anything right now. I couldn't get a straight answer from her agent, or anyone at Global. Not available, that's all I heard. Of course, she was in *Sudden Fear* last year. Maybe she didn't want to be in another picture with a train. I suggested Lana Turner or even Lizabeth Scott. And for the male lead, Dana Andrews or Dan Duryea. But Peter Vesey picked the cast. He's the studio exec. He holds the purse strings. He looked at a list of actors who were available and picked the cast. End of story."

Wade snorted in derision. "So we get the third team, not even the second. Global doesn't want to pay the kind of money it would take to get big stars. And we wind up with Leona Alexander? She's decorative, I'll grant you that. But she's no femme fatale. I'll bet she's sleeping with somebody to get parts. She'll wind up in the pages of *Confidential*."

Drake sighed. "Lots of people wind up in that scandal sheet. I'd just as soon the star of the picture didn't."

"And Neal Preston playing the detective?" Wade said, continuing his tirade. "When it comes to acting, that guy is as stiff as a board. And he's typecast as a cowboy. He's been in a bunch of Budd Boetticher oaters. For crying out loud, his last part was in

The Cimarron Kid with Audie Murphy."

He took another puff on his cigarette and flicked it to the ground, stamping out the butt with his shoe.

"I have some news," Drake said. "Stu Felton is coming to town. He'll be on the set Monday."

The screenwriter made a face. "Felton. Stuart-goddamn-Felton. Vesey's right-hand man. Hatchet man is more likely. What a tight-fisted son of a bitch. What the hell does he want? If he's demanding any more changes to my script, I swear, I'll make him eat it, page by page."

"Tight-fisted he certainly is. But we have to keep these studio people happy in order to get this picture made. After all, you've got money invested in this project, too, just like me and Dewitt."

"What does Felton want?" Wade demanded again.

"I don't know. Eve's going to ask around, and so will I. He gets in sometime tomorrow evening and he visits the set Monday morning. I guess we'll find out then."

Wade was not yet done complaining. "I've had it with Felton and his interference. Every time I turn around, he's doing something to put a stick in the wheels. We have to do something before he totally destroys this movie."

Drake dropped his cigarette butt into the coffee can. "Unless we can find out why he's here before he arrives, we'll just have to wait and see. I just hope I'm not expected to entertain him this weekend."

"Entertain him?" Wade snapped his fingers as though keeping time to some internal rhythm. "But yes, entertain him is exactly what we need to do. I've got an idea. Felton gets in tomorrow night, you say? Where's he staying? Not here in Niles, surely. It's the back side of beyond."

"San Francisco, that's what I was told. At the St. Francis."

"Perfect." Wade grinned. "We give Felton a party. No, don't look at me like that. Why not? Dewitt is the big-shot money man with the fancy house in Pacific Heights. Here's how it works. Dewitt hosts the shindig and we invite everyone, the cast and crew. We schmooze, we massage Felton's ego, and maybe, just maybe, we'll find out what's going on in that lizard brain of his."

"Saturday?" Drake frowned. "That's the day after tomorrow. But it's a good idea. I'll talk with Dewitt. I'm not sure Adelaide will buy into it. That's a lot of work for her, putting something together in such a short time."

"Oh, come on," Wade said, his tone dismissive. "Adelaide's a rich society lady. She's got maids and butlers and cooks to do all the work. Listen, Dewitt wants to be a big important Hollywood producer, he has to act the part. So he tells his wife to get in line and do what's required to make things happen."

"I'll talk to him." Drake sounded doubtful. "But you don't just tell Adelaide to get in line. Believe me, she's got a mind of her own. Besides, what if we give the party and Felton says no, he doesn't want to come?"

"We've got that covered," Wade said. "I hear Felton collects art. Has a whole bunch of paintings in his house in Beverly Hills. Dewitt also collects paintings. From what he says, he's got great stuff hanging on the walls all over his house. Dangle that in front of Felton. I'll bet he'll jump at the chance to look at all that art."

Drake nodded. "Good idea, a very good idea. Listen, I'll call Dewitt right now. After I talk with him, I'll get back to you."

Both men walked away, Drake heading for the warehouse and Wade going back across the street to the hotel.

Jill moved away from the parked cars, walking slowly to the front of the building. She had learned some interesting things. The director, his assistant and the screenwriter were all nervous about this upcoming visit by Stuart Felton, the man from Global Studios.

No wonder she'd seen such dismayed looks when people found out that phone call was from Felton.

Chapter Five

JILL WAS IN one more scene that afternoon. It required three takes to shoot the scene to Drake's satisfaction, then she was done for the day.

She headed for the trailer that served as a dressing room for the female bit players and extras who played train passengers. It was the size of a small bedroom, furnished with several tables and chairs that looked as though they'd been rescued from a thrift shop, with a bathroom at one end. Stretched across one wall was a closet rail for costumes and street clothes.

There was no one else in the dressing room. She removed her Zephyrette costume, so much like her own uniform, with a few modifications made by the designer, and hung up the costume. Then she put on a short terrycloth robe that had been provided to her. It had once been orange and was now faded to a pale color that reminded her of sherbet. She sat down at one of the tables and reached for a jar of cold cream. Using tissues and a soft cloth, she removed the heavy makeup that had been applied that morning when she reported to the set.

The set, she thought. How odd to think of this musty old warehouse in Niles as a movie set. She had trouble thinking of it as such, but it was. She'd only been part of this movie-making enterprise for a few days and she understood that her participation would be needed for another week or so. By the time she got used to being on a movie set, the location shooting would be over and the cast and crew would return to Hollywood. And Jill would be able to go back to her routine, riding the *California Zephyr* from the Bay Area to Chicago, and back again.

That movie makeup looked so garish, especially when she was looking at it up close in the mirror. She was glad to wipe the last of it, and the cold cream, from her face. At the bathroom sink, she washed her face thoroughly with soap and warm water. That felt good. After patting her face dry with a towel, she dusted it with a light powder from her own compact and added a trace of color on her eyelids and a touch of lipstick. Much better, she thought, examining her image in the mirror.

She put on the clothes she'd worn to the warehouse—the set—that morning. The short-sleeved cotton dress had a tailored bodice and a wide skirt, blue with a pattern of yellow and pink flowers. Over this she wore a lightweight blue cardigan, the ensemble perfect for a warm evening. She added earrings and checked her watch.

As she left her dressing room, Neal Preston emerged from his trailer at the back. He'd changed from his costume, the tailored suit, and wore more casual attire, a pair of gray slacks, a checked shirt and a sports jacket. Without makeup, he looked older, with lines in his lean, tanned face. He was a man of few words, unless they were in the script, but now he smiled and wished her a pleasant evening. She thanked him and they both walked toward the parking lot near the Niles depot. On other evenings she'd seen him walk across Front Street to the hotel, but this afternoon he got into a Buick Skylark convertible—cream-colored, with red upholstery—and drove away.

Jill's parents had recently bought a second car, a 1953 Ford Customline four-door sedan. That meant Jill had use of the family's older car, a green-and-white Ford Victoria. Jill had been driving the Victoria to and from work at her new temporary job.

This evening, however, she was not going directly home to Alameda. She had a dinner date.

Jill had met Mike Scolari last December when he and his grandfather were passengers on an eastbound *California Zephyr*, heading to Denver to spend Christmas with members of their extended family. Since then, Jill and Mike had been seeing each other frequently. He was a student at Jill's alma mater, the University of California in Berkeley, where he was using his GI benefits to get a degree in Geology. She liked Mike a lot, and the feeling was mutual, but so far both of them had resisted the matchmaking attempts that came from all sides. Mike wanted to finish school and get established in his career before any such move. Jill liked being a Zephyrette and she knew she'd have to leave the job if she got married. Though it happened a lot. The joke among her fellow Zephyrettes was that the shelf life for their profession was about two years. The young women who rode the rails were constantly leaving to get married. Either they met a passenger, as Jill had, or accepted a proposal from a fellow crew member, as had one of Jill's coworkers who earlier in the summer had married a brakeman.

At the wheel of the Ford, Jill drove to Oakland. When she arrived, she turned onto Broadway and drove toward the waterfront, crossing the tracks on Third Street, heading for the waterfront. A couple of years ago the Port of Oakland had renamed the neighborhood after a famous Oakland writer, calling it Jack London Square. The area's boundaries were Broadway, Webster Street and First Street, which was also called the Embarcadero. When Jill had looked up the definition of the Spanish word, she found that it usually meant a landing place, especially along an inland waterway. That fit the description of the estuary, which was also known as Oakland's inner harbor, the body of water that separated Oakland from Alameda.

Jill parked the car in a nearby lot and walked along the waterfront, enjoying the fall evening. There were several popular restaurants in the area, such as the Sea Wolf and the Bow and Bell, located at the foot of Broadway. The Showboat was a floating restaurant aboard a converted sternwheeler, tied up between the Sea Wolf and the Oakland Seafood Grotto. She strolled past the Grotto and Fisherman's Pier, at the end of Franklin Street. She was meeting Mike at the foot of Webster Street, outside a local landmark, Heinhold's First and Last Chance Saloon. The bar had been on the Oakland waterfront since 1883 and it was said that Jack London was a frequent patron. He even mentioned the place in his novel *John Barleycorn*. It was a shack, really, constructed from the timbers of an old whaling vessel. And it had a crooked floor, a result of the 1906 San Francisco earthquake that skewed the pilings under the building.

She glanced at her watch. Mike was a few minutes late, but that wasn't surprising. Fall semester had started and he had a late afternoon class. He may have run into some traffic on the drive from Berkeley to Oakland. She stood outside the bar, watching the people around her. She heard music coming from somewhere, "How High the Moon," by Les Paul and Mary Ford. Then the music faded away, replaced by laughter and loud conversation from a group of people passing by.

Jill looked toward Heinhold's bar and was surprised to see Neal Preston again, just an hour after she left the set. The actor was leaving the bar, accompanied by a young man with a shock of white-blond hair and a slender frame clad in blue jeans and a green shirt. Preston, who always looked quite serious on the set, was laughing as he put his hand on his friend's arm. The two men turned and walked toward the corner of First and Webster streets. At the corner, they disappeared from view.

Jill turned and strolled toward Fisherman's Pier, where several boats were tied up at a small marina. There was a small parking lot here, and she was again surprised, this time by Wade Ratliff. The screenwriter, still in the gray slacks and shirt he'd been wearing earlier that afternoon, was getting out of a dark blue Buick Roadmaster hardtop. The afternoon sun glinted on his red curls as he leaned on the car and took cigarettes and lighter from his pocket. As he smoked the cigarette, he looked around, as though he was waiting for someone. He must have spotted the person, because he straightened and pitched the butt into the water. He walked toward Heinhold's, stopped and spoke with an older man in a blue suit. The two men were about ten feet from where Jill stood, and she heard scraps of their conversation.

"Of course I've got it," Wade said. There was something about the way he stood, with both arms over his chest and his feet apart, that seemed challenging. She didn't hear what the other man said, but she could hear Wade, who cut off the other man with a dismissive gesture. "Are you interested? If you're not, say so. I haven't got time to waste. You're not the only fish on the line."

The other man didn't like Wade's attitude, or his words. He leaned forward, a frown on his face, and said something to the screenwriter. Then he turned and walked away.

Eavesdropping, Jill thought. I've done a lot of that today. Something's going on, but I'm not sure just what it is.

She headed back the way she had come. Then she saw Mike walking toward her. He quickened his pace and joined her, giving her a quick kiss on the cheek. "Thanks for meeting me for dinner. First of all, I really want to see you. And second, I'm definitely in the mood for seafood tonight."

"Same here," Jill said. "Both seeing you, and the seafood."

Mike waved a hand toward the waterfront restaurants. "Where shall we eat? How about the Grotto? Or would you rather go to the Sea Wolf?"

"The Grotto's fine. The food's good."

They started toward the restaurant. Then Jill heard someone speak her name. It was Wade, alone now, the other man nowhere in sight. He flashed a friendly smile. "Miss McLeod? It is you. What a surprise to see you here. And..." His voice trailed off as he eyed Mike. "Scolari? Mike Scolari?"

Mike hesitated for a second, so briefly that Jill thought she might be imagining it. "Hello, Wade."

"Well, it's been a long time." Wade shoved a hand in Mike's direction.

"Yes, it has." Mike hesitated, again, then he shook hands.

That wasn't like him, Jill thought. Normally Mike was friendly, affable, ready with a smile. But the smile was nowhere in evidence now. As for Wade Ratliff, the smile on his face didn't quite extend to his hazel eyes.

There was something between the two men; she could feel it, and it wasn't good. She'd have to wait to get the story from Mike.

"What a coincidence, seeing you here," Wade said. "Miss McLeod, I had no idea that you knew my old army buddy."

"No reason for you to know," Jill said. "So you were in the Army Air Force with Mike?"

"That's right. I'm sure Mike has told you all about that."

Jill smiled and nodded. Actually Mike hadn't told her much. Like her cousin Doug, who had fought in Italy and who'd been wounded, Mike was reluctant to talk about his experiences during the war.

Wade looked as though he could talk a while longer, but Mike said, "If you'll excuse us, we have dinner plans."

"Oh, sure," the screenwriter said. "We'll have to get together, talk over old times. I'm in town for the next two or three weeks."

Mike didn't respond. He took Jill's arm and they walked toward the Grotto. Once inside, they were led to a table overlooking the estuary. As they consulted their menus, Mike said, "I'm going to have some wine. How about you?"

She nodded. "A glass of chardonnay would be nice."

When the waiter appeared at their table, Mike ordered the wine. Jill scanned the wide selection of entrées. Then she looked up at Mike, across the table. "You don't like him."

Mike glanced at her over the menu. "You picked up on that, did you?"

"Right away. You hesitated before you shook his hand."

He didn't say anything as the waiter returned with the bottle of chardonnay, pouring a dollop into Mike's glass so he could taste it. He nodded and the waiter poured wine into Jill's glass.

"Are you ready to order?" the waiter asked.

Jill nodded. "I'll have a cup of clam chowder and the swordfish. And let's share a tossed salad."

"Half a dozen oysters on the shell, and the salmon." As the waiter left the table, Mike teased, "You can have one of my oysters."

Jill made a face. "No, thank you. I like them cooked, but not raw." She sipped her wine. "I know you were in the Army Air Force and you flew bombers during the war. That much you've told me."

"Medium bombers, B-26 Martin Marauders. I went to England in 'forty-three. I was with the 323rd Bombardment Group. Initially we were a part of the Eighth Air Force and later the Ninth. We were at a couple of bases in England, northeast of London. Later we went to France. And then Germany."

Jill took another sip of her chardonnay. "I didn't know you'd gone to Germany." He didn't say anything, glancing out at the estuary, where a sailboat was going by. "I know you don't like to talk about the war. Neither does my father."

He sighed. "Someday I'll tell you. But not right now. I certainly don't want to spend the evening talking about the war. Or Wade Ratliff. But I do want to hear all about your experiences as a movie actress."

Jill smiled. "Me, an actress? I wouldn't go that far. I have a few lines in a few scenes. The man who's playing the conductor, Bert Gallagher, he's really nice. He's what they call a character actor and he's been doing this for years. He's been in movies with all sorts of people. In fact, he was in *Meet Me in St. Louis,* in the trolley scene, he says. After this movie is done, he's going to be in a Western. He calls those oaters. Anyway, he's been telling me all sorts of stories, translating the movie lingo for me. The lead actress is a woman called Leona Alexander, and the man who is playing the role of the detective is Neal Preston."

"Preston," Mike said. "I think I remember him from an Audie Murphy movie. An oater, as you say. He was playing a cowboy."

"I think in the past he's mostly played cowboys. He looks as though he'd rather be wearing blue jeans, instead of the suit he was wearing in the scenes they were shooting today. I hear he has a ranch near Chatsworth, in the San Fernando Valley near Los Angeles, where he keeps horses."

"This movie they're making, it's a thriller, right?"

"Yes." Jill paused as the waiter delivered her clam chowder and Mike's oysters. "What they call a film noir. A French term, because the subject matter is dark. Although Bert—Mr. Gallagher—calls it a heist movie. As a matter of fact, *The Heist* is the working title. I say working title because that could change. I understand there's some disagreement about what to call the finished product."

"*The Heist.* That's an appropriate title." Mike lifted one of the oysters from the plate. "I gather somebody steals something."

Jill nodded and dipped a spoon into the chowder. "I've read the whole script and I think it's pretty good. Neal Preston is playing a hard-boiled private detective called Stan Gray. He's been hired by a rich man to recover a valuable painting that's been stolen. He's tracking down a mystery woman named Dolores Bain—that's the character played by Leona Alexander. She was originally in cahoots with a man called Creswell, who is something of an art connoisseur, as well as a crook. He's played by Charles Bosworth. Anyway, in the plot, Dolores and Creswell steal the painting together. Then Dolores decides to take the painting and sell it herself. So her former partner is after her, and so is the detective. Only he's falling in love with her."

"Romance, of course," Mike said with a grin.

"Certainly. When it comes to Hollywood, there's always romance." Jill spooned up more chowder. "So the two men have followed the femme fatale onto the eastbound *California Zephyr*, heading from the Bay Area to Chicago. They're looking for the painting, which she's hidden somewhere on the train. And that's where my character comes in. The Zephyrette sees something that winds up being a clue."

He smiled. "That sounds like it's right up your alley. You've solved a couple of mysteries in the time that I've known you."

"Not because I wanted to, I assure you." Jill finished the chowder as Mike slurped down more oysters. "This week we've been shooting at that warehouse in Niles. Today we were filming on the set that's supposed to be a dome-lounge car. It really does look accurate, up to a point. It doesn't have a Vista-Dome, of course. Mr. Preston, the leading man, seems nice, though a bit distant."

"What about the leading lady?" Mike asked, pushing aside the plate that had held the oysters.

Jill considered this before answering. "She seemed a bit stuck up at first. And she has a habit of looking down her nose. But I honestly think it's because she's nearsighted. I'll bet she wears glasses and can't see very well without them. She acts like she doesn't care for Mr. Preston, which is a problem because in the movie they're supposed to be attracted to one another. But I'm not seeing any chemistry there. I know she's not a big star yet, but I get the feeling Global Studios is hoping she will be. She's played some supporting roles over the past few years, according to Mr.

Gallagher. She was in a movie recently with Kirk Douglas, he said. But this is her first leading role. So she has a lot riding on it."

The waiter delivered their entrées and the salad they were sharing. Jill picked up her fork and scooped some lettuce onto her plate. Then she squeezed lemon juice onto her swordfish.

Mike took a fork to his salmon. "If they're filming the movie inside the warehouse, why didn't they just make it down in Hollywood? I mean, they have all those big soundstages, don't they?"

"They do," Jill said. "I understand the crew has already filmed some scenes at Global Studios in Hollywood. Then they came up here to do what they call location shooting, filming at the Oakland Mole and the rail yard. One of the producers, Mr. Collier, owns the warehouse in Niles and I think he has some clout with the Western Pacific Railroad, which is how they were able to film in the rail yard, shooting exterior scenes with actual locomotives and railcars. I guess they want to make it look as real as possible. The warehouse is right next to the Niles depot, which will be used in a couple of scenes. And they are planning to shoot some scenes in Niles Canyon as well. And up in the Feather River Canyon."

She paused. As she cut off another piece of swordfish, she thought about the conversation she'd overheard earlier that afternoon. Drake Baldwin had said that someone at Global Studios had been opposed to shooting on location. She supposed it was more cost-effective to film the whole thing in a soundstage. But as a moviegoer, she liked the authentic look of location filming.

"It sounds like I might get invited to a party on Saturday," Jill said, recalling Wade's idea to invite the studio executive to Collier's house. "The director and that screenwriter were talking about having a get-together at Mr. Collier's house in San Francisco, because an executive from Global Studios is coming to town. I think they want to get on his good side. We don't have any plans for Saturday afternoon, do we?"

Mike shook his head. "Not the two of us. I've got that class field trip all day on Saturday, remember. At Mount Diablo."

"Oh, yes, you told me about that."

"Sorry I'll miss the party. When are your parents due home?" he asked.

Jill paused, a forkful of swordfish on its way to her mouth. "They haven't said. They're still in Monterey and I'm sure they're having a good time."

In late September, Jill's younger sister, Lucy, had married her fiancé, Ethan, then the newlyweds had sailed on a Matson liner headed for Hawaii on their honeymoon. Once the out-of-town relatives had left, Lora McLeod had declared that she needed a break from the rigors of being mother of the bride. Her husband, Amos, had whisked her away for a well-deserved vacation. They had loaded up the family's new car for a drive down the coast to Monterey. Jill and her younger brother, Drew, were the only ones at home at the McLeod house on Union Street in Alameda, but Drew was frequently out. He had followed through on his plans, announced last summer, to drop out of school after his first year at the University of California. He played guitar in a blues and jazz band that had been touring in some West Coast cities, but he'd come home for the wedding. Now he and the band were doing some gigs here in the Bay Area.

Jill and Mike chatted companionably as they finished their dinners, then left the restaurant and walked out to where they'd parked their respective cars. After a lingering kiss, Jill got into the Ford and drove to Alameda.

Home was a two-story Victorian house on Union Street in Alameda, the island city that was separated from Oakland by the inner harbor. The comfortable old house, built in the Queen Anne style, dated to the 1890s. It was a few blocks from Alameda Hospital, where Dr. Amos McLeod was a general practitioner. Blue with bright yellow trim, the house had a porch that wrapped two sides of the house, big enough for a porch swing, a glider and several outdoor chairs. Though it was autumn, the Cécile Brünner rose climbing out of its trellis and up one side of the house still held plenty of soft pink blossoms. The dahlias, fall bloomers the size of plates, were a riot of purple, pink, yellow and red, complementing the bronze chrysanthemums. The sun was going down, painting the sky in the west bright gold and copper.

Jill fetched the mail and carried it inside, finding a postcard from her parents. Sophie, her calico cat, came down the stairs, mewing for attention. The cat trotted ahead of Jill to the kitchen and stood expectantly next to her food bowl.

"All right, all right," Jill said over the demanding meows. "You're not going to starve in the next five minutes." She reached for the can opener and a can of cat food. Once the cat was eating, purring loudly, Jill turned off the kitchen light and headed for the stairs, stifling a yawn.

Time for bed. She'd been up at six this morning, and had another early call tomorrow.

Chapter Six ———————————

WHEN JILL ARRIVED in Niles on Friday morning, she parked the Ford at the end of the row of cars on the west side of the warehouse. She got out of the car and stood for a moment, looking beyond the railroad tracks, where the bright blue sky of this October morning contrasted with the velvety golden-brown of the hills to the north and east, surrounding the entrance to Niles Canyon.

She heard a voice coming from the back of the warehouse. A door at the rear of the building opened onto a small concrete pad, cracked and uneven, between the warehouse and the railroad right-of-way. The perimeter was overgrown with crabgrass and weeds, shaded at one end by a scraggly-looking juniper. Usually, the back door to the warehouse was kept closed, to reduce the noise coming from trains passing by. But it was open during breaks, providing much-needed ventilation to the cavernous interior of the building.

Curious about the source of the voice, Jill walked along the uneven brick sidewalk and peered around the corner.

Neal Preston paced up and down the length of the yard. He held a dog-eared script in his left hand. As Jill watched, he consulted the pages and then looked up, staring out at the tracks. He tossed the script onto an overturned milk crate near the door and ran a hand through his dark hair.

He laughed, then he spoke, his tone light and bantering, "You may think you know what's going on, but you don't." He stopped, shook his head, then said the line again. This time the laugh had an edge to it, and so did the words, somehow darker and loaded with contempt. He stopped again, looking thoughtful. Then he leaned forward, chin jutting out and his right hand up, as though he was pointing at an adversary.

"You may think you know what's going on," he sneered, his voice rough. Then he shook his head. "But you don't."

He nodded, seemingly satisfied with this last interpretation of the dialogue. He reached for the discarded script and Jill backed away, not wanting to disturb him.

She wondered if Preston felt comfortable in the role he was playing in this movie, that of a hard-boiled private detective. As she'd heard yesterday, the actor had made his name in Westerns. Perhaps he was more attuned to the role of a cowboy.

A whistle signaled the approach of a freight train, from the west. Jill watched as the train rumbled slowly past the Niles depot, the diesel engine disappearing from view. The freight stopped, brakes squealing. A man stood in the open door of one of the boxcars at the rear of the freight. He jumped off the train, a canvas bag swinging from his shoulder, moving quickly across the tracks.

A hobo, Jill thought. She had seen these so-called "knights of the road" many times during her years as a Zephyrette. Hobos picked crops in the farming areas. In the mountains they worked in mines or logging camps. The cities offered them casual labor, such as digging ditches or factory work. They inhabited the shabby areas of towns and cities, the so-called skid rows or "hobo jungles" that sprang up on the edges of town. In San Francisco, they congregated in the cheap hotels south of Market Street. They worked for a time and then they would hop freight trains, riding the rails to different places.

They were itinerant workers. Men, most of them, but she'd seen a few women riding the rails. People who kept moving, with no fixed address, no friends, no family. But it wasn't always so, not back in the Depression years. At times the railroad police, who were supposed to keep trespassers off railroad property, had often turned a blind eye, or simply been overwhelmed by the numbers of people on the boxcars.

When she first began working as a Zephyrette, a talk with a brakeman had given Jill a different perspective on hobos. The brakeman was originally from western Kansas, which had been hit hard by the Dust Bowl.

"I was only ten years old," he told her. "I remember how my mother would wet the sheets and put them over the windows and doors, trying to keep out the dust. But she never could. My little sister died of what they called dust pneumonia, from breathing in all that dirt. When we lost our farm, we walked all the way to Dodge City, forty miles or more. From there we rode boxcars all the way to California, found work in the fields down by Bakersfield. It's been more than twenty years, but I'll never forget. Whenever I see a hobo, I think of those days. I know what it's like to be down on your luck."

The man who'd just jumped off the boxcar was of medium height, with a powerful, muscular torso. He was dressed in worn denim pants and a faded green jacket over a checked shirt. His chin was covered with dark stubble and his hair was tucked under a short-brimmed green cap, the kind she'd seen worn by newsboys in old photographs. The train began moving again as the hobo stopped and took a pack of cigarettes from his pocket. He stared at Jill as he shook a smoke from the pack and lit it with a match. He gazed at her for a long moment, then he broke off his stare and began walking at a brisk pace. He crossed Front Street and headed up H Street, into the Niles residential district.

Looking for a meal? Jill wondered. A place to stay? Or a temporary job? Odd that he would stop in such a small town as Niles. There were more choices to be had in Oakland or San Francisco.

Maybe Niles was a good place for a hobo to stop. There was a whole lexicon of symbols called hobo sign. That's how they left messages for one another. A picture of a cat meant "Kind lady lives here." An X surrounded by a circle meant "Good for a handout." Perhaps there were hobo signs on houses and fences in Niles; it was a railroad town. This man seemed to be walking with purpose, as though he had a destination.

Enough lollygagging, Jill told herself. It was time she got to work. She stepped onto the sidewalk that ran along the side of the warehouse and immediately stumbled as her foot encountered the loose brick, the clay one with NILES stamped on it. It was even looser now, halfway out of its space. She nudged the brick into place with her shoe, then turned and headed for the front of the building. She walked past the warehouse entrance to the makeup trailer.

There were usually two makeup artists, a young woman named Nancy, who wore her long brown hair in a ponytail, and an older woman named Venita, with a helmet of gray-blond hair and a perpetually cheerful expression. Nancy was working on one of the actors who was playing a passenger. Venita beckoned Jill to a chair. "Have a seat, hon. Now, let's get you ready." She swept a protective cloth around Jill and reached for her pots and brushes.

Venita was usually something of a motor-mouth, and today was no different. "I hear next week we're going to do some location shooting up in the canyon. That will be a change from the routine. The last time I did a location shoot it was a movie Neal Preston was in. We were at one of those movie ranches out in the valley. Oh, that's the San Fernando Valley, since you're a Northern California girl. Neal is such a nice fellow. I just love that man. I think he's going places. Now, he's usually playing a cowboy. The last movie he did, that was with Audie Murphy."

"I really like Audie Murphy," Jill said, getting a few words into Venita's chatter, which sometimes left her breathless.

"Oh, hon, I do, too. Did you read that book of his, *To Hell and Back*?" Venita barely waited for Jill's nod. "What a story. If only half of it's true, he was some hero. They say he won every medal there was, including the Medal of Honor."

Jill managed to get in a few more words. "French and Belgian medals, too. The *Croix de Guerre*."

"Well, I hear they're going to make a movie of his book. That should be some picture." Jill nodded in agreement, only to be scolded by Venita. "Now hon, don't you move or I'll mess up your makeup for sure."

Once she was done, Jill headed for the dressing room and put on her Zephyrette costume. She reported for duty on one of the sets, a credible facsimile of a ten-six sleeper, with the sides cut away to show the corridor and the interiors of the roomettes and a bedroom. She took her place and waited for shooting to begin.

———

Drake Baldwin must have contacted Dewitt Collier on Thursday, shortly after Jill overheard him and Wade Ratliff talking about entertaining the visiting executive from Global Studios. On Friday afternoon, after a completed scene, the director called the cast and crew together and made an announcement.

As the buzz of conversation died down, he said, "Listen, everyone. As you know from the phone call I got yesterday afternoon, Stuart Felton of Global Studios is coming to town. He arrives this evening. He'll be visiting the set on Monday." As soon as he said it, Jill heard a low hum as the import of his words took hold. The studio executive was coming and that wasn't good news.

Drake went on. "In the meantime, our producer, Mr. Dewitt Collier, and his wife, Adelaide, are hosting an open house for Mr. Felton tomorrow afternoon, at their home in San Francisco. The cast and crew are invited. I hope to see all of you there. The party starts at two o'clock and goes to whenever," he added, punctuating his comment with a laugh. He gave the address, on Broadway, and added that the cross street was Broderick.

Pacific Heights, Jill thought. Yes, Mr. Collier would live in that part of San Francisco.

The low hum got louder. Jill had been watching faces as Drake spoke, remembering how the cast and crew had reacted yesterday when they learned that the phone call was from Felton. She had wondered why people looked dismayed, then the conversation she'd overheard told her why.

Now the faces around her held a whole range of emotions, including annoyance and resignation. She certainly didn't see anyone who looked happy at the thought that the studio executive would be visiting the set on Monday. Nor was there any enthusiasm about attending a party in Felton's honor. There was more to this than irritation at the thought of giving up some well-deserved downtime after a busy week on the set, for a party that people apparently were reluctant to attend. For it seemed to Jill that the spoken invitation had included overtones that said the cast and crew, especially the ones who were most important in the hierarchy, were expected to be at the party. Leona Alexander's pique showed on her face and Neal Preston was frowning.

The only one who appeared to be happy about the prospect

was Charles Bosworth. "A party. How nice. I look forward to seeing Mr. Collier's art collection. I understand it's quite extensive. I have a modest collection of my own."

Billy Dale, the actor who was playing the waiter, snorted derisively. "I'm the wrong color for a party in Pacific Heights. I show up, they'll hand me a tray and tell me to serve drinks. Besides, I got things to do this weekend. I got family in the Fillmore."

"Is that where you're from?" Jill asked.

"Yeah. The Western Addition. I left when I was eighteen, to try my luck as a song and dance man. But my grandmother still lives in a big old Victorian near Fillmore and Fulton." His mouth turned down in a frown. "The city's been talking about tearing down houses in that part of town. They call it urban renewal. Hah! I call it Negro removal."

Billy was one of several Negroes in the cast. The others were bit players or extras, taking the roles of Pullman porters, cooks, and waiters like the one Billy was playing. However, his was the only role with a substantial speaking part.

"How long has your family lived there?" Jill asked now.

"A long time," Billy said. "Since the Thirties, when my grandpa came out here from the South. Back before the war, there was a lot of Japanese folks living in that part of town, the people they rounded up and sent to the camps. I don't know where my family would go if they do all this tearing down they're talking about."

"I hope that doesn't happen," Jill said. But she had her doubts. If the city of San Francisco wanted something, it was probably inevitable. "So you were a song and dance man. Like the Nicholas Brothers?"

"Not nearly as good as the brothers," he said with a laugh.

"Oh, yes. That number from *Stormy Weather* was wonderful. Speaking of brothers, mine has a band, and they're playing in the Fillmore this weekend."

"He's a musician?" Billy looked interested. "What does he play?"

"Guitar. His band is called the Blues Timers. They're going to be at a club— What is the name of it? I know it's on Fillmore Street." She thought for a moment and came up with the name.

"I know the place," he said with a nod. "Friend of mine tends bar there. I'll drop by and see if your brother knows how to play the blues."

"He's pretty good. At least I think so. He's expanded my listening horizons to include Bessie Smith and Billie Holiday."

He laughed. "Well, good for him."

Bert Gallagher joined them at the back of the set and voiced what Jill was already thinking. "This party has all the earmarks of a command performance."

"Not for me, it doesn't." Billy pulled a pack of cigarettes from the pocket of his waiter costume. "Excuse me, I'm going outside for a smoke." He headed for the rear door, the one that led out back near the train tracks.

Jill and Bert moved toward the door, at a slower pace. "Mr. Dale thinks he'd be out of place."

"Unfortunately, he's probably right," Bert said. "Though I suspect for some of us, attending this party is expected, at least for some of the cast and crew. The people above the line, so to speak."

They reached the doorway and stepped out onto the concrete pad that separated the building from the railroad right-of-way. Jill looked up at her companion. "Above the line? I heard someone say that before. I assume it's a moviemaking term. What does it mean?"

Bert nodded. "Yes, it's movie jargon. Dates back to the early days and the silent era. Initially it had something to do with budgets. Above the line means the people who oversee the creative process, such as the directors, the producers, the screenwriters and the principal actors. The budget connotation stems from the days when the budget sheet would have a line drawn to separate the costs. Above the line and below the line, get it?"

"I do." Jill glanced back into the warehouse, where the crew was setting up for the next shot. "So in this case, the above-the-line people would be Drake Baldwin, the director, Wade Ratliff, who wrote the script, and Mr. Collier, since all three of them are producing the film. And the leading actors, such as Miss Alexander, Mr. Preston and Mr. Bosworth."

"That's right," Bert said. "A character actor like me, well, I've never been much above the line. But I'll go to the party. It's a courtesy. After all, Mr. Collier is investing heavily in this film and providing us with this warehouse to use as a studio. Besides," he added with a laugh, "who am I to turn down free food and booze?"

Jill smiled. "I'm just a bit player, as you call it. So I'm probably not invited. Though I'd like to go."

She certainly didn't have anything planned for Saturday, since Mike would be busy with his class field trip. Yes, she would love to attend a party in a Pacific Heights mansion. She'd seen the exteriors of homes in that district of San Francisco, with its hills looming over the city. It would be a treat to see the inside of such a place.

"You should definitely put in an appearance," Bert said. "I insist. After all, you're our Western Pacific Railroad representative."

"All right. You've convinced me to go. And while you're explaining things, who is this Mr. Felton? And why does the mention of his name strike what appears to be fear in certain quarters?"

"Ah, you noticed that," Bert said. "You notice lots of things."

"I'm curious. It's part of my charm," she added with a laugh.

"And your skill." Bert looked thoughtful. "Stuart Felton is a studio executive at Global Studios. And he is definitely above the line. Felton works for Peter Vesey, who is even higher up the ladder. Vesey is the executive in charge of several productions, including this one. That means he is in charge of the money for this particular movie. Keeping on the good side of the men who control the money is always a good idea. As studio executives go, Vesey is for the most part a nice guy, easy to deal with."

"And Stuart Felton is not," Jill guessed.

"You got it in one. Not the easiest person in the world to get along with. I haven't had many dealings with him, but from what I can see, and what I've heard, Felton frequently goes out of his way to antagonize people. In other words, you wouldn't want to get on his bad side. The fact that he's paying a visit to the set can't be good news. And I don't think this party is going to do anything to alleviate whatever crisis seems to be in the wings. Still, I welcome the opportunity to get free booze and food at Dewitt's house in San Francisco. How does that hoary old saying go? 'Eat, drink, and be merry, for tomorrow we die.'" Bert punctuated the words with a smile, then he turned as someone called his name. He was in the next scene, which also involved both the leading man and his adversary.

Jill wasn't in the scene, and neither was Leona Alexander. After the announcement about the party, the actress had disappeared. Jill thought she must have gone back to her dressing room. She was already outside, so she went around the back corner of the building to the lot where the cars were parked. She stood for a moment, enjoying the afternoon sunshine. A movement caught her eye. There, on the Front Street sidewalk, she saw Rose, the woman she'd met the day before, with her little dog, Bella, exploring the grassy verge. She wore slacks again today, blue, with a yellow blouse. It looked as though she was waiting for someone. Perhaps it was the elderly man who stopped to pet the dog and speak to the woman.

Jill turned to her right and walked toward the bench under the oak tree. To her surprise, Leona Alexander was there. The star was still in costume, a floral print dress for the scene she would be shooting later. And she had a book in her lap.

I was right, Jill thought. She does wear glasses.

The star of the movie looked up, her blue eyes magnified by the lenses in the harlequin frames.

"Hello, Miss Alexander."

"Oh, please. Call me Leona. And I'll call you Jill. We might as well be informal, since we're all actors together."

"I don't know that I consider myself an actress. It's just a small part."

The actress smiled. "You're doing very well. We do need you for verisimilitude. Please sit down."

Jill joined her on the bench. "Will you be at this party tomorrow afternoon?"

Leona's expression echoed the sour look Jill had seen earlier, when the party was announced. "I suppose I have to. I know Drake expects it. Sometimes the socializing goes with the territory." Her expression relaxed. She put a bookmark in the pages of her book and held it up so that the cover was visible. "Have you read this? It's quite good."

The book she held was a novel called *The Bridges at Toko-ri*, by James Michener. The book about Navy pilots during the Korean War had been published in July of this year, just as the Armistice in Korea was being announced.

"Not yet," Jill said. "I've heard it's good. I really enjoyed Michener's book *Tales of the South Pacific*. But I haven't been able to bring myself to read this one. My fiancé was killed in Korea. In December 1950. At Chosin Reservoir."

A sad smile crept over Leona's face. "My husband was killed in September of that year, at Inchon."

"I'm sorry for your loss," Jill said. She certainly had no idea the actress had been married and that she was a widow.

"Most people don't know. I keep myself to myself. Always a good idea in Hollywood." She paused and thawed a bit more. "My husband and I have a daughter. She's four now. My mother is looking after her while I shoot this movie. She doesn't remember her daddy. She was barely a year old when he left for Korea. Anyway, I'm reading about the war so I can understand. At least I hope I can."

"It's hard to understand," Jill said. "Somehow World War Two seemed more black-and-white than this war in Korea."

"I agree." A troubled expression played over Leona's face, and she touched a ring she was wearing. Jill hadn't seen it before. The actress certainly didn't wear the ring during filming. It was on the fourth finger of her left hand. Was it an engagement ring? It didn't look like the typical diamond. This was a round ruby with a smaller diamond on either side, in a gold basket setting.

"That's lovely," Jill said. "Is it an engagement ring?"

Leona hesitated, then she smiled. "Good guess. Yes, it is. I'm getting married later next month."

"My sister just got married a couple of weeks ago," Jill said.

"How about you?" the actress asked. "Not that it's any of my business, of course."

"I'm seeing someone. I met him on the train last year. But I'm not quite ready, and neither is he."

"I wasn't either," Leona said. "But I was filming a movie in Denver last spring and I met this man." She smiled and held up the ring, the jewels sparkling in the afternoon sunlight. "And he's such a wonderful man that when he asked me, I said yes."

"Congratulations. Will you live in Denver?"

"We're working that out. I'd like my acting career to go somewhere, and if this movie's a success, it just might. So we'll see. Are you familiar with Denver?"

"I was born there," Jill told her. "And lived there until the end of the war. My mother and brother and sister and I lived with my grandmother until my father got out of the Navy. He's a doctor, and was on a ship in the Pacific. Then we moved to California. I went to college at the university in Berkeley. I was going to teach school, but after my fiancé died, I became a Zephyrette."

"And here you are," Leona said, "playing a Zephyrette in a movie. Tell me about Denver. My fiancé is an attorney and he lives in a neighborhood called Cheesman Park."

"That's where my grandmother lives," Jill said.

They talked about Denver for the next few minutes, then they were interrupted by Eve Stillman. The assistant director waved. "Leona. There you are. You're wanted on the set."

"Oh, thanks. I'll be right there." Leona stood and tucked the book under her arm. "I enjoyed talking with you, Jill. I suppose I'll see you tomorrow at the party."

"Yes, you will." Jill watched as the actress walked back toward the warehouse. At first glance, Leona Alexander had seemed standoffish and chilly. But under that mask was a warm and pleasant woman who could become a friend.

You never knew about people.

Leona went inside the building, but Eve didn't. Instead she walked toward Front Street, where she stopped to talk with someone. It was Rose, the woman Jill had seen earlier, with her dog, who was wagging her tail, eager for a pat. Eve reached down to scratch the dog's ears.

Interesting, Jill thought. Did Eve and Rose know each other? Or was Eve just being friendly? Something about the older woman and her black-and-white terrier invited attention. Eve turned and walked back toward the warehouse, going inside.

Jill sat for a few minutes longer. But it was time for her, too, to go back inside. If they were getting ready to shoot Leona's scene, that meant Jill's scene was next on the schedule. She rose from the bench and headed for the warehouse. If the crew was between scenes, she could get in through the back door. As she drew closer to the concrete pad, she saw three people gathered there—Drake, Eve, and Wade Ratliff, the screenwriter.

"Did you find out anything?" Drake asked.

Eve nodded. "It took me a while, but yeah, I did. A friend of mine who works as a cutter at Paramount says she's been hearing that Vesey is leaving Global, and going to Paramount. It's just a rumor, but you know how it goes. No smoke without fire."

Drake shook his head, looking dismayed. "Oh, no. That's bad news. I would hate to lose Vesey. He liked my first movie, and he likes this one. He's been behind me from the start. But Felton, not so much. He doesn't like this project. He hates location shooting, says it's too expensive and we could make the movie for less money in Hollywood. And he was upset when Vesey gave us the go-ahead to shoot the movie here in Niles."

Wade had a disgusted expression in his face as he threw his cigarette to the ground and stamped on the butt. "Bad news? Hell, it's terrible. Felton hates the script. He was demanding all kinds of changes before we started shooting, And even now, earlier this week, he was after me to change a scene. We went round and round about it. And Vesey overruled Felton."

"Felton's a piece of work, all right." Eve ran her hands through her short dark hair. "I hear when someone crosses him, he likes to get even. I've heard stories."

"We all have," Drake said. "Felton is Vesey's second in command. If Vesey really is leaving Global, it's a good bet that Felton will move up into Vesey's job. Then we're in trouble." He glanced at Wade. "He could force us to make those changes in the script. Or even worse, make us shut down the location shooting and go back to Hollywood."

"We're getting ahead of ourselves," Eve pointed out. "We don't know what Felton wants until he gets here. We don't even know for sure if the rumor about Vesey moving to Paramount is true."

"Agreed," Drake said. "We'll have to wait and see what

happens. In the meantime, I'd better let Dewitt know what's going on. All the more important to make nice with Felton at the party tomorrow."

"Or get some leverage," the screenwriter said, firing up another cigarette. "I might just have something Felton wants."

Eve looked mystified. "What could you possibly have that Felton would want?"

"Besides a new script," Drake said. Wade glared at him. "Hey, that was supposed to be a joke."

"Very funny." Wade took another drag on his cigarette. "Just wait. I have a few cards in my hand and I know how to play them."

Chapter Seven

JILL STOOD IN her small walk-in closet, barefoot and wearing a white slip. She pushed hangers along the closet rail, searching for something suitable to wear to a cocktail party at the Colliers' house. She was sure that Mrs. Collier and the other women attending would be wearing elegant attire.

She didn't have anything that resembled a cocktail dress. The fanciest outfit in the closet was the long pale pink gown she'd worn as her sister's maid of honor at the wedding, but that wouldn't do for cocktails and hors d'oeuvres in San Francisco. She wondered if she'd ever wear that dress again. Maybe if I shortened it, she thought, and did something different with those sleeves.

She pushed it aside and turned back to the section of her closet containing dresses, taking one, then another off the rail. No, not that one. Hmm, maybe. That one was a possibility. Oh, but that hem needed mending.

In a few minutes, she had winnowed her choices to three, each dress clean, in good repair and suitable for a party. The checked taffeta was nice, green plaid with touches of blue and red, sleeveless and with a cut-out neckline. The full skirt rustled as she held it up and examined herself in the long mirror on the wall. Then she hung it back on the rail and reached for the second dress. This one was crepe chiffon with a boat neck and long sleeves. Pretty, but the dark plum color seemed suitable for winter, not autumn. That left the silk organza. It was a blue-and-yellow floral pattern, with a fitted bodice, scooped neckline and a wide skirt. That would work well. She had a pair of high-heeled pumps in the same shade of blue.

She carried the dress into the bedroom, draping it on her bed. She put on nylons, smoothing them on her legs, then the dress. Yes, it looked just fine, dressy, but not too much. She slipped the shoes onto her feet, then put on a pair of gold earrings and a thin gold chain that held a tiny gold heart. The necklace had been a birthday gift from Mike. She took a pale blue shawl from a bureau drawer. In San Francisco, it was a good idea to take a wrap of some sort. The closer one was to the water, the more likely the chill.

She dabbed a bit of lilac-scented perfume behind her ears and fluffed her hair, which she wore short, in the style popularized by Audrey Hepburn in the recent movie *Roman Holiday*. Then she draped the shawl and her handbag over one arm and went downstairs. The household's car keys were kept in a bowl on the hall table. Jill picked up the key ring for the Ford Victoria and left the house. Outside, her brother, Drew, had backed his 1949 Mercury coupe into the driveway and he was loading his gear into the car's trunk. He was nineteen, tall and lanky, with Jill's blue eyes and brown hair. Today he was dressed in faded jeans and a white T-shirt.

Drew had spent last year as a freshman at the University of California in Berkeley. But his first love was music. He played electric guitar in a band called the Blues Timers. He had decided to drop out of school to play music, a decision that didn't sit well with his parents. But the family had decided to give him the chance. The band was working with an agent who'd gotten them some out-of-town gigs, going down the California coast, playing in Monterey and San Luis Obispo, then on to Santa Barbara, Los Angeles and San Diego. He'd also promised them some playing dates in Nevada and Colorado, but there had been a delay. Or the promised engagements had fallen through. Jill didn't know the details and Drew hadn't shared much about the situation. All part of being a musician, he said with a shrug. At least his return to the Bay Area meant that he was here for Lucy's wedding, taking on the role of groomsman. Now he and the band were playing gigs in San Francisco as well as their old haunts in the East Bay.

"You look fancy," he said now, surveying Jill in her finery.

"The cast and crew has been invited to a party. One of the producers lives in San Francisco, in Pacific Heights."

"Well, have fun. I'll be in a different part of town. We have a gig at a place on Fillmore Street, over in the Western Addition."

As Billy Dale had pointed out yesterday when they'd talked, before the war, the neighborhood had been populated by the Japanese immigrants and their American-born families. The war had sent most of them to the relocation camps. The houses and apartment buildings in the neighborhood had emptied out, then filled again with new residents. The Bay Area's Negro population had boomed as workers came from the South to find well-paying, war-related jobs. Drew had told her that the area, like Seventh Street in Oakland, had lots of blues and jazz clubs, where patrons could listen to stars like Ella Fitzgerald and Louis Armstrong.

Since Drew was leaving as well, Jill made sure the front door was locked and went down the steps to the front walk. The Ford was parked at the curb, where she'd left it the night before. She drove to the Bay Bridge. Traffic was heavy this Saturday afternoon and it took some time for her to reach the toll booth, where she handed over a quarter.

The Colliers' house was on the western end of Broadway. Jill headed up the wide street, through the Broadway tunnel under Russian Hill, and crossed Van Ness Avenue. Jill drove slowly up Broadway, looking at addresses. When she neared the block where the Colliers lived, she turned right onto Broderick, the nearest side street, and parked in the first available space. She got out, draped the blue shawl over her shoulders, and walked to the corner, then up the slope to the middle of the block.

The house was impressive, three stories high, built in a style reminiscent of a French château, with cream-colored stucco topped by a blue-shingled mansard roof. The driveway was wide enough for three cars, leading to a sizable garage on the street level. Jill went up the front walk to the double front doors, made of ornately carved wood. She pressed the brass door bell. Almost immediately, one of the doors opened. A man wearing a black suit and tie over his gleaming white shirt waved her into a tiled foyer that held a narrow table and a pair of chairs. A coat rack had been set up at one end.

"The living room is up those stairs, miss," he said, directing her to a wide staircase. "May I take your wrap?"

"Yes, thank you." Jill handed over the shawl. He draped it on a hanger and hung it on the rack.

She walked up the staircase, her hand on the wooden banister. The living room was huge, the walls a cool white, all the better to display paintings, mostly landscapes, with ornate gilt frames. All the paintings looked old and European, Jill thought. And valuable. The furniture was polished to a shine, with sofa and chairs upholstered in a rich-looking royal blue fabric. Small items such as bowls or jars, made of silver, cloisonné or porcelain, were scattered here and there on the tables. Thick Oriental rugs in shades of blue and red covered the floors. The fireplace mantel was marble, white veined with silver and flecks of gold, with Corinthian columns on each side and intricately carved flowers in a row on the top. On the mantel was an ornate clock made of brass and wood, its base adorned with carved leaves and vines. French doors bracketed by ice blue draperies were open, leading out to an expansive terrace that looked down on the Presidio and the Golden Gate Bridge, with San Francisco Bay shimmering in dark blue and gold.

Jill looked around the room, feeling like a country mouse. Leona Alexander stood across the room, looking spectacular in an off-the-shoulder black satin dress that hugged every curve of her statuesque frame. Now, that was dressy. On the other hand, Eve Stillman, the assistant director, might as well have been on the set. She wore slacks as usual, gray and pleated. Her tailored shirt was blue, open at the neck. In honor of the occasion, she had added a pale green scarf, knotted loosely around her throat.

Jill smoothed the skirt of her silk organza and straightened, throwing back her shoulders and tilting her chin upward. I'm wearing a nice dress, she thought. I won't worry about it.

In the center of the room stood an attractive, elegant woman of medium height, blond and in her late forties. She wore a midnight blue eyelash taffeta dress with a full skirt and three asymmetrical gold buttons. The jewelry she wore, a necklace and matching earrings, were sapphires set in gold, their deep blue color complementing the dress. Jill recognized her immediately, having seen the woman's photo in the society pages of the San Francisco newspapers. This was Adelaide Collier, Dewitt Collier's wife and her hostess.

"Well, look who's here. The Zephyrette-turned-movie star." The familiar voice was tart as a lemon.

Jill turned and smiled. "I didn't expect to see you."

Mrs. Grace Tidsdale, known to her friends as Tidsy, winked. "I invited myself. After all, I'm in the neighborhood."

At this, Jill raised an eyebrow. Tidsy lived in the Brocklebank Apartments on California Street at the top of Nob Hill. The Colliers' house was at least two miles away. But then, she'd heard San Francisco really was a small town.

Tidsy toasted Jill with a glass full of her favorite tipple, Scotch on the rocks. She was on the far side of forty, with a caustic, take-no-prisoners tongue to go with her raucous sense of humor. She had a head full of brassy blond curls and liked to wear red. Today it was a red silk cocktail dress with elbow-length sleeves, a full skirt, a fitted bodice and plunging neckline. Her fingernails were exactly the same shade of red as the dress and her jewelry was gold, lots of it, with rubies and diamonds to spare.

"This is some neighborhood," Jill said.

"Ain't that the truth. I never was that fond of mansions. Too much upkeep. I like my apartment just fine." Tidsy took a sip of her Scotch. "For crying out loud, get yourself a drink. I'm already a glass ahead of you."

Jill looked around and saw a maid carrying a tray of wineglasses, some containing red and the others white. She reached for a glass of the white and took a sip. It was a dry chardonnay and she approved. "Why are you here, really?"

Tidsy chuckled. "Addie and I go a long way back."

"Addie?" Jill looked perplexed.

"Adelaide Collier." Tidsy waved one carmine-tipped hand in the direction of their hostess. "She's actually Adelaide Baldwin, born and raised in Gustine, which is somewhere out in the wilds of the Central Valley. Near Modesto, I think."

"Baldwin," Jill echoed. "The director's name is Baldwin." She looked across the room and saw Drake Baldwin. He was out on the terrace now, holding a glass and smoking as he talked with Wade Ratliff.

"He's Addie's nephew. That's how Dewitt got talked into investing in this picture. Part of the reason, anyway." Tidsy tipped back her glass and swallowed a mouthful of Scotch. "Dewitt always wanted to be a mogul of some sort, Hollywood or otherwise. Lord knows he has fingers in lots of pies here in the Bay Area. Banking, real estate."

Jill nodded. "Railroads. Mr. Collier has some connection with the Western Pacific Railroad. They've given us access to the WP rail yard and rolling stock as well. We're shooting scenes in a warehouse Mr. Collier owns down in Niles." She had earlier told Tidsy all about meeting Drake Baldwin on the train and how she'd gotten involved in this movie. "So how do you know Mrs. Collier? From your university days in Berkeley?"

"From my days in Washington," Tidsy said.

Tidsy, a San Francisco native, had grown up in the city's Mission District. After college, she'd married. Then came the war, and she soon became a war widow. Her husband had died during Doolittle's 1942 raid on Tokyo. Tidsy wanted to do something for the war effort, so she went to Washington, D.C. to be what she called a government girl. She hadn't elaborated about what being a government girl entailed, but Jill had the impression that there was something more to it than typing and filing. There was the whiff of the clandestine about those times. Jill hoped that some day Tidsy would tell her more.

"Addie's first husband died in the war, same as mine," Tidsy continued. "She moved to Washington about the same time I did and worked in the same place. We even roomed in the same boarding house. Then she headed for Los Angeles to work in the Office of War Information. That's where she met Dewitt. He was down there on business, something to do with war department contracts. Very hush-hush, or so I understand. Anyway, it was a second marriage for both of them. His first wife had died. He has a son and daughter from that first marriage and they were out of the house and on their own. Addie moved to San Francisco and we reconnected. So that's how I know Addie and Dewitt."

"You know everyone," Jill said.

Tidsy's blue eyes sparkled with a touch of wicked humor. "I also know where most of the bodies are buried. And I've been known to bury a few of my own." She swirled her glass, rattling the ice cubes. "So who is this Felton guy? And why does everyone hate him?"

"You picked up on that," Jill said.

"Of course. You could cut the atmosphere with a damn knife. The party is supposed to be for him but I get the distinct impression some of these birds could gladly strangle the guest of honor."

"He's a studio executive. From what I hear, he is in charge of the money. And he has the ability to cut it off. Nobody knows why he decided to come up here, but he's scheduled to be on the set Monday morning. Everyone seems to be quite nervous about that. I guess we'll all find out then."

"Dewitt has his heart set on being a movie producer. Addie's hoping it's a phase and he'll outgrow it. She thinks it's another toy, like his collection." Tidsy waved a hand at the paintings on the wall. "He collects art. Addie collects doodads."

Jill smiled. "What sort of doodads?"

Tidsy gestured at the living room tables. "Those gewgaws taking up space on the tables. Like that silver bowl over there. Addie loves to go to antique stores and buy little things, like snuffboxes and cigarette cases. Compacts and vanity purses, too."

"Compacts? For powder? I didn't know things like that were collectible."

"The old ones are," Tidsy said. "Addie has several from the Victorian era, little silver purses with wrist chains. I know she paid a bundle of money for some of those things. She also has some pieces that are Art Nouveau and Art Deco. And the snuffboxes are quite valuable, she tells me. Some of those date back several centuries. A lot of the stuff is in display cases in the hallway." She waved in that direction.

"I'll take a look." Jill had a powder compact in the small purse she carried. She wondered if someday it would be collectible.

Tidsy took another swig of Scotch. "Dewitt, on the other hand, goes for paintings, mostly European, though I think he does have some American artists. He's got a few Impressionists and Post-Impressionists, but he is fond of the older stuff. Dutch and Italian. He's loaned a few of them to the de Young Museum. As you can see, a lot of them are on display here in the living room. And his library. That's at the end of the hall, so go take a peek."

"I will."

"Incoming," Tidsy said, with a nod at the approaching Bert Gallagher, looking dapper in his dark blue suit.

"Jill, good to see you." He smiled at Jill, then turned to Tidsy. "Who is this lovely lady?"

"This is my friend, Mrs. Grace Tidsdale," Jill said. "And this is Bert Gallagher. He's one of the actors, playing the conductor in the movie."

"Delighted, Mrs. Tidsdale."

"Nice to meet you." Tidsy appraised him with her eyes, as though she liked what she saw. She took a cigarette from her gold case and let him light it. "I'm sure Jill is giving you lots of tips on how to accurately portray a Western Pacific conductor."

"She's invaluable," he assured them. "I know you're Jill's friend. Since you're here, I assume you're also acquainted with the Colliers?"

"Indeed, I am." Tidsy didn't elaborate concerning her relationship with their hosts. Instead she narrowed her eyes and looked Gallagher up and down. "I believe I've seen you on the silver screen, Mr. Gallagher. Weren't you in a Frank Capra movie back in the Thirties?"

"You're a quick study." His smile grew broader. "I was in *You Can't Take It with You*. My part was so small I'm surprised you noticed."

"I have a good eye," Tidsy said.

"I've been fortunate to work with some great directors—Capra, Billy Wilder, John Ford." He glanced out at the terrace, at Drake Baldwin. "And some not so famous. But it's all in a day's work. I'm glad to be employed on a regular basis, no matter what the role."

They chatted a while longer as Jill looked around the room.

It looked like most of the cast and crew was here this afternoon, though she didn't see Neal Preston. Billy Dale, the actor who was playing the waiter, was absent as well.

There was a buzz of talk from the front of the room as Neal Preston finally arrived. He wore a suit, similar to the costume he'd been wearing on the set. The tall, rangy actor still looked as though he'd be more comfortable in blue jeans and cowboy boots. He walked over to greet Adelaide Collier, smiling as he took her hand and inclined his head. Then he glanced to his left and saw Dewitt Collier with another man. A strange expression crossed Preston's face. He quickly excused himself, took a glass of wine from the maid's tray and headed out to the terrace.

I wonder what that was all about, Jill thought. It's as though he wanted to avoid Mr. Collier. Or was it the other man he didn't want to see? Who was the other man? Stuart Felton? It looked as though she was about to find out. They were headed this way.

Jill had seen Dewitt Collier before, but this was the first time up close. He was tall, about six feet, and bulky through the shoulders and torso, though his impeccably tailored dark gray suit flattered his frame. He had close-cropped gray hair over a square face. He was older than his wife, by ten or fifteen years, Jill guessed, which would put his age as late fifties or early sixties.

Collier made the introductions. "Mrs. Grace Tidsdale, a dear friend of ours. And this is Mr. Stuart Felton, of Global Studios in Hollywood."

Felton was shorter and thinner than his host, with stooped shoulders inside his dark blue suit, and bony wrists visible under the cuffs of his white shirt. He had a narrow face with a hawk-like nose. His short brown hair was streaked with gray, thinning at the top. He had pale blue eyes, cold and calculating, his gaze constantly shifting around the room. He reminded Jill of some sort of predator, maybe an actual hawk, those eyes searching for weakness, ready to pounce on his prey at the slightest hint of vulnerability. It was a quality that could be useful in the business world, Jill thought, but it made her feel uncomfortable. Especially since Felton's gaze crawled all over her, taking in her figure before he looked at her face. She had experienced that gaze before, from male passengers on the train. Men she called wolves, the ones who figured the Zephyrettes were fair game. She was quite relieved when he looked away from her and focused his attention on Tidsy.

Tidsy had Felton's number. She gave him a cursory look and turned to Collier. "Dewitt, this is my good friend, Jill McLeod. She's a real Zephyrette on the *California Zephyr*, and she's in your movie."

Collier smiled and took Jill's hand. "A real Zephyrette. It's very nice to meet you, Miss McLeod. I'm delighted to have you in the cast of our movie. You're giving us a touch of authenticity, along with our location in Niles and the rolling stock the Western Pacific is letting us use. When Drake was casting the movie, he said he'd met just the right Zephyrette on the train. That was you, of course. He insisted that you had to be in the film. So I pulled whatever strings I could down at WP headquarters to make that happen."

"It's an honor, sir," Jill said, though in the back of her mind she wasn't sure that it was. Now that she knew that Mr. Collier was the director's uncle, and had friends in the higher echelons of the Western Pacific Railroad, she understood how her routine had been interrupted so that she could be in the movie.

"Are you enjoying the filming?" Collier asked.

"It's instructive. I had no idea how movies are made. I'm learning a lot. I understand we have another week or so of shooting at the warehouse in Niles, and then the crew is going to shoot some exteriors in Niles Canyon and head north to do some filming in the Feather River Canyon."

"Yes, that's the plan," Collier said.

Jill had been looking at Felton when she mentioned the Feather River Canyon. The studio executive narrowed his eyes and pressed his thin lips together, frowning. Why? She recalled the conversation she'd overheard on Friday, when Drake Baldwin said Felton didn't like location shooting, because of the cost.

Collier smiled at Jill. "It sounds like you're looking forward to getting back to work. At your real job, I mean."

Jill nodded. "Well, yes. I've gotten used to riding the trains. It seems odd to be at home for such a long time." She didn't want to seem ungrateful for the opportunity to be in the movie. After all, she was a nine days' wonder with her family and friends.

"This is the first time I've invested in a movie, so I'm taking a close interest in what's going on," Collier said. "By the way, I'm no stranger to trains. My father worked for the Chesapeake and Ohio."

The Chesapeake and Ohio Railway was an old company that operated in Virginia and the Ohio Valley, running trains from Norfolk and Richmond to places in Ohio, such as Cleveland and Toledo, and on to Chicago. She had traveled on the C&O during a trip to the Midwest with her mother and sister. During that trip, she'd purchased a set of small souvenir plates featuring the famous logo of Chessie the cat, the C&O's advertising mascot. The railroad's brochures featured the cuddly striped kitten sleeping under a blanket, with a paw extended. "Sleep like a kitten," said the Chesapeake's advertising, which was so successful that Chessie souvenirs were popular. Chessie had two kittens, Nip and Tuck, who also put in appearances in the advertisements. During the war, the C&O ads showed Chessie's "husband" Peake as a returning soldier with a bandage on his paw.

"What did your father do?" Jill asked now.

"He started out as a brakeman, Then he moved up. He was a conductor when he retired. Based out of Cleveland. That's where I grew up. Came out to California before the war."

"I want to see your collection," Felton said, impatient.

"Of course. But first I want you to meet someone." Collier whisked the studio executive away, introducing him to a man Jill didn't recognize. Tidsy knew him, of course, saying he was an executive with the Bank of America. While the banker and Collier talked, Felton didn't bother to disguise his annoyance at the delay. His eyes darted around the room. Just then, Charles Bosworth, who was playing the villain in the movie, walked up to Felton, a smile on his face. It looked as though he was introducing himself to the executive, but Felton waved his hand and said something Jill couldn't hear. She got the distinct impression Felton was brushing off the actor, who looked somewhat put out as he stepped back. Bosworth turned and walked away, frowning as he smoothed his mustache with his forefinger, something Jill had seen him do repeatedly when he was on the set.

Now Felton stared across the room at Leona Alexander, who was talking with Bert Gallagher. When Bert moved away, she looked up and saw Felton. She set her wineglass on a nearby table and left the living room, walking out onto the terrace.

Tidsy rattled the ice cubes in her glass. "What do you know, all the Scotch is gone. Time for a refill. How about you?"

"I'm still working on my wine," Jill said. She stayed where she was while Tidsy walked over to the bar that had been set up in the living room. Then she saw Stuart Felton approach the bar. He stood on Tidsy's left side, very close. He appeared to be engaging her in conversation, then Jill's eyes widened as she saw Felton's right hand touch Tidsy. He ran his fingers down her arm and then laid his hand on her hip.

Jill didn't hear what Tidsy said to Felton. She didn't have to. The body language told her everything. Felton dropped his arm and stepped back from the bar. Then he did an about-face and walked quickly toward the hallway, pulling a handkerchief from his pocket. Was he mopping liquid from his chin? Dewitt Collier followed, quickening his steps.

Tidsy stalked back to where Jill stood, carrying a fresh glass of Scotch on the rocks. "Did you see that?"

Jill nodded. "I did. Looks like Felton got wet."

"Wet." Tidsy snorted, the look in her blue eyes hot enough to strip paint off the wall. "That son of a bitch. He's lucky I didn't hand him his balls. The only thing that stopped me is that I don't want to make a big scene at Addie's party."

"A small scene is okay, though."

At that, Tidsy laughed. "Oh, yes, a small scene is just about right. So Mr. Studio Executive is a creep. No wonder people are avoiding him. Especially the women. For example, the icy blonde in the black dress. I saw Felton staring at her, and she went outside."

"That's Leona Alexander," Jill said. "She's one of the stars. And that dark-haired man, Neal Preston, he's the other star. He's trying to avoid Felton. He went out to the terrace, too."

And she could see why. Felton seemed to dislike Preston. It

was plain in the way he looked at the actor, staring at him with narrowed eyes tinged with contempt. It was as though Preston felt menaced by the gaze.

Just then, their hostess walked up and greeted them, putting her arm around Tidsy. Adelaide Collier had a pleasant voice, smooth as the silk of her elegant dress. "Thanks for coming. We have to put on a show for this Hollywood guy, for Dewitt's sake. Which is why I had to throw this party together on forty-eight hours' notice."

"You did great," Tidsy said, returning her embrace. "Addie, this is Jill, my friend."

"The Zephyrette." Adelaide Collier took Jill's hand, a warm smile on her face. "Drake has told me so much about you."

"It's a wonderful party," Jill said. "I've never been inside a Pacific Heights mansion before."

Addie laughed. "Well, it is a big pile. Certainly a lot bigger than the farmhouse I grew up in down in Gustine. Who knew when I was picking apricots on my dad's farm that I'd marry up and wind up in a big house on a hill in San Francisco."

"Collecting art," Jill said. "Tidsy tells me I should take a look at your collection."

"By all means." Addie gestured toward the hallway. "I collect little things, like snuffboxes. Tidsy calls them doodads. Mostly they're small. If I'm going to collect things, they should be small, not take up too much room. And they don't cost as much as Dewitt's paintings. They're in cases all up and down the hall. I think eventually I'll donate them to one of the museums here in town."

Jill excused herself, leaving the two friends to talk. Neal Preston had just come back inside. He left his empty glass on the bar and looked around. Avoiding Felton, Jill thought, as she followed the direction of the actor's gaze. Felton and Collier had reappeared from the hallway. Preston turned and walked the other way, joining Tidsy and Addie Collier. He had a rare smile on his face as he chatted with his hostess.

Time for some fresh air. Jill went out the door to the terrace.

Chapter Eight

OUTSIDE, SHE FOUND LEONA with her arms propped on the terrace railing, leaning forward as she gazed out at the view. The fog was coming in through the Golden Gate Bridge. Closer to hand, a curved staircase led down from the terrace to the Colliers' backyard, which contained a kidney-shaped swimming pool at one end. Next to this was a patio with an assortment of furniture covered with colorful floral cushions and a number of flowers in terra-cotta containers. A live oak anchored one corner of the yard and tall rhododendrons covered the wall at the back of the property. A breeze stirred the leaves. Several partygoers were down on the patio, their voices an indistinct buzz as they talked.

Jill stood next to Leona and put her elbows on the terrace railing. "Is everything all right?"

Leona turned and gave her that nose-in-the-air look that Jill had initially mistaken for haughtiness rather than nearsightedness. Although today it could be the former, even if the actress wasn't wearing her glasses.

"I'm sorry," Jill said. "Did I speak out of turn?"

Leona shook her head, her lips curving in a faint smile. "I'm just surprised you noticed. You're very observant, Jill. Is that part of the Zephyrette job description?"

Jill considered this, then nodded. "I suppose it is. My job is to be attentive to the passengers' needs, ready to respond to anything that comes up, whether it's a child with a skinned knee—or a derailment."

"I'll bet you're good at it," Leona said.

"I've been told I am." Jill supposed if Leona wanted to talk about whatever was bothering her, she'd make the first move.

It didn't take long. "You're right. Someone was staring at me, not in a good way. That's why I came out here."

"Felton," Jill said.

Leona gave her a sideways look. "You are good." She sighed. "Felton and I have some history."

"Ah." Jill left it at that. She was assuming that something unpleasant had happened. It was up to Leona whether she wanted to share that.

Silence stretched for a moment. The look on Leona's face said she was debating whether to provide more details. Then she shook her head. "I'd rather not talk about it."

"That's fine. It's your business. By the way, that's a beautiful dress."

The actress smiled. "Thanks. My little black dress, the one I wear to parties. It's always useful to have a black dress."

"I don't have one," Jill said. She smoothed the full skirt of her silk organza print. "This is what I have for dress-up. Blue is my favorite color."

"It's a good color on you," Leona said. "You look lovely."

"Both of you do. Two lovely ladies." Charles Bosworth, in full mellifluous voice, saluted them with the glass of red wine he carried. "Have you tried this cabernet? It's quite good. I had a feeling our producer would have a good cellar."

Jill had a feeling it wasn't his first glass. His broad florid face was even redder than usual.

"I wonder how long I have to stay before I can get out of here," Leona said.

"Oh, we have to stay," Bosworth told her. "We have to be polite to Stu Felton."

Leona frowned. "I don't have to. I have no intention of being polite to him."

"Of course you do, my dear," he said. "If the rumors are true that Peter Vesey is leaving Global, Felton now holds the purse strings. My next picture is with Global and so is yours, I believe.

Now, now, Leona, it doesn't take much to be nice to the man. Just give him a smile and flash some leg."

Leona glared at him, offended. "If you'll excuse me." She turned and headed for the living room. Jill followed. Leona looked around the room. "I see that Neal Preston has already left. Smart man."

"Last time I saw him, he was talking with our hostess," Jill said.

"Probably saying good-bye. Neal hates these things." Leona turned as one of the crew members hailed her.

Jill handed her wineglass to a maid who was passing by with a tray. "Could you please direct me to the bathroom?"

"Yes, ma'am. The guest bath is down that hallway and then to your right. It's just past a long table. You can't miss it."

"Thanks." Jill headed out of the living room and down the hallway. Here were the display cases Tidsy had mentioned, four in all, two each arranged on either side of the hall. All the cases were different, one constructed with Shaker simplicity, another in the Mission style. Both of these had square corners. The other two had bow fronts, crafted in more traditional styles such as Chippendale or Sheraton. All of the cases had glass on three sides, the better to display the contents.

Jill slowed her steps, examining the items inside. Tidsy was right, Adelaide Collier had quite a collection. Jill had once heard an antique collector refer to these items as "smalls," and indeed they were. Most of them would have fit in the palm of her hand. Here were the compacts and vanity cases, mixed in with cigarette cases and pillboxes, many of them silver or enameled. The next pair of cases displayed the snuffboxes. Some were quite plain and others ornate. Jill leaned forward and admired an oval-shaped box about two inches long, made of gold set off with dark blue enamel. On the lid was a miniature of a woman, ringed by diamonds.

She looked up as someone came out of a room farther down the hallway. It was Eve Stillman. "Looking for the bathroom? It's right here."

"Thanks," Jill said. "Are you enjoying the party?"

Eve smiled. "Let's say I'm enjoying the excellent food and beverages." She continued down the hallway.

Jill turned to her right and entered the small room, a half bath with a toilet and sink, its walls decorated with pale green wallpaper that complemented the darker green hand towels. Inside, she shut and locked the door. When she was finished, she came outside, intending to head back to the living room. But she lingered. While she had looked at the display cases earlier, she hadn't really examined the paintings in the hallway. Now she did, mindful of what Tidsy had said about Dewitt Collier's collection. Her eye was caught by one in particular, a still life, one of those depictions of inanimate objects such as flowers, fruit, and other food items, including dead game animals. The one she was looking at had the dark background and meticulous detail she associated with the Dutch painters. This painting was at the end of the hall, next to a door that was slightly ajar.

The library, Jill thought. Tidsy told me to take a look at the library.

Curious, she pushed open the door. Two walls held shelves with books. A closed rolltop desk stood in one corner, with a wooden chair on casters. A red-and-blue Oriental carpet covered the polished wood floor. In the middle of the room was a comfortable-looking sofa upholstered in brown leather. Between this and a matching chair was a table holding what looked like a Tiffany lamp. It had a bronze base and the glass shade was green at the top, with a lower rim decorated by dragonflies with blue wings. Given the amount of wealth on display in the Collier house, it was probably an original. She leaned over and peered at the lamp. Sure enough, she saw a stamped legend on the base, reading TIFFANY STUDIOS NEW YORK.

She looked up, taking in the paintings on the wall. She counted eight of them, landscapes, portraits and a couple more still lifes. She walked to the nearest painting and examined it. It showed an untidy kitchen, with four women crowded together as they prepared a meal. A ginger cat sat on the end of a wooden table. Below this, a black-and-white dog was eating food that had been dropped on the littered floor. The palette was one of bronze, red, orange and yellow, with golden light coming through a window, washing over the domestic scene.

"Dutch," she said, almost to herself.

"Correct." The voice came from behind her. She turned and saw Dewitt Collier standing in the doorway. He stepped into the room.

"Sorry, I didn't mean to intrude."

"Tell me, Miss McLeod, do you like art?"

"Very much," she said. "I enjoy visiting museums. The de Young and the Legion of Honor here in San Francisco. And I've been to the Met in New York City and the National Gallery in Washington. I took several art history classes when I was in college."

"Are you educated enough to recognize some of these paintings?"

"Well..." She drew out the word, then looked around her. "Dutch, as I said earlier. The Dutch Golden Age. The time of Rembrandt and Vermeer."

"Dutch Golden Age. I really like the period. As you say, among the most famous artists of that era are Rembrandt and Vermeer." His hazel eyes took on an avaricious gleam as he mentioned the two artists. "I'd do anything to get my hands on a painting by either of them. I almost had a Rembrandt earlier this year. But I was outbid at the last minute." He paused. "I do have a good representation of the era here. This painting you were looking at, the kitchen scene, is by Jan Steen. That portrait over there, the man with the hat, is by Frans Hals. The still life by the window was painted by Willem Kalf. And this one is quite a find." He indicated another still life, showing a lush arrangement of roses and poppies, the colors vivid pink and orange against the green foliage. "This is by Rachel Ruysch, one of the few women painters who was famous while she was still alive. I have another painting of hers, and a landscape by Pieter Bruegel the Elder. They're both upstairs. Would you like to see them?"

Jill was torn, wanting to see the paintings but not at all sure she wanted to go up to the private areas of the house. She was saved from making that decision when Tidsy appeared in the doorway. "Dewitt. So this is where you disappeared to. Showing off your art collection? Watch out, Jill. He'll talk your ear off about his paintings."

He smiled. "Of course. I'm quite proud of my collection."

"It's lovely," Jill said. "I haven't seen this many Dutch paintings outside of a museum."

"At least he displays them," Tidsy said. "I know of some collectors who keep the stuff locked away so that they're the only ones who look at them."

"How do you two know each other?" he asked, looking from Tidsy to Jill.

"We met on the train," Jill said.

"And Jill and I have been getting up to no good ever since." Tidsy walked over and put her hand on Collier's arm. "You need to come out to the living room and rescue Adelaide. That guy from Wells Fargo—"

"Oh, him." Collier shook his head. "He's such a bore. I invited him just to fulfill an obligation." He followed Tidsy out of the library. Jill lingered. She wanted one last look at the paintings, especially the still life by Rachel Ruysch. It was fascinating to see a painting of such antiquity by a woman artist.

Having looked her fill, she headed for the library door. Collier hadn't closed it all the way, and as she reached for the knob, she saw Wade Ratliff, coming out of the guest bathroom. He didn't see her. He started down the hallway, then he stopped in front of one of the display cases containing snuffboxes. He leaned closer, examining the boxes on the shelves, just as Jill had done earlier. Then he reached for the handle of the display case. Surely it's locked, Jill thought. But it wasn't. As she watched, Wade jiggled the handle and the case opened. He reached inside and took one of the boxes from the middle shelf. He stood for a moment holding the box in his hand, then he held it up to the light, looking at it from all angles. Jill could see that it was the one she'd been admiring, gold set off with dark blue enamel and, on the lid, a miniature of a woman, ringed by diamonds. Wade opened the lid and sniffed at the interior, as though searching for some residue of tobacco. Then, with a glance in either direction down the hall, he pocketed the snuffbox. Before closing the display case, he moved the other boxes on the shelf, to disguise the fact that one was missing. Then he turned and walked down the hallway.

He stole it! Jill thought. Just like that, as bold as you please. If she hadn't seen it with her own eyes, she wouldn't have believed it.

She went out to the hallway. When she reached the living room, Jill looked around for Tidsy. There she was, in the doorway leading out to the terrace, talking with Charles Bosworth. Jill walked over to join them. Bosworth nodded in greeting, then excused himself and headed for the bar.

"I have to talk with you," Jill said. "In private."

Tidsy nodded and downed the rest of the Scotch in her glass. She handed the glass off to a passing maid, then steered Jill out onto the terrace. People were clustered at the railing, or sitting in chairs around an outdoor table. Tidsy led the way to a corner where a big planter held bright yellow chrysanthemums.

"What's going on?" Tidsy asked.

"I was coming out of the library just a few minutes ago," Jill said. "And I saw a man help himself to one of Mrs. Collier's snuffboxes. He just opened the door, took it out and put it in his pocket."

Tidsy frowned. "I thought the cases were locked. Those doodads are worth a pile of money."

"I thought so, too, but he jiggled the handle and it opened. Maybe the lock didn't engage properly."

"He. So it was a man. Who was it?"

Jill looked to her right. Wade Ratliff was visible in the doorway that led into the living room. He was smoking a cigarette, using it to punctuate his words as he talked with Bert Gallagher.

"Wade Ratliff, the screenwriter. That's him, standing with Bert Gallagher. He's more than just the writer, though. He's a co-producer, along with Drake Baldwin and Dewitt Collier."

"And a very good friend of Drake, if I'm not mistaken. The nerve of the guy," Tidsy said, her eyes flashing. "If it was up to me I'd call the cops on the son of a bitch. Or plant the toe of my high heel in his backside. But it's not up to me. Addie would hate any kind of blow-up or scandal. She wants to be the upper-crust San Francisco society matron and it wouldn't do to have the cops show up at this soirée. The wrong kind of publicity for Dewitt and this celluloid epic he's investing in. So the case of the purloined snuffbox has to be handled with care. The screenwriter, huh. I'll speak to Addie. She can talk with her director nephew and tell him to put the screws to the screenwriter. One way or the other, the snuffbox will be returned."

"I certainly hope so."

Tidsy stared at Wade as she took a cigarette from her case and lit it. "I wonder if this Wade character makes a habit of helping himself to things that don't belong to him."

"I was wondering the same thing," Jill said slowly. "I met Mike for dinner the other night, over at Jack London Square. We saw Wade there, just before we went into the restaurant. It turns out they were in the same unit during World War Two. And Mike doesn't like him, I could tell. He didn't say why and I didn't push it. But now I'm definitely going to ask him about it, as soon as possible."

"Let me know what he says," Tidsy said. "Now I'm curious. Let's go back inside. I need another drink."

They left the terrace. Once inside, they walked toward the bar. "Anything for you?" Tidsy asked as the bartender poured her another Scotch.

Jill shook her head. "I'll pass."

They stepped away from the bar as Wade Ratliff came up and asked for a refill. Tidsy gave the screenwriter a withering look, but he didn't notice. Then he moved away, toward the front of the living room, where he joined a group of crew members.

Dewitt Collier walked up just then, and the bartender replaced his empty glass with a full one. "And how are you lovely ladies? I hope you're having a good time."

"Excellent party." Tidsy saluted him with her glass and downed some Scotch.

"Good, good. I think it's turning out well." Collier tipped back his glass. Then he turned as one of the maids tapped him on the shoulder and said something Jill couldn't hear. "Now? Oh, all right, I'll take the call in the library." He excused himself and walked down the hallway.

Jill looked at the clock on the Colliers' mantel. She'd stayed at the party longer than she had intended. Time to go home. But before she got on the road, she would pay another visit to the bathroom. She headed down the hallway once again.

She was coming out of the lavatory when she heard Dewitt Collier's voice. He must still be on the phone, she thought. Once again the door was ajar and she glimpsed Collier standing at his desk, then he disappeared from view. "Of course I want to see it, as soon as possible." He paused. "No, no, Sunday won't work. Adelaide and I have plans during the day and a dinner engagement. It will have to be Monday. That makes more sense. I'm going to be in the neighborhood anyway." He paused again. "I know it's not ideal, but it can't be helped. We'll make it work."

I really shouldn't be listening, Jill thought. I've turned into such an eavesdropper.

As the library door opened wider, she slipped back into the bathroom so Collier wouldn't see her. As she closed the bathroom door, she glimpsed her host as he stepped out of the library and walked toward the living room. Now it was safe. She left the bathroom and then she froze. She'd heard another sound. Was there someone else in the library? Had Collier been talking on the phone? Or to a person, right there in the room with him?

She hurried down the hallway, past the display cases, and rejoined the people milling around the living room. The party was pleasant—on the surface. But the undercurrents were strong. Keeping up with everything that was going on was tiring. It looked as though Charles Bosworth had succeeded in getting Felton's attention, though. The two men were standing near the bar, talking. Every now and then, Felton turned, his eyes darting around the room, as though he was looking for someone. He stopped for a moment and stared, hard, at Wade Ratliff. The screenwriter was in another corner of the living room, where the hallway branched off. As he glanced at the display cases, Jill wondered if he was looking for another opportunity to steal something. She said so to Tidsy.

"I know that's the guy with light fingers," Tidsy said. "Don't worry about that. Before I leave, I'll talk with Addie and alert her to the wandering snuffbox. Call me tomorrow for an update."

"I will. And now I'd better say my good-byes to our hosts."

Jill saw Dewitt Collier at the bar with Felton and Bosworth. She didn't want to interrupt their conversation. However, Adelaide Collier stood near the piano, talking with Leona Alexander. Jill walked over and said, "Mrs. Collier, I'm leaving, and I want to thank you for a lovely afternoon."

"Thanks for coming, Miss McLeod. I enjoyed meeting you." She laughed. "I had no idea you and Tidsy were such good friends."

"Tidsy is a wonderful friend."

Adelaide nodded. "She is. The best."

Leona Alexander took Adelaide's hand. "I have to be on my way, too. A lovely party, thanks." Then she turned and took Jill's arm. "I'll walk out with you, Jill." As the two women headed down the staircase to the ground level, Leona lowered her voice and added, "I want to get away while Stu Felton is otherwise occupied. So far I've been successful at avoiding him, but I'm afraid he might try to corner me while I'm alone."

"I'll walk you to your car." Jill collected her shawl from the coat rack. Leona did the same, slipping her arms into a soft black jacket that covered her bare shoulders. They left the house and headed down the driveway to the street.

"Thanks, Jill." Leona pointed to her right. "It's that Chevy Bel Air across the street, the blue one with the white top."

The two women crossed Broadway. Leona took a set of keys from her small purse and unlocked the Chevrolet, sliding under the steering wheel. She started the engine.

"Enjoy the rest of your weekend," Jill said. "I'll see you on Monday."

She watched as Leona pulled out of the parking space and headed down Broadway. Then she crossed back over to the Colliers' side of the street. When she reached the sidewalk, she heard someone calling her name. When she turned, Stuart Felton was walking down the driveway toward her.

"You and Miss Alexander left together," the studio executive snapped. "Where is she? I have to talk with her."

Jill smiled and shrugged. "She just left."

Felton leaned toward Jill, shoulders hunched, an intense expression in his pale eyes. "Did she say where she was going? It's

really important that I talk with her. There's something she and I
have to discuss."

Jill found herself backing away from the studio executive. "No,
I'm sorry. I don't know where she was going." Jill assumed Leona
was going back to the hotel in Niles, but she didn't say so. During
the past hour or so, the actress had done everything she could to
avoid Felton, so the less said, the better.

Felton mumbled something that might have been "Thank
you," but Jill doubted it. He turned abruptly and left. He walked
up the street to a Cadillac Fleetwood sedan, metallic green with
a white top. He got in, started the engine, pulled out and made a
U-turn, driving down Broadway.

Well, that was interesting. Jill recalled what Leona had said
about having some history with Felton. She had seemed quite
irritated at Bosworth's suggestion that she "flash some leg" at the
studio executive.

Was that what happened between Leona and Stuart Felton?
Or was it that the man had tried to force his attentions on
Leona? Had he made a pass at her, the way he had earlier with
Tidsy? She remembered what she'd heard Wade say, implying
that Leona had sometimes provided sexual favors in exchange
for career-enhancing parts. But she couldn't see Leona doing that.
Maybe Felton had tried something and she had rebuffed him, just
as Tidsy had. If that was the case, Felton could damage Leona's
career. No wonder she wasn't happy to be in the same room with
the man.

Jill took the car keys from her purse and walked down Broadway to Broderick Street, where she had parked the Ford. She drove
down Broadway and crossed Van Ness Avenue. Ahead of her, at
Polk Street, a light flashed yellow and then red. She stopped and
then glanced to her right.

Was that Neal Preston? Yes, it was. He had indeed left the
party early. Now he stood in the doorway of a corner bar, and he
was with the same young man that he had been with on Thursday evening, when Jill had seen him coming out of Heinhold's
saloon at Jack London Square. Jill recognized the other man by his
white-blond hair, which stood out against the dark blue tile on the

bar's exterior wall. And it was plain that the two men were more that friends. As Jill watched, Neal put his arms around the young man and then leaned in to kiss him.

The light had changed and the driver of the car behind Jill honked his horn, impatient for her to move through the intersection. She made her way through the streets of downtown San Francisco, heading for the approach to the Bay Bridge, and thinking about what she'd seen.

The cowboy star was a homosexual. She wasn't shocked. After two and a half years as a Zephyrette, she had seen all sorts of people in all sorts of situations, such as the male couple who had traveled together in the drawing room of the dome-observation car on a recent run from Chicago to the Bay Area. And earlier this year, there were two women who had appeared to be in a relationship.

It wasn't Jill's place to make judgments about passengers. But she was sure that Hollywood wasn't as forgiving, particularly for an actor who made Westerns. No wonder Neal Preston looked at the studio executive with trepidation. He had something to hide.

Chapter Nine ———————————

JILL WOKE THE NEXT MORNING, lying on her side, with her cat, Sophie, tucked into the small of her back. She shifted position and propped herself up on one elbow. Sophie sat up and stretched, the way cats do. Then she moved to Jill's pillow and settled in for another snooze.

It was nearly eight, according to the clock on Jill's nightstand. It felt good to sleep in this morning, since she'd been getting up so early to go to work on the movie set. It looked like a nice day, judging from the sunshine coming through the white eyelet cotton curtains on her bedroom window.

The house was quiet. Normally on a Sunday morning, her mother would be down in the kitchen, fixing a big breakfast for the family. But Amos and Lora McLeod were still out of town, not due back until the middle of the week. Her sister, Lucy, who'd lived at home until her marriage, was off on a Hawaiian honeymoon with her new husband. And Jill's younger brother, Drew, was probably still asleep. He had never been much of an early riser and now that he was playing gigs with his band, late mornings were the rule. The band had played last night at a club in San Francisco, and she hadn't heard him come in, though she guessed it was early this morning.

Jill sat up and swung her legs off the bed and to the floor. Time to get up. She'd had some trouble getting to sleep last night, thinking about what she'd seen and heard at the party. It was time she had a talk with Mike about Wade Ratliff.

After a shower, she dressed in dungarees and a cotton blouse.

Jill made her bed, dislodging the calico cat from her warm nest on the pillow. Sophie grumbled in protest and retreated to the nightstand where she nearly knocked over the purple African violet next to the clock.

"What a fussbudget you are." Jill rescued the plant and straightened the rose-colored chenille bedspread on her white wrought iron single bed. The cat meowed and jumped down from the nightstand, following her downstairs. In the kitchen, she stood expectantly at her food bowl as Jill fed her and refreshed her water.

With the cat attended to, Jill added water to the stainless steel GE percolator on the kitchen counter, then opened the nearby can of Maxwell House coffee, scooped grounds into the basket and plugged in the appliance. As the coffee perked, she took a loaf of bread from the breadbox and put two slices in the toaster. The butter was already on the counter. Her mother had made jam during the summer, both peach and apricot. There was an open jar of peach jam in the refrigerator. She took that out, along with a bottle of cream for her coffee.

Reaching for a mug from the nearby rack, she poured her first cup of coffee and doctored it with cream, then buttered the toast that had popped up from the toaster. A small breakfast, but that's all she wanted. She ate it sitting at the kitchen table, which was covered with utilitarian oilcloth, a colorful print of pears and cherries. When she was done, she topped off her coffee, stirred in more cream and carried the mug to the living room. Then she retrieved the newspapers from the front porch. Sophie joined her on the sofa, curling up for a post-breakfast nap.

The McLeods took three local newspapers—the *San Francisco Chronicle*, the *San Francisco Examiner*, and the *Oakland Tribune*. The headlines and lead stories were all about Earl Warren, the governor of California. President Eisenhower had appointed him to the Supreme Court, to fill a vacancy left by the recent death of the chief justice. The Key System strike had been settled, which was good news. The privately owned transit company ran buses all over the East Bay. People in many communities relied on the system to get where they were going, particularly to work. The carmen had been on strike since July and the lack of public transit during that time period had put more cars on the streets as people sought alternative transportation. And in the sports section, the news was all about the World Series.

Jill skimmed the first paragraph of an article concerning a dispute about the repatriation of prisoners of war from the war in Korea. With the armistice of last summer, that conflict had come to an end. But reading anything about Korea triggered feelings of loss. Her fiancé, Steve, had been killed in that war. Most of the time she thought she had moved on from those old plans to be a wife, mother and schoolteacher. Still, seeing anything about Korea in the headlines always made her wonder about what might have been.

Jill put aside the *Tribune* and turned to the *Chronicle*. After reading the front section, she got up to fetch another cup of coffee. She glanced at the clock on the mantel and decided to call Mike first. The downstairs phone extension was on a narrow table in the front hallway. She picked up the receiver and dialed Mike's number. "I hope I didn't wake you."

"No, I'm up. I'm on my second cup of coffee. How was that party yesterday?"

"That's why I called you. Come over and I'll fix lunch. You can tell me about your field trip and I'll tell you about the party."

He laughed. "Why do I have the feeling there's more to it than that?"

"You read me very well," she said with a chuckle. "Yes, I do want to discuss something with you and I'd rather do it in person. Come over and we'll have a picnic in the backyard."

"All right. I'll be there around noon."

Jill's next call was to Tidsy. After they'd exchanged good-morning greetings, she asked, "Did you talk with Adelaide Collier?"

"I did. She was shocked that one of her guests would steal something. As we left it, she was planning to give her nephew an earful, so she can get the snuffbox back from the light-fingered screenwriter. What about that conversation you were going to have with Mike, about why he doesn't like Wade? Must have something to do with their time together in the Army."

"Mike's coming over for lunch. I'll talk with him then. When I have more information, I'll call you."

"I look forward to the next installment in this drama," Tidsy said.

They ended the call and Jill replaced the receiver. She heard footsteps coming down the stairs and looked up to see Drew, barefoot and clad in plaid pajama bottoms and a white T-shirt.

"Is there coffee?" His voice sounded as bleary as he looked.

"In the percolator," she told him. "How was your gig last night?"

"I'll tell you after I've had coffee." He shambled down the hall and into the kitchen, crossing the checked linoleum floor to the counter where the percolator sat. He grabbed a mug and filled it to the brim. After his first sip, he closed his eyes and said, "That's more like it." He pulled out one of the kitchen chairs and sat down, propping his feet on the rungs of the next chair. "The gig was great. That place in the Fillmore, they want us to come back."

"Glad to hear it." Jill poured herself another cup. "Mike's coming over for lunch. As soon as I finish reading the paper, I'm going to make a batch of cookies. Maybe chocolate chip."

"Definitely chocolate chip. I guess I'll go shower." Drew got to his feet and left the kitchen, heading back upstairs with coffee in hand.

Jill carried her coffee back to the living room and spent the next hour reading the rest of the Sunday newspapers. Then she returned to the kitchen. I'll make sun tea, she thought. She dropped tea bags into a clear glass pitcher and filled it with water, then covered it with a paper towel. She carried it outside and set it on the patio table. Over the next few hours, the warm sun would slowly steep the tea into a mellow-tasting brew.

Back in the kitchen, she took a well-used cookbook from a shelf. She turned to a favorite cookie recipe and set the book on the counter, then took the utensils and ingredients she needed to make cookies. She stood at the counter and measured flour and sugar, then creamed the butter with the stand mixer.

By that time, Drew had come back downstairs and was rummaging through the refrigerator, in search of breakfast. He put bread into the toaster, then grabbed the bag of semi-sweet choco-late chips and shook out a few, tossing them into his mouth. Jill slapped his hand as he reached for another handful. "If you eat all of them, there won't be any left for the cookies." She moved the bag of chips out of reach and added some to her dough mixture. Drew grinned, unrepentant, as he slathered his toast with butter and jam. He sat down at the kitchen table to eat.

Jill used a spoon to scoop dough onto a baking sheet and put it in the oven, setting the timer. When the chime sounded a short time later, she removed the first batch from the oven. Drew appeared again, lured by the enticing smell. He set his coffee mug on the counter and made a beeline for the cookies cooling on a trivet.

"Careful, they're hot," she said.

"Doesn't matter to me." He used a spatula to filch a cookie from the sheet. Melted chocolate oozed onto his hand. "Ouch!"

"You get no sympathy from me."

Jill put the second batch of cookies into the oven. She looked out the kitchen window to the backyard, where the apple tree was heavy with fruit. It was a Rome Beauty, the apples red with streaks of green. Windfalls littered the grass.

Apple pie, she thought. That sounded good. Maybe she'd make one for tonight, to go with the chicken she'd taken out of the freezer earlier. She saw splashes of red and yellow in the garden at the back of the yard. Good. Even though it was October, that meant there were still tomatoes ripening amid the green foliage, along with bell peppers and squash.

She headed out the back door, carrying a colander. It was a beautiful sunny day, with a cloudless blue sky above and that bright light she associated with autumn in the Bay Area. A slight breeze stirred the branches of the apple tree. She heard the growl of a lawnmower from a nearby yard, overlaying the sound of chil-dren playing. A dog barked somewhere in the distance. The rose bushes that ranged along the redwood fences on either side of the yard, underplanted with succulents, still held a few flowers. The chrysanthemums were putting on a show, loaded with blooms of yellow, bronze and white. Somewhere in the apple tree a bird sang, and she saw a blue jay swoop down, landing on a telephone wire. A squirrel scampered along the back fence, then stopped, its tail twitching. Then it resumed its journey, leaping from the fence onto the trunk of the oak tree in the back corner of the yard.

Jill set the colander on the patio table and grabbed two pails, heading into the yard. She picked up apples, putting the usable fruit into one pail. The apples that had been pecked by birds or munched on by squirrels and bugs went into the other. Then she retrieved the colander and walked back to the garden to pick tomatoes. She also found a few ripe peppers and yellow crook-neck squash. That would do for dinner this evening. And the apples would go with the impromptu lunch she was planning. She dumped the unusable apples into the compost pile and carried the pail and colander into the house. She rinsed the apples in the kitchen sink and transferred the fruit to a large bowl.

Then she turned her attention to lunch. There was ham in the refrigerator, as well as cheddar and swiss cheeses. Jill constructed sandwiches, putting them on a platter. She added olives and pickles as well as a bowl of corn chips, and sliced some apples and a few tomatoes. Might as well make lemonade to go with the tea. There was a bowl of lemons on the counter and she reached for it.

Half an hour later, the doorbell rang. She heard Drew open the front door and call, "It's Mike."

"I'll be right there." Jill rinsed her hands at the sink and headed for the front hallway. She hugged Mike. "Thanks for coming over. I've got sandwiches and other goodies. Including chocolate chip cookies, if we can keep my brother away from them."

"You could leave some for me," Drew said as he stretched out on the sofa with the newspaper.

"I did. I left a plate with sandwiches and cookies in the kitchen."

Jill led the way to the kitchen, where she and Mike put their repast on a big tray. Mike carried the food out the back door to the patio. Jill followed with the pitcher of lemonade and two glasses filled with ice. The sun tea had brewed to a deep golden brown. They set everything on the round table. "Tea or lemonade?" she asked.

"I'll take lemonade."

Jill filled his glass and poured tea for herself. They pulled up two metal lawn chairs and settled in. Mike bit into a ham sandwich and they ate in companionable silence, until Jill asked him about yesterday's field trip to Mount Diablo, some thirty miles to the east, in Contra Costa County. The peak, over 3,800 feet above sea level, was one of the three tallest mountains in the Bay Area, along with Mount Tamalpais in Marin County and Mount Hamilton near San Jose. Compared to the mountains in Colorado, where Jill grew up, Mount Diablo was small. But for this region, it was tall enough. Long ago, numerous Indian tribes had lived in the countryside around the base of the mountain, notably the Ohlone, the Miwok and the Yokuts tribes. The Spanish had later called the peak *Diablo*, meaning devil.

As a geology student at Cal, Mike's interest was the mountain itself. "It was great. A beautiful clear day. We could see all the way to the Sierra Nevada. Mount Lassen was just barely visible," he added, mentioning the southernmost peak in the Cascade chain, a volcano that had erupted in 1915. "That's about a hundred and eighty miles north." He paused for another bite of his sandwich, washed it down with lemonade and refilled his glass. "Diablo is kind of an anomaly. It was created by compression and uplift. It's between a couple of earthquake faults and it's still growing."

"I didn't know that." Jill reached for a dill pickle. "Not by much, surely."

"Three to five millimeters a year, that's what the professor said. Uplift and erosion have exposed the ancient rocks, from the Jurassic and Cretaceous ages. And of course, there's sandstone, with lots of fossilized seashells. Sandstone, chert, basalt and shale."

"Was it ever a volcano? It looks like it, from the shape."

Mike shook his head. "Nope. I agree, it looks like it. It's a double pyramid." He finished his sandwich and reached for another. "I'm sure that's more than you wanted to know about the mountain. Tell me about the party."

"It was fun," Jill said, deciding to keep the description light and airy. At least before she got into the serious stuff. "I enjoyed myself more than I thought I would. Mr. Collier is a producer, one of several, I think. And it turns out that Mrs. Collier is the director's aunt."

"That's keeping it all in the family." Mike popped a couple of olives in his mouth.

"The Colliers have a big fancy house at the top of Broadway. From the terrace there's a great view of the Golden Gate Bridge. All the women were in their best outfits. I felt a bit dowdy when I saw Leona Alexander's dress. Very chic. So was Mrs. Collier's dress. Well, I know that women's fashion means as much to you as sandstone and chert do to me." She smiled. "They did have all sorts of fancy food, including caviar. Stuffed mushrooms and that runny French cheese. Lots of wine and an open bar." She paused and took a slice of plain old cheddar, layering it on an apple slice. "Tidsy was there, by the way. It turns out she knows Mrs. Collier."

Mike laughed, grabbing a handful of corn chips. "Tidsy knows everyone."

"I gather from what she said that she and Mrs. Collier met during the war. When Tidsy was a government girl. Which in Tidsy's case probably means more than typing and filing."

"I'm sure it does," Mike said. "I'll bet she was a spy, or something clandestine."

"You're probably right. One of these days I'm going to ask her about it."

"You said the party was for some guy from Hollywood, right?"

Jill nodded. "His name's Stuart Felton. He's an executive with Global Studios. From what I've learned, he is one of the people who is in charge of the money. He's been asking for lots of changes in the script and I've heard he doesn't like location shooting, thinks it's too expensive. He called, or someone from his office did, on Thursday, to say he was coming up here and that he would be on the set tomorrow morning. That news seemed to upset everyone. The party was intended to get on Felton's good side. Though I have reason to believe he doesn't have one. He seemed very disagreeable and he made a lot of people uncomfortable. Especially a couple of the actors." She paused, thinking of the way Leona Alexander and Neal Preston had reacted to the man. "He actually made a pass at Tidsy. Of course, she shut him down."

Mike laughed. "I'll bet she did. I would have paid money to see that." He had finished his second sandwich. Now he wiped his hands and swallowed more lemonade. "Are you going to tell me why you wanted to have this conversation today?"

She paused, reached for a cookie and broke it in half. "You read me very well."

"Not all the time, but I'm getting there. Something happened, right?"

"I want you to tell me about Wade Ratliff. You don't like him. I want to know why. Was it something that happened while you were in the Army?"

Mike frowned. "Why are you asking?"

"The Colliers have quite an art collection. There are paintings everywhere. Mr. Collier particularly likes Dutch paintings. I saw several of those in his library. And Mrs. Collier collects small valuable things, like snuffboxes. She has them arranged in cases all down the main hallway. I assumed the cases were locked. I guess they're supposed to be. Anyway, I was in the library, looking at the paintings. I started to leave, and I saw Wade in the hallway. I thought he was just looking at the boxes, but he jiggled the handle of one case and it opened. He took a box and put it in his pocket. Then he closed the door and walked away." Jill paused and took a sip of iced tea. "I told Tidsy. She said she'd tell Mrs. Collier. She is going to talk with her nephew, the director, and he'll talk with Wade, hopefully to get him to return the snuffbox. If that doesn't work, I don't know what will happen."

Mike didn't say anything at first. He rattled the ice cubes in his glass and then reached for the pitcher, topping off his lemonade. As the silence stretched, Jill heard music. Drew must have gone back upstairs to his room. He was playing records on his hi-fi, Bessie Smith singing "St. Louis Blues."

"You've asked me about my experiences during the war," Mike said finally. "So far I haven't wanted to talk about it." Nor did he want to see movies that dealt with the war. Two of them had been released this past summer, *Stalag 17* and *From Here to Eternity*. When Jill suggested seeing them, Mike demurred.

"I understand," Jill said. "A lot of people don't. And if you don't want to say anything now, that's fine. I just thought you could tell me something about Wade."

"I can. And I will. Let me give you some background first. Call it the broad overview of my war." He took a sip from his glass, then began his story. "I was with the 323rd Bombardment Group. First with the Eighth Army Air Force and later with the Ninth. We flew medium bombers, B-26 Martin Marauders. We attacked airfields, industrial sites, military installations. Targets all over France, Belgium and Holland, especially in February of 1944. That was a big campaign against the Luftwaffe and the German aircraft industry. We attacked a lot of coastal defenses and airfields in France right before D-Day, and on June sixth we were bombing roads and coastal batteries. So aerial barrage, that's what we did. I'm getting ahead of myself, though."

Mike reached for a cookie and broke it in half, then in fourths. Then he continued. "I did my training here in the States, of course. Then I shipped out for England in 1943. The first base I was at was Horham. That's in Suffolk. Then we went to Earls Colne, in Essex. Both of them were northeast of London. A couple of months after D-Day, in August of 1944, the group moved to France. We were at several bases there." His eyes took on a faraway look as he recited the names. "First we were at a place called Lessay in Normandy. We were there for a month. Then a few weeks at Chartres, southwest of Paris. I was able to visit the cathedral. In the middle of October we went to Laon-Athies. It was northeast of Paris and it had been a Luftwaffe airfield. We were there through January of 1945, flying missions during the Battle of the Bulge. We were hitting transportation installations, to prevent the Germans from bringing up reinforcements. After that we flew missions over the Ruhr and attacked German communications stations. In February we moved to Denain. It was farther north, closer to Calais. We ended combat operations in April. In May, right after V-E day, we moved to Germany."

He paused, this time so long that Jill wasn't sure he'd start talking again. "We were in Germany to help with disarmament, that's what they called it. We were based in Gablingen. It's north of a town called Augsberg, which is northeast of Munich. Gablingen had been a Luftwaffe training base. There was also a plant where the Germans built Messerschmitts, and tested them. We found out later that the plant was built with slave labor from Dachau."

His face turned somber at the mention of the infamous concentration camp located near Munich, one of hundreds scattered all over Germany and occupied Europe. Jill had seen the photos taken after liberation, disturbing images that would stay with her for the rest of her life.

"Did you see the camp?" she asked.

Mike shook his head. "I didn't. The pictures I saw were enough. A guy I went to high school with, he was with the 42nd Infantry Division. That's one of the units that liberated Dachau. When I saw him in Germany, later that year, he told me stories— I can't even imagine. He said the pictures, the ones the newspapers decided they could print, just told part of the story. The reality was much worse. All those people, murdered like that." He took a deep breath. "I was a pilot, dropping bombs. I know the things I did during the war caused deaths on the ground."

"But it was war," Jill said, putting her hand on his arm.

"I know. The war did all sorts of things to people." He hesitated and took a drink from his glass. "Anyway, you want to know about Wade Ratliff. He joined the group when we were at Earls Colne. We were thrown together a lot. I didn't much like the guy from the minute I met him. There was something about him that seemed off. I don't know if you've noticed, but he can't keep still. He's always moving. I wondered if there was a reason for it. Some of the guys, well, I heard about drugs that some of the pilots and airmen used."

Jill's eyes widened in surprise. "You think Wade was using drugs?" It was possible, she supposed. She'd noticed his energy, the fact that he always seemed to be moving.

"I don't know for certain," Mike said. "But I do know one thing for sure. Wade Ratliff is a thief."

"You saw him take something?" Jill asked, startled. "When? And where?"

Mike nodded. "Yeah. I saw him take things. Usually small things. The first couple of times, I wondered if it was some sort of compulsion. Like maybe he'd see an opportunity and just take something."

"Little things," Jill said. "Like that snuffbox."

"Easy to conceal and transport. It wasn't only little shiny things, though. Once, when we were in France, another officer had a stash of poker winnings. He kept some of the money in a tobacco tin, tucked under his mattress in his quarters. The money went missing. I don't know for sure what happened, or how. But I'd seen Wade in the vicinity. Seeing him there wasn't enough to accuse him of anything. But I had a feeling it was him. No proof of course. And when we were in Germany, I saw him take something from an empty house. It was a little painted miniature. I called him on it, threatened to tell the commanding officer about it. Wade said it was spoils of war. To me, it was outright theft. But he wasn't the only one doing it."

"Did you report him?"

"I was going to." He looked frustrated. "Then the commanding officer was injured, we had to go on a mission, and all my good intentions went by the wayside. I never did tell anyone. Until now."

"This is serious," Jill said.

He nodded. "It is. So when you tell me he took something from your host's house, well, I hope Mrs. Collier is able to get back her snuffbox. There's something else. Have you ever heard about all that art that's missing? When I was in Germany, I met this officer who was an art historian before the war, at one of those big universities in the east. He was in the army, in a special section called Monuments, Fine Arts, and Archives. They called themselves Monuments Men. They were Americans, Brits, French, and guys from other countries. Their job was to protect all those cultural treasures, like art and old buildings. Which was tough, with all the bombing and fighting, especially at the end of the war. Lots of art was destroyed. But the Germans stole plenty. The Nazis looted artwork from all over Europe, just helped themselves and shipped it back to Germany. Many of the pieces have never been recovered. Private collections maybe, or Soviets got the stuff. But our guys found a lot of it."

"That's fascinating," Jill said. "But what does it have to do with Wade?"

"Maybe nothing. But maybe looting, of a different sort. Maybe it wasn't only the Germans who stole art. Right before we left Gablingen, I saw him packing something into his duffel bag. It was wrapped up, small and flat, maybe twelve or fifteen inches square. I don't know what it was. It could have been a book, a big one. Or a tapestry, folded up. Or it could have been a painting. All I know is that it was something Wade didn't want anyone to see. I didn't give it much thought when I first saw Wade slip that package into his bag. It was only after I talked with the guy who was with the Monuments Men that I wondered what Wade was taking back to the States."

Chapter Ten

JILL THOUGHT ABOUT her conversation with Mike as she drove to Niles on Monday morning. After he'd left, she tried calling Tidsy, but there was no answer at her friend's San Francisco apartment. But Mike didn't have much in the way of facts, just suspicions.

She remembered what Wade had said in the conversation she'd overheard on Friday, talking about leverage to use against Felton. "I might have something he wants," that's what he'd said. And he'd mentioned that Felton collected paintings. Was it possible? No, it was too tenuous. Besides, the war had been over for eight years. If Wade had managed to smuggle a painting out of Germany, would he hold onto it this long? Surely he would have sold it by now. What a strange tale this was.

She parked the Ford near the back of the lot next to the warehouse, then got out of the car and stood for a moment in the sun. It was another beautiful fall day, and she was going to spend most of it inside that dark warehouse, a Zephyrette pretending to be a Zephyrette.

At the makeup trailer, she didn't see Nancy, but her middle-aged counterpart, Venita, greeted Jill with a smile. "There you are, hon. I'm ready for you." When Jill settled into the chair, the woman covered her with a cloth and began applying pancake. "I tell you, there must be an outbreak of Monday blues. Everybody I've had in here this morning has been as jumpy as a cat in a roomful of rocking chairs. Leona Alexander snapped at me when I was doing her makeup. Usually she's the sweetest, most agreeable person in the world. She apologized, of course. But I can't imagine what set her off. Neal was kinda grumpy, too. Of course, with him, it's hard to tell. He really is the strong, silent type. Never know what's going on inside his head. But he was definitely off this morning, that's for sure."

Jill listened to Venita talk, thinking, I know why everyone is jumpy. It's because that man Felton is going to be on the set this morning. Just the thought of that is setting everyone on edge.

A few minutes later, Venita set down her brushes and paints and said, "All done, hon. You go knock 'em dead."

"I will," Jill said with a laugh.

In the shared dressing room, she said hello to a couple of the bit players who had roles as train passengers. She took off her blue twill skirt and seersucker blouse and put on her Zephyrette costume.

The scene Jill was in was to be shot on the dome-observation car set. Nancy, the other makeup artist, was there, standing on the sidelines as she applied a powder puff to Neal's nose.

Jill took her place at the rounded end of the car and watched as the set dresser and the property manager arranged small objects on the set. The round tables arranged in front of the chairs held drinks and ashtrays, just as they would on a real observation car. As Jill watched, the set dresser put a pack of cigarettes on one of the tables. He stared at it for a second, then moved it an inch to the right. The man in charge of props put glasses in the recessed holders of three different tables, then poured in strong tea to substitute as whisky. A newspaper was draped over a chair, looking as though it had been discarded by a passenger.

Jill had a few lines to say in this scene, and she was rehearsing them with Ella, a round-faced, comfortably upholstered actress who was playing a wealthy, older passenger. "Miss Casey," Ella said in a snooty-sounding East Coast accent, "I do wish you'd speak to the conductor. That man in the compartment next to mine is impossible."

"I'd be happy to help," Jill said, "if you'll just tell me what's going on."

The actress raised a hand and fluttered it at Jill. "He's getting drunk at all hours, and creating such a disturbance. I've spoken to the porter, to no avail."

"I'll mention it to the conductor," Jill assured her.

Ella broke character and her accent switched to her usual Midwestern tones. "I hate this outfit. This blouse itches like crazy." She tugged at the collar of the white blouse she wore under a severe-looking gray suit. Perched on her head was a garish concoction covered with fabric flowers. "And this hat looks like a fruit salad died on top of my head." She laughed. "Now, why couldn't my character dress like Leona?"

"It is a gorgeous dress," Jill agreed. The dress Leona wore for this scene was a sleek, dark blue sheath, accented with silver beading at the scooped neckline. It was a spectacular fit with the actress's figure and her blond, ice-queen looks. "At least you have a costume. I might as well be on duty aboard the train, in my real-life Zephyrette uniform. Of course, this one was made by the costume designer, not the place where I usually get them." She pinched her costume skirt. "The fabric's different."

"Oh, well," Ella said with a shrug. "Leona's got the figure for that kind of dress, and I don't. The lot of a character actor. I'm just supposed to fill in the background, looking like your average well-heeled matron. With bad taste in hats."

Drake was talking with his lead actors, referring to them by their characters' names. "Dolores is coming down the stairs from the Vista-Dome. I want you to take it slow, you're making an entrance. As soon as you start coming down the stairs, everyone's eyes are on you." Leona nodded and climbed the stairs to the platform that was supposed to represent the dome. Drake turned to Neal. "Stan's coming from the front of the car. You've just had a confrontation with Creswell and you're upset. Now you're looking for Dolores. You want to get her alone and talk with her. But she's been avoiding you. When you round the corner here, she's just starting to come down these stairs. You look up. The two of you lock eyes."

"One quick question." Neal leaned toward Drake, though Jill couldn't hear what he was saying. After they conferred, Neal took his place on the set and Drake sat down in his canvas director's chair.

At the top of the platform, Leona smoothed her skirt, threw her shoulders back and her chin up. She stood motionless, waiting for the cameras to roll. Then her expression changed.

Jill glanced back, at the periphery of the set, and saw why. Stuart Felton was now on the set. The studio executive's face held the same sour expression it had during the party on Saturday. He was accompanied by Dewitt Collier, who looked more cheerful, as though determined to put the best face on the situation. Both men took seats near the cameras. Despite the heat of the Klieg lights beating down on the set, it was as though the temperature of the room had dropped twenty degrees.

What was it about Felton that had everyone on edge? Nobody liked him. He was certainly making everyone nervous.

Drake called for the actors to take their places. The camera began to roll as the clapperboard came down. But things weren't going well. After entering the car and spotting Leona's character on the stairs, Neal was supposed to say, "I've been looking for you. We need to talk, and soon." During the first take, he flubbed his lines. They started over. It happened again. On the third botched take, Drake yelled, "Cut!" He sounded exasperated as he got up from his chair and moved toward the actors. "Let's take five, and try again."

Neal walked off the set, disappearing from view. It's Felton, Jill thought. The studio executive had been staring at the actor through each take. And there was something unpleasant in the gaze he was directing at the leading man. Neal was aware of the scrutiny, and it bothered him.

It was as though Felton was deliberately trying to rattle the actor.

Why? Was he trying to sabotage the production?

Jill knew that Drake and the other producers were concerned about Felton's unexpected trip to the Bay Area, and his visit to the set. Especially with what they'd learned on Friday. Now that Felton was in charge, they've have to dance to his tune. And nobody liked that prospect.

What about Neal Preston, though? His involvement in the production was as an actor. From his behavior today, it was as though he was afraid of Felton. What could he possibly—?

Suddenly she knew. It had to do with what she'd seen on Saturday, after leaving the party, while her car was stopped at a red light: Neal, in the doorway of a corner bar, kissing another man. She guessed that Neal was a homosexual, and that Felton knew it. Neal was afraid of exposure. His public image of the stalwart cowboy actor, or in this picture, the rugged private detective, didn't jibe with his personal life. Jill suspected that could kill his career.

As Jill mulled this over, Leona came down from the platform. She gave Felton a wide berth as she moved off the set, passing below the merciless Klieg lights into a darkened area behind them. A pitcher of water and several glasses were on a nearby table. Leona poured herself a glass of water and took a sip. Now that Neal was off the set, Felton's eyes were on Leona, and it was making the actress uncomfortable as well.

On Saturday, Leona had hinted that she had some sort of history with Felton, but she hadn't wanted to discuss it. After her own experience of unwanted ogling from the man, and his attempt to force himself on Tidsy, she suspected something similar had happened to Leona—or worse. No wonder the actress had been so eager to get away from the party.

"Let me show you the rest of our setup," Dewitt was saying to Felton. Trying to get him away from the set, Jill guessed. The studio executive let himself be persuaded. Once both men had left, the sigh of relief was almost audible. Neal returned from wherever he'd been hiding. After a quick touchup by the makeup artist, Leona once again climbed the steps to the platform. This time, the take went off without a hitch.

Jill was in the next scene, also shot on the dome-observation car set. The script called for her to exchange dialogue with Charles Bosworth, as the actor pressed her to spy on Dolores, the character played by Leona.

"I'll pay you," he said, leaning close. He reached into the inner pocket of his suit and pulled out a slim leather wallet. "How much would it take? Consider it a tip."

Jill recoiled and stepped back, giving her lines an indignant edge. "Really, Mr. Creswell. I couldn't. Your suggestion is inappropriate. Now if you'll excuse me." Jill turned and made her exit as the actor and the extras played out the rest of the scene.

Drake, from his chair, called, "Cut! That was good. Let's take a break."

"Damn straight," the cameraman said. "Turn on that TV. The Series started at ten and it's after eleven already."

Someone had already turned on the set, tuning in the sixth game of the World Series. Jill wasn't particularly a baseball fan, so she hadn't been paying much attention to the matchup between the New York Yankees and the Brooklyn Dodgers. But she knew the Yankees had won four World Series in a row. As she navigated her way over the cables and past the cast and crew members clustered around the television, she heard a lot of good-natured bantering about Yankees Yogi Berra and Mickey Mantle and Dodgers Jackie Robinson and Duke Snider.

She went to the dressing room and put on her comfortable shoes, heading outside for a short walk. At the side of the building, she saw a Cadillac Fleetwood sedan, metallic green with a white top, parked at the end of the row next to her own Ford. It was the same car Felton had been driving on Saturday.

She headed for the depot. It was late morning and the *California Zephyr* that had left Oakland had already come and gone, heading up Niles Canyon. She stood for a moment on the platform and then stepped off. She stopped walking when she heard voices. Angry voices. She peered around the corner of the depot building. Stuart Felton was there, with Wade Ratliff.

Wade was leaning toward Felton, a pugnacious look on his face. "You can't talk to me like that. Remember, I have something you want."

Felton sneered at him. "Who the hell do you think you are? A penny-ante screenwriter. I wipe my feet on guys like you. And if you want to stay on my good side, you'll—"

At that point, Felton leaned toward Wade and said something Jill couldn't hear. But she could tell the screenwriter didn't like it. He said, "You miserable excuse for a—"

Felton cut him off. "You do as I say, or you won't work in Hollywood again. If I put the word out you're a damn Commie, you'll be blacklisted."

Wade's eyes blazed. "Don't you threaten me, you son of a bitch. I'm a decorated war veteran with medals to prove it. Who the hell do you think you're dealing with?"

"The same kind of pumped-up fool I deal with every day," Felton said, with a contemptuous laugh. He turned away from Wade and then stopped as he saw Jill. He glared at her. "What the hell are you doing here?"

"Just out for a walk," she said. "I'm sorry. I didn't mean to interrupt."

The studio executive muttered an expletive, then said, "I'm surrounded by idiots." He brushed past her, walking briskly toward the warehouse,

Jill looked at Wade but he didn't say anything. He smoothed all expression from his face and stalked away, heading across Front Street toward the hotel.

Something you want, Jill thought. That was the same thing Wade said on Thursday, when Jill had overheard him talking with Drake. No, not quite. He'd said that he had something that Felton *might* want.

What could that be?

A dog barked. Jill realized someone else had observed the altercation between Felton and the screenwriter. Observed and possibly overheard. Rose, dressed casually as usual in dark green slacks and a lighter green shirt, with Bella on a leash, stood near the spot where Felton and Wade had been arguing.

Rose smiled. "Well, I wonder what that was about? I couldn't hear everything they were saying, but I heard enough. And their body language spoke volumes. Who were those two? I know I've seen the younger man, the redhead, over at the hotel and in the café."

Jill leaned over to pet Bella, who was wagging her tail. "The younger man is our screenwriter, Wade Ratliff. The older man is some studio executive named Felton. He's come up from Hollywood. Just having him on the set is making everyone nervous.

I gather he's made a number of changes in the script and Wade doesn't like it."

Rose smiled. "Probably not. From what I know of writers, they don't like anyone messing with their golden prose. How is the movie going?"

"Pretty well, I think. We're going to do some location shooting in the canyon later this week."

The older woman leaned down and plucked a leaf from her dog's fur. "Well, I need to be heading home. Nice talking with you."

It's time I got back to the set, Jill told herself.

She moved away from the depot. As she reached the warehouse, she saw Felton coming out the front door, with Dewitt Collier. "I've got us a private room at the hotel restaurant," the businessman said. "The food's pretty good and we can talk business there. Drake will join us as soon as he's finished shooting this scene."

She watched the two men cross Front Street, heading for the hotel. Drake and Dewitt, she knew, were concerned about Felton. But why had Wade been arguing with Felton? It must have something to do with the movie. Did Felton want still more changes to the script?

The blacklist. Felton had threatened Wade with the blacklist. Jill had heard of it. She knew about the Red Scare and she'd read the news stories claiming that Hollywood was rife with Communist sympathizers, that the film industry's unions had been infiltrated, that certain actors, directors and writers were tarred with that brush.

The blacklist, insuring that those people on it couldn't work, was no idle threat. No wonder Wade Ratliff was so angry. But why would Stuart Felton make such a threat?

As she approached the warehouse, she saw Drake leaving. He quickly crossed the street, walking toward the hotel. A moment later, Eve came out of the building. She pulled a wallet from the pocket of her tan slacks and walked across Front Street. Was Eve going to join the men for lunch? Probably not. Today she stopped and looked in the drugstore window, as though she'd seen something interesting. Then Jill saw a familiar figure, Rose walking up Front Street with her dog. She spoke to Eve, who leaned over and scratched the dog's ears. A casual conversation with a passerby? That's what it looked like at first glance. But something about the way the two women were talking, the length of their conversation and the expressions on their faces, made Jill wonder if Eve and Rose knew each other.

The two women parted. Rose and her dog walked up the street, and Eve stepped inside the drugstore.

Jill's stomach rumbled. She was hungry. She headed for the catering trailer. People were lined up to get lunch, while others sat at tables, eating. Or doing other things. Billy Dale, in his waiter's costume, sat at a round table with four other men, all bit players. Billy shuffled a deck of cards as the other players tossed coins into the middle of the table. A poker game, and it looked like Billy was winning. He began dealing a hand of seven card stud, two cards down and one card up. "Five of clubs, three of hearts, jack of diamonds, deuce of spades, and the dealer gets a nine of clubs. Okay, bet your jack." The other players examined their hole cards and the man who held the jack tossed a quarter into the pot. The other players did the same, and Billy dealt another round. He reached for the bottle of 7 Up near his left hand and watched as the other players consulted their cards again.

Jill lined up and got a chicken salad sandwich and a glass of iced tea. She looked around for a place to sit and saw several crew members grouped around a small radio, listening to the World Series. Neal Preston was by himself, sitting on the steps of the trailer that served as his dressing room. He was studying his script. A small tray table held a glass of tea and a plate with a half-eaten ham sandwich and a few cookies. She didn't see Leona, then she caught a glimpse of the star in the doorway of her own trailer, wearing a cotton robe over her costume. She turned from the door and disappeared from view.

Jill found a spot at a table and ate her sandwich. When she was finished, she went back inside the warehouse. She was in the scene that was supposed to be shot at one P.M. At least that's what was on the call sheet. But so far this morning, shooting was running behind. She wondered if it was because of Felton's looming presence, even though he hadn't been on the set for the last scene.

As she reached the dome-observation set, cheers erupted from the crowd huddled by the TV set in the back corner. "What's all that?" she asked Harvey, the tall, skinny key grip who was standing nearby.

He grinned. "The Yankees won the Series. That's five years in a row." He waggled a finger at his friend Dave, the gaffer. "You owe me five bucks. Pay up."

Dave gave a gusty, good-natured sigh. "I really thought the Dodgers had a chance this year. Son of a—" He pulled out his wallet and opened it, handing over a five-spot. "Here. Take your blood money."

Other crew members were settling bets as well, money changing hands. Bert Gallagher was handing several bills to Charles Bosworth. "I knew the Yankees were going to take it," Bosworth said, chortling.

"Don't rub it in," Bert said. "Say, where's Drake? I thought we were going to start shooting at one. We're behind schedule today."

Bosworth shrugged. "I suspect they're still at lunch with Mr. Felton, the dragon from Hollywood. I do hope he's not coming back to the set. I suspect things will be smoother if he doesn't."

"Oh, they're back from lunch," one of the cameramen told them. "Drake and Mr. Collier, anyways. They're having a confab, over there on the Pullman set." The cameraman waved his hand toward the mock-up of the sleeper car.

"Wonder what that means." Bert looked toward the door, frowning.

So do I, Jill thought.

She skirted the crew members and made her way toward the set, moving as close as she dared. Drake Baldwin and Dewitt Collier stood close together in the mock-up of a Pullman compartment, their expressions somber. Then a third person joined them. It was Wade Ratliff. "Well, what did you find out?" the screenwriter asked.

"It's worse than we thought," Dewitt said. "Felton wants to close down the whole production."

Wade erupted. "Damn it, he can't do that!"

"Quiet, keep your voice down." Drake gestured as he looked around at the crew and cast members on the other side of the warehouse, still celebrating the conclusion of the World Series. "I don't want everyone to know, at least not now." The director ran a hand through his short blond hair. "He can shut us down and he will, unless we can figure out a way to stop him."

"He's been against the project from the start," Dewitt said. "He tried to persuade Peter Vesey to give it a pass. But he was overruled."

"The bastard." Wade spat out the words. "Felton hates the script. He's hated it all along. Demanding changes every other day. I'd like to wring his scrawny neck."

"So would I." Drake's eyes were hot behind his glasses. "The smug son of a bitch. He told us that Vesey is gone, already. As of this morning, he's working for Paramount. Felton is in charge now and he's going to axe the whole thing. For crying out loud, we're into our second week of shooting. We've got film in the can."

"We've got to talk to him," Wade declared. "Take another shot to see if we can change his mind. Where is he?"

"We left him at the hotel," Dewitt said. "He said he had to make some phone calls. Then he was headed back to the airport to turn in his rental car and catch a flight back to LA." The producer shook his head. "There's no point in talking with him. His mind is obviously made up. I don't know what else to do."

"I do," Wade said. He turned to go.

"Wade, don't make a bad situation worse," Dewitt cautioned. "There must be someone else at Global we can contact. It will have to be later for me. I have a meeting in Oakland. Drake, I'll check in with you later."

"We can't wait," Wade argued. Then all three men were talking at once and Jill couldn't heard what was being said.

"Eavesdropping?"

Jill jumped, startled. She backed away from the Pullman set and turned to see Billy Dale. "I didn't mean to. It's just that they were so loud, I was curious to find out what they were arguing about."

"Whatever it is, ain't no skin off my nose," he said with an unconcerned shrug. "Hey, I've been meaning to tell you. I went over to that club in the Fillmore this weekend. Heard your brother and his band. He plays a pretty good blues guitar for a white guy."

"Thanks. I'll let him know you said that."

The actor moved away and Jill turned again. The three men had left the Pullman set and Drake was walking this way. "All right, everyone," he called. "Let's get set up for this next scene."

No doubt Dewitt had left, to keep his appointment. As for Wade, she thought, it was just like the hotheaded screenwriter to go looking for Stuart Felton. But where? It sounded as though the studio executive had already left for the airport.

Without Felton's malevolent presence looming over them, shooting the next scene went smoothly. Jill was in the scene after that, here on the dome-observation car set, in the background during a confrontation between Neal and Bosworth. Drake didn't like the first two takes so they were shooting a third. The afternoon had turned quite warm and it was hot under the Klieg lights. Jill was glad when the third take met the director's approval. She was done for the day, and past ready to get out of that costume and remove the heavy makeup.

It was about a quarter after three when Jill left the dressing room and walked outside. It would be good to get home, ahead of whatever afternoon traffic there was on the way back to Alameda. As she passed the front door leading into the warehouse, she smiled and said hello to Harvey and Dave, the key grip and gaffer who'd had a bet on the World Series. Both men smelled like cigarette smoke so she guessed that they'd been having a quick break out by the oak tree.

As she rounded the corner of the warehouse, she heard a train whistle and saw the flash of sunlight reflecting off the shiny stainless steel cars of the westbound *California Zephyr*. It rumbled past the Niles depot without stopping. Evidently there were no passengers disembarking in Niles today. Today's consist had the Silver Solarium as the dome-observation car at the end of the train. It was good to see the real thing rather than the set inside the warehouse.

The train moved out of sight. Jill heard another whistle. Must be a freight, she thought.

She walked up the narrow brick sidewalk toward the spot

where she had parked her Ford. She was surprised to see the green-and-white Cadillac parked where it had been this morning, at the end of the row near the overgrown bushes.

That's the car Mr. Felton was driving, she thought. Surely he'd gone by now. It was just after one o'clock when she'd heard Dewitt Collier say that Felton was heading to the Oakland Airport to turn in this very rental car and catch a flight to Los Angeles. That was two hours ago. Why was the Cadillac still here? Had he come back to Niles? Or had he never left?

Jill saw someone near the front of the Cadillac. A man. The figure moved. But it wasn't Felton. It was the hobo who'd jumped off the freight Friday morning.

Was he trying to break into the Caddy? She hurried toward him. Then she gasped.

Chapter Eleven

S TUART FELTON LAY CRUMPLED on the ground, a large, bloody wound on the back of his head. His suit coat was open.

The hobo looked up, staring at Jill. Then he straightened and shoved something into the pocket of his dungarees. He turned and ran into the rail yard, just as the whistle sounded again. A slow-moving freight came into view. The hobo headed for it. He sprinted past the diesel locomotive and stopped for a second, looking for an open door in one of the boxcars that were now moving past him at a good clip. He spotted one and ran toward it, putting on a burst of speed. Then he leapt for the boxcar.

But he didn't make it. He fell heavily onto the gravel beside the tracks, dangerously close to the train's huge wheels. Jill let out the breath she didn't know she was holding. The man scrambled to his feet. He looked down the length of the train, which was by now moving too fast. Besides, another man had come out of the depot. He was pursuing the hobo, who ran back toward Jill.

He's hurt, Jill thought. He's limping.

The hobo pivoted, changing direction. He sped away from the depot, eluding the man who was trying to intercept him. Injured or not, the hobo moved fast. He ran across Front Street, dodging a couple of cars that honked at him. As he ran up I Street, Jill lost sight of him.

Now she turned and looked down at Felton. The chicken salad sandwich she'd had for lunch turned in her stomach. She certainly didn't want to throw up and compromise the scene of the crime.

But she had to be sure the man was dead. She knelt and gingerly reached for the man's neck. No pulse.

Jill rose and backed away. She shook her head as though to clear it. Then she noticed that the clay brick she'd stumbled over this morning was no longer in place. She looked around and saw it, visible under the bushes. It was stained with gore.

She headed for the warehouse. Another scene was being shot on the dome-observation car set, this time with Leona Alexander, Neal Preston and Charles Bosworth. The actors were in their places, waiting, as the cameras were getting ready to roll. Drake was talking with Eve Stillman and the cameraman, both arms moving as he outlined what he wanted in the next scene.

Jill walked up to Drake and grabbed his arm in mid-gesture.

"What are you doing?" he demanded, annoyed at the interruption.

"Mr. Felton is dead. He's been murdered."

It was as though her words sucked all the air out of the room. The rest of the cast and crew stood motionless, mouths agape.

Drake's irritation gave way to consternation. "Is this some kind of joke? It's not funny. Felton left, he's on his way back to Los Angeles."

"He's outside. And I assure you, he's dead."

Jill didn't wait for a response. She crossed to the phone, the one that had rung on Thursday afternoon and set all of this in motion. She grabbed the receiver, dialing the operator. "Get me the police in Niles, or the sheriff, whoever's in charge."

At that, everyone began talking at once, firing questions at her. Jill put her hand over her left ear to block out the noise and focused on the voice she heard coming from the receiver. She tersely reported the death and gave the location. She hung up the phone, ignoring the outcry, and went back outside to wait for the police, taking a position near Felton, determined to keep people out of the way.

"Where's the body?" Drake demanded. He crowded close, and so did the others who'd followed her outside.

"Just the other side of the Cadillac. But don't go near it. You might interfere with evidence that the police will need."

He stared at her. "What do you know about police and evidence?"

"I've found bodies before. Of people who have died on the train." Jill's voice was steely. She was giving the orders now. "Please move over there, out of the way. The police will be here soon."

Eve raised her hands, palms outward. "She's right. Everyone, move back. Stay out of the way."

Jill heard sirens in the distance, the sound getting closer. Then several vehicles, lights flashing, sped down Front Street and turned into the parking lot.

———

"Tell me again about the hobo," Deputy Carlucci said.

Niles was such a small town it didn't have its own police force. Instead, law enforcement was provided by the Alameda County Sheriff's Department, which had a substation in the nearby town of Centerville. A crowd had collected on Front Street and near the depot, townspeople and railroad employees, drawn by the sirens and the emergency vehicles. The deputies had been accompanied by an ambulance and later other vehicles containing the medical examiner, technicians and a photographer. They had cordoned off this section of the parking lot, which meant Jill's Ford was off limits for the time being. The photographer was taking photos of the crime scene while the professionals examined the body and the surrounding area, looking for physical evidence.

Carlucci was in charge. He was of medium height, with dark hair going gray and dark brown eyes in a world-weary face. His partner was a man named Gruber, with thinning blond hair and the big, beefy look of a football player.

Jill finished her second recitation of what she had seen, adding, "The man headed into town after he fell off the boxcar. He was limping. I think he was hurt. But he was moving as fast as he could." She pointed. "He ran up I Street. I saw him go past the library and then he disappeared. He may still be in town. I don't think there have been any more freights through here since then. I certainly haven't heard any train whistles."

"Still in town," Gruber repeated. "Waiting for the opportunity to hop another freight. Could be he'll come back this way, to the rail yard, hoping to catch the next one. I'll talk to the dispatcher about the schedule, and get in touch with the railroad police."

"Or he could figure another way out," Carlucci said. "Hide out in the back of a truck. Or catch a bus. We need to do a search, right now. Call in some reinforcements." He turned to Jill. "You can go now, Miss McLeod. We have your address and phone number in case we need to get in touch with you."

Jill watched as Gruber walked away, heading in the direction of the depot, while Carlucci conferred with another deputy. She turned and walked back toward the warehouse. Several members of the cast and crew stood near the building, looking at the crime scene and talking among themselves.

The hobo was the prime suspect, she thought. Of course, that was logical. Felton was dead, the hobo had been going through his pockets, and he'd run away when Jill saw him.

But she wasn't so sure. Stealing the dead man's wallet was a crime of opportunity. That didn't necessarily mean that the hobo picked up the brick and struck the fatal blow.

Drake Baldwin stood near the park bench, with Eve Stillman and Wade Ratliff. The screenwriter had emerged from the hotel on the other side of Front Street as the emergency vehicles arrived. He'd darted across the street to join the members of the cast and crew, demanding to know what had happened.

"This is a disaster," Drake said. "Not that there was any love lost between us. He was opposed to the project from the start. With Vesey leaving, he was planning to shut us down."

"We have to call the studio," Eve said. "They need to know what happened. They'll designate someone else to be the executive in charge."

Wade Ratliff shook his head. "Let's wait until we have more information. Maybe the cops will catch this guy, the hobo. I mean, it makes sense. Felton leaves the building, he's well dressed, he's driving a Cadillac. It's obvious he's got money. Maybe he's even flashing his wallet. This railroad bum figures Felton for an easy mark and bashes him over the head. With a brick, you say? Lots of those lying around. Anyway, if the hobo did the deed, that would be tidy, wouldn't it?" He smirked as he said this last.

"Maybe that's the way it happened," Drake said. "I don't know. I'm leaving that to the cops. But we have to let the studio know Felton is dead, at a minimum. Dewitt went back to the city after we had our talk earlier. I'll call him first. Then the studio."

Eve nodded, agreeing. "Maybe a new exec will let us continue shooting."

"Suit yourself," Wade said. "I'm going back to the hotel. Let me know if you have any news." He turned and headed back across Front Street. Drake and Eve walked the other direction, toward the warehouse.

Jill walked over to where Bert Gallagher stood with a group of bit players. "Hell of a thing," he said. "When Felton wasn't on the set this afternoon, I figured he'd left, heading back to Hollywood."

"So did I." So did a lot of people, Jill thought.

"Quite a shock," he said. "You finding the body like that."

"It's not the first body I've found. Although the others have been on the train."

"Natural causes, I expect."

She shook her head. "Murder."

He raised his eyebrows in surprise. "Really? I never would have thought. Sort of a locked room mystery. I guess it's hard for a killer to get off a moving train."

"It is at that," Jill said. "I'm getting a reputation, according to my father. The Zephyrette who finds dead bodies."

She heard a dog bark, looked up and saw a woman in green slacks and shirt. Rose, her black-and-white terrier on a leash. She's here again, Jill thought. Earlier she'd been outside the depot, close enough to hear the altercation between Stu Felton and Wade Ratliff. Now she was part of the crowd that had gathered on this side of Front Street. On the surface, it appeared that the woman was just a local resident, drawn to the site by the moviemakers who'd come to town. And this afternoon, drawn by the sirens and the spreading news of the murder.

Or was there something else? She certainly walks that dog a lot. Come to think of it, Rose and her dog had been hovering near the warehouse and its environs so much that Jill now wondered if the woman had more than a passing interest in the movie being shot here in Niles, and the moviemakers themselves. In fact, Rose was close enough to the crime scene that she must have heard Jill's conversation with the police.

"Why are you here?" Jill mused, half to herself.

"Who?" Bert asked.

"The woman with the dog. I've seen her several times. She told me her name is Rose."

Bert looked at the woman and drew a startled breath. "What in the world? I'll be damned."

"Do you know her?" Jill asked, as Rose turned, disappearing into the crowd. "Who is she?"

"Her name is Rose Laurent," Bert said, rubbing his hand on his chin. "She was in Hollywood for years and then she left. So she came back here. That makes sense. She was originally from Niles, or one of these little towns in the area. You see, she got her start right here, working for Essanay Studios. As an actress and stuntwoman. When she went to Hollywood, she kept acting and became a screenwriter. And then a director. A good one."

When Jill had first encountered Rose and her dog on Thursday, the older woman had said that she remembered Essanay's days in Niles very well. She hadn't said that she worked for the studio. That would explain why Rose Laurent had an interest in the latest movie to be shot in Niles. But there had to be more to it than that.

"Why did she leave Hollywood?"

Bert looked uncomfortable, reluctant to answer. "I'm not sure. You'll have to ask her."

"I may do just that. Come on, Bert. You must know. Or you heard things."

He sighed. "Rumors. Nothing concrete. I heard she was set to direct a movie for one of the studios and she got fired. Rumors about—" He hesitated. "About the blacklist."

"I've read about the blacklist. What is it all about?"

His words came slowly. "You can't work. Blacklist, graylist, just the hint that the FBI is taking a look at you. Doesn't even have to be true. All it takes is for someone to accuse you of being a lefty or a Communist and you can't work. Your livelihood is gone. The studios won't hire you. It's happened to a lot of people. The

Hollywood Ten, that's a group of screenwriters that was called to testify before the House Un-American Activities Committee. Not only are they not working, they've gone to jail. This thing has people spooked."

"Is that what happened to Rose Laurent?" Jill asked.

"The way I heard it, someone accused Rose of being a Commie and that's why she got kicked off a project. In 1948, I think it was. She couldn't find work so she packed it in and left town."

Jill opened her mouth to ask another question, but before she could say anything, Charles Bosworth bustled up to them. "Well, this is a fine kettle of fish. Stu Felton, of all people. Who would have thought? I gather they think this hobo Miss McLeod saw is responsible. It looks like they plan to search the town. I'm sure they'll catch him." Bosworth's hand reached up and he absently stroked his mustache. "Bert, if you have a moment, I'd really like to talk with you about that scene we're doing tomorrow."

"Of course." Bert turned toward Bosworth, as though glad to end the discussion he'd been having with Jill, and the two men stepped away.

I need to talk with Rose, Jill thought. Was it too late? The woman and her dog had moved into the crowd when Bert had seen her. Now the crowd was dispersing and Jill scanned the people on Front Street, looking for the black-and-white dog and the woman in green slacks. No sign of her.

Jill sighed with frustration and disappointment. Then her spirits lifted. Rose and Bella stepped out of the drugstore in the middle of the block between H and I Streets. Rose carried a brown paper shopping bag cradled in her left arm, with the end of the dog's leash in her right hand.

Jill sidestepped a man who was standing nearby, drinking a Nehi grape soda from a bottle, and went past a woman in a house dress. She dashed across Front Street in front of a Chevy, earning a blast from the car's horn.

Rose and her dog crossed H Street and continued down Front Street, passing the old movie theater. At G Street, she turned left. Jill followed. When Rose reached Second, she crossed the street and walked up the sidewalk leading to the corner house.

The one-story house, painted pale green with yellow trim, was an Essanay house. From her earlier conversation with Rose, Jill knew that this was one of those bungalows built by Broncho Billy Anderson to house himself and several of the actors and crew of Essanay Studios. When Rose entered the house, Jill crossed the street and stood on the corner, examining the bungalow. It was small and close to the street, with bronze chrysanthemums blooming in the front flowerbed. The big living room window was framed with yellow curtains and to the left of that, steps led up to a small front porch, where a planter held more flowers.

Jill walked slowly along G Street. On this side of the house, a rose bush climbed the exterior wall next to the brick chimney that went up the side of the house and extended a few feet above the roof. Beyond this were two windows. The smaller window at the back of the house must be the kitchen, with terra-cotta pots and plants visible on the windowsill. This side of it was a larger window that must be the dining room. When she was nearly opposite that window, she saw movement. There were two people visible on the other side of the glass. Rose, and a man. It was the hobo.

No, it couldn't be. But it was. At least it looked like the man she'd seen kneeling by Felton's body. He had the same tall, powerful frame and dark hair. The two people visible through the window turned, so that the man's face was fully visible. Yes, it was the hobo. She was sure of it now.

Now what? He knew Rose and he was hiding here. For how long? Surely the woman would spirit him out of Niles as soon as it was dark.

Jill took a moment to consider her options, then she made a decision. She left the sidewalk and angled across the lawn, heading for the porch. She went up the steps and rang the bell.

Chapter Twelve

ROSE OPENED THE front door and stood on the other side of the screen. She looked out at Jill, surprise evident in her bright blue eyes. Then Bella appeared, greeting Jill with a friendly bark and a wag of her tail.

"You followed me," Rose said.

"I did. I know he's here. I saw both of you, through the window."

The older woman moved her hand, as though she was planning to shut the front door in Jill's face. Then she stopped and ran the hand through her short silver-streaked hair. The defiance in her words matched the look in her eyes. "You know I'm going to drive him out of town as soon as possible."

"That's why I rang your bell, At least let me talk with him."

Rose shook her head. "What good would that possibly do?"

"Better me than the police. They know he hasn't left. I told them what I saw, that he tried to jump into the boxcar but he fell and ran into town. They're searching Niles. And they're looking at the possibility that your friend there might hide in the back of someone's car or truck. So if you were planning to hide him in the trunk of your car, that's risky."

Rose hesitated, staring at Jill. The dog barked again.

Then, from somewhere in the back of the house, Jill heard a man's voice.

"Let her in."

Rose frowned. She reached down and took the dog by the

collar. Then she opened the screen door and beckoned for Jill to enter.

The living room had a comfortable, lived-in look, furnished with several easy chairs and an old sofa upholstered in faded green, with a patchwork quilt draped on the back. Bookcases on either side of the fireplace held books as well as framed photos. Posters hung on the walls, but Jill didn't have time to examine them. She followed Rose past the dining room table, into the old-fashioned kitchen, which had a linoleum floor of black-and-white squares, a tiled counter, and cabinets painted a cheery yellow. The kitchen window was open, admitting a breeze. The plants Jill had seen on the windowsill were African violets, in vibrant shades of pink and purple.

The man stood near the back door, as though ready to flee at the first sign of trouble. Her two previous glimpses of him had been fleeting, but now she had the opportunity to examine him more closely. He was well-built and appeared to be in his forties, with powerful shoulders. He had deep-set brown eyes, thick brows over an aquiline nose, and a wide mouth in a long face. His hair was thick and dark brown, shot here and there with gray. The dark stubble she'd seen on his face when he got off the train on Friday was gone. He'd shaved that morning, but he looked as though he had a heavy beard and the whiskers would be visible again by nightfall. His clothes had been washed and he looked cleaner, as though he'd had a few days with a bathroom in close proximity, as well as a bed and plenty to eat. Which made sense, Jill thought, if he'd been staying here with his friend, Rose.

A first-aid kit sat on the kitchen table, open to reveal an array of bandages and over-the-counter medicines. A bottle of antiseptic was open on the table, next to a pair of scissors and a roll of gauze. She was right, he'd been injured when he fell from the boxcar. A length of gauze had been wrapped around his left ankle and his left hand was covered with a bandage. Blood had seeped through the gauze.

She smiled, hoping to put the man more at ease. "My name is Jill. I'm a Zephyrette."

He stared at her from those dark eyes, as though he didn't

trust her. But he had told Rose to let her in. His voice was deep, a baritone, and it sounded rusty, as though he didn't talk much. When he did, though, he sounded like an educated man, which intrigued Jill.

"I thought you were just playing one in the movie."

"It's both. I'm a real Zephyrette and I'm playing one. What's your name?"

He took his time answering. "My 'bo name is Onions. Because I worked in the onion fields down in the Central Valley. Rose calls me Hal."

"Because that's your real name," Rose said, her voice sounding exasperated. "I wish—"

Hal cut her off with a gesture. "You wish a lot of things."

Now Rose looked sad. "I wish we could go back to the way things were."

"Not gonna happen. Too late for that."

Rose started to say something else. Then she thought better of it. Instead, she leaned against the kitchen counter, her face tired.

Hal—she'd rather think of him as that than call him Onions—angled a look at Jill. "I didn't kill him."

"No, I don't think you did. But you're a very convenient suspect. Tell me what happened, before I saw you."

He was favoring his injured leg. He moved away from the back door, pulled out a kitchen chair and sat heavily, stretching the left leg out in front of him.

"The man was already dead. I saw him lying there. Then you came along." He shrugged and ran his uninjured hand through his full, dark hair. "I ran. I figured I'd better get out of town as soon as I could. I was planning to catch that freight. I'd have made that boxcar, too. But my timing was off. It felt like the train sped up just as I made my play."

"Was there anyone else around?" Jill asked. "When you saw the man lying there? Did you see or hear anyone?"

He shook his head.

Jill paused. Then she said, "I'm not sure I believe you. From what I know, a hobo has to be aware of his surroundings and the people around him, so as not to get caught."

He stared at her for a long moment. "I hear that's part of being a Zephyrette, being aware of your surroundings and the people around you."

"It is. I'm observant. I have to be."

He didn't say anything. A standoff, then, Jill thought. She wondered how she could get him to tell what he knew. Because she was sure he had seen or heard something. He seemed reluctant to tell her anything that might clear him of the accusation of murder. But she suspected that he was used to running, used to getting on the next freight and heading out of town.

He spoke first, with a sigh. "Can I have another cup of coffee?"

Rose nodded. She turned and Jill saw a percolator on the counter next to the sink, with two pale green coffee mugs next to it. She poured a mugful and handed it to Hal. "You want some?" she asked Jill.

Jill shook her head. Rose poured coffee into the second mug and resumed her stance, leaning back against the counter as she took a sip.

Hal took a long swallow from his mug, his head tilted back. Then he set the cup on the table.

"There's a place in the back of that warehouse. It's hidden by the trees and the brush."

"I know the place," Jill said. It was the area where she'd seen Neal Preston rehearsing his lines Friday morning, and it was indeed out of sight, private, but accessed by a door from the warehouse as well as from the sides.

"That's where I usually go when I'm going to catch a freight," he continued. "The people in the depot can't see me from there. When a freight comes along I can look out and see if there's an open boxcar I can catch. That's where I was headed. I know the schedule, knew there's a freight due about that time. Of course, that warehouse had been empty for a couple of years, nobody around. And now all those movie people are there. Makes it harder to stay out of sight." He took another sip of coffee. "I never got to the place behind the warehouse. The man was just lying there. I wondered if he was drunk or something, just passed out. Then I got closer, I saw the blood on the back of his head. That brick had blood on it, too. Somebody bashed him in the head with it. He was dead, that's for sure. Not very long. He was still warm when I touched him."

"So you thought you'd take his wallet," Jill said.

"Why not?" Hal shrugged. "He didn't need it anymore."

"I had just given you some cash," Rose interrupted. "You have plenty of money. You should have just kept going. You could have been on that freight and long gone from here."

Resignation colored his voice. "Let it go, Rose. I see an opportunity, I take it. It's how I live."

"And then I came along," Jill said.

"That's right." A ghost of a smile played on his lips. "I heard the freight blow its whistle, right when you saw me, and I figured I'd better run like hell to catch it. I'm sorry I didn't. Now this is a mess."

"It won't be for long," Rose said, her face determined. "I'll get you out of town. Maybe if we wait until it gets dark."

Jill turned to Hal. "Tell me what happened and start from when you left Rose's house. Take it slow. Remember details. Maybe something important will come to the surface."

Hal cradled the coffee mug in his hands and thought about it for a moment. He set the mug on the table and began speaking again, using his hands as he talked. "All right. I left the house and walked up G Street to Front." He pointed in that direction with his left hand and moved his right hand in the opposite direction. "Headed up Front past the movie house. Kept on the store side of the street, until I got past H Street. Then I crossed Front, heading toward the warehouse. Not the depot." He shook his head. "I didn't want to get too close to the depot. Don't want to be seen by the people that work there. They don't like hobos hopping freights."

"Who did you see on the street?" Jill asked.

He tilted his head to one side. "People. Same as always. Going in and out of the shops there on Front Street. There was a woman with a kid, a boy about six, I'd guess. They were walking toward me. And a man. He was dressed like a farmer, leaning on the fender of a pickup truck. Drinking a soda, talking to another guy. And that café next to the hotel. There was a couple of women, older, dressed up. Looked like they'd just had lunch and were coming out. Stopped just past the doorway and talked for a minute, then they parted company, one of them walking toward me, the other heading the other way."

Hal stopped for another sip of coffee. He began talking again. Jill nodded in encouragement, visualizing the scene, trying to see what he had seen and was now describing.

"I walked across Front Street, heading in the direction of the depot. I was going to skirt around the cars parked this side of the warehouse and go into my hide, that place behind the building. Then I saw two guys walking my way. Turns out they were heading to that bench near the big oak tree. I didn't want to run the risk of them seeing me go behind the building, so I waited. Stood maybe twenty feet from the depot, while those two fired up some smokes."

"The men who were smoking, what did they look like? How were they dressed?"

Hal shrugged. "Just a couple of guys. Older from the look of them. They were wearing pants and shirts, no jackets."

Members of the crew, Jill guessed. In fact, she wondered if the two men Hal had seen were the two crew members she had encountered in front of the warehouse as she left that afternoon. Both of them had smelled of cigarette smoke.

"I saw another man," Hal continued. "He was dressed in a suit. I saw him standing by that two-tone Caddy."

Jill traded looks with Rose, and she knew the older woman was thinking the same thing she was. The man in the suit had to be Felton.

"Did you see him come out of the building?" Where had Felton come from, since everyone on the set assumed he had left the warehouse long before his body was discovered?

Hal shrugged again. "I didn't see him come from anywhere. I looked at those two guys smoking and then I glanced toward the back of the building, the place I wanted to get to, to see if the coast was clear. He was there, on the driver's side of the Caddy. I guess he was about to get in, but he stood there for a bit, maybe fiddling with the keys." He furrowed his brow, remembering something else. "The guy in the suit, he turned away from the car. He was facing that corner that goes round the back of the building, to the place where I was gonna wait for the next freight. It was like somebody called to him. Yeah, I saw somebody. Just for a second. Another man, I think."

Jill gave a start. Could it be that Hal had seen the killer?

"Then I heard a noise," he said. "I looked toward that. It turned out to be a truck backfiring. It was up ahead, a panel truck, pulling away from the curb. When I looked back at the warehouse, I didn't see anybody by the Caddy. Those guys who were having a smoke by the bench were walking back toward the building. Once they were out of sight, I crossed Front Street and walked over to those cars parked by the side of the building, trying to get to my hiding place. That's when I saw the man in the suit. Like I said, when I saw him lying there, I thought maybe he'd passed out. Then I saw his head, all bloody, and the brick had blood on it, too. I knew he was dead. But not for long. I touched him. He was warm. Then I saw his wallet, right there, in his inside coat pocket. I figured, why not? He's not going to need it. I'd just pulled it out of his pocket. Then you showed up and I ran."

Jill voiced what she had been thinking. "You saw someone, at the back of the building."

He nodded. "Briefly. A glimpse, that's all. Then I turned to look at the truck that had backfired."

"Think about it," Jill urged. "Impressions. You thought it was a man. Why?"

"The clothes," he said. "Looked like slacks and a shirt. And short hair." He looked surprised. "I guess I saw more than I thought."

"How tall?"

"About the same height as the guy in the suit," he said slowly.

Jill thought back to her encounters with Felton. How tall was he? Not as tall as Drake Baldwin. The director had about five or six inches on the studio executive. So did Neal Preston, the male lead. He was about six feet tall, or more. She guessed Felton must have been about five feet eight inches tall. There were plenty of people about that height. Male and female, she told herself. And a woman could wear slacks and a shirt and have short hair. Rose, for example, she thought, glancing at the older woman.

"What about hair color?" she asked.

"Hell, I don't know." He threw up his hands, a gesture full of frustration. "I'm doing good to remember that much."

Now Rose looked past Jill toward the living room, alarm on her face. Someone was opening the front door. The dog bounded up from the rug where she'd been sleeping and raced for the front of the house, barking.

"Hey, Bella." A woman's voice, sounding familiar. Jill was startled to see Eve Stillman. She was dressed in her usual attire, slacks and a shirt, her short dark hair swept back from her face. The assistant director stared back at her. "Jill. What are you doing here?" She took in the other two people in the kitchen. "Rose, I have to talk with you. And— Hal? Why are you still here? The police are all over town, looking for you."

"It's not safe to leave," Rose said. "Not until it gets dark."

"I guess you two know each other," Jill said, looking at Eve.

"Rose is my aunt," the assistant director said. "But you didn't answer my question. Why are you here?"

"I'm curious as to why I keep seeing Rose hanging around the warehouse," Jill said.

Rose narrowed her eyes. "I saw you talking to Bert Gallagher. Did he say anything about me?"

"He recognized you. And yes, he told me a bit about you. That you'd worked for Essanay and then in Hollywood. That you left about five years ago. And why."

"That's a conversation for another time," Rose said.

Jill turned to Eve. "I followed Rose here from the drugstore and saw Hal through the window. I have questions. I figured this was a good opportunity to get some answers."

"Someone at Western Pacific told me about you," Eve said. "When we were looking into you being in the movie. You found a body on the train, he said. A man who'd been murdered. And you helped figure out who did it."

Jill smiled. "Three bodies, as a matter of fact. Not all at the same time, of course. I'm getting quite a reputation. As for figuring out who killed those people, it was a combination of luck and my ability to observe and put things together. I think we're all agreed that Hal didn't kill Stuart Felton. Then who? Someone from the cast and crew? Hal saw someone, briefly. Wearing pants and a shirt. It could have been a man. But it could have been a woman."

She glanced from Rose to Eve. Both women routinely wore slacks and shirts. And both had short hair.

Rose stared at Jill, as though she knew what she was thinking. She folded her arms over her chest. "It wasn't me. And it wasn't Eve. We're done talking for now. You'll have to look elsewhere for a suspect."

Chapter Thirteen

JILL LEFT ROSE'S HOUSE and walked back to Front Street. As she approached the warehouse, she saw emergency vehicles and police cars still parked at the murder scene. It looked as though it would be a while before Jill could get to her car.

Just beyond the drugstore, she saw a phone booth. Stepping inside, she shut the door to filter out the noise. She picked up the receiver with one hand and rummaged in her change purse for some coins to drop into the slot. She dialed a familiar number, that of Tidsy's apartment in the Brocklebank on San Francisco's Nob Hill. Her friend picked up the phone on the second ring.

"Tidsy, it's Jill."

"I thought it might be. I know about the murder."

Jill was both astonished and bemused. "How could you possibly know? I found the body not more than an hour ago."

"Word travels fast. Drake Baldwin called Addie from the set. He was frantic to get in touch with Dewitt, who was in some meeting in Oakland. After that, Addie clued me in. She wants me to look into it. But she doesn't want Dewitt to know I'm involved. Men," Tidsy added with a derisive snort. "They have such tender egos." She paused and Jill heard the flick of a lighter as Tidsy lit one of her ever-present cigarettes. "I need details, everything you saw, everything you know."

Someone tapped on the glass door of the phone booth. Jill looked up. An elderly man hovered nearby, his impatient expression and body language telling her he was waiting for her to hang up and leave the booth.

"I'm in Niles right now and someone wants to use the pay phone. So this isn't the time or place to have that conversation. I'm heading home soon. When I get there, I'll call you. Besides, there are some other things you need to know, from yesterday's conversation with Mike."

"I've got a better idea. I'm heading over to Berkeley in half an hour or so, to have drinks with an old friend who's staying at the Claremont Hotel. How about I come over to Alameda afterward?"

"Good idea."

Jill gave her the address of the McLeods' house on Union Street. She hung up the receiver and opened the door of the phone booth. As she stepped out, the old man glared at her and muttered, "It's about time." She hadn't been on the phone that long, but there was no pleasing some people. She gave the man a pleasant smile and walked back across Front Street.

Bert Gallagher, still wearing his conductor's costume, stood at the corner of the warehouse, with a group that included members of the crew as well as some of the bit players. "I was wondering if you'd gone home," he said. "You might as well. We're not getting any more work done today."

"I can't leave just yet." Jill pointed at the ambulance. "My car is still blocked. I had to make a phone call. No more work this afternoon, but what about tomorrow?"

Bert shrugged. "Business as usual, I would imagine. It takes more than a murder to stop filming, unless the body in question is a lead member of the cast. In that case they'd scramble around to recast the part. But in this case, well, he was only a studio executive. I'm sure Global will move someone into Felton's position soon."

"Tell me about Stuart Felton."

"You've heard that saying, the one that goes, you're not supposed to speak ill of the dead."

"I have. But in this case, I'd really like it if you would. Maybe not speak ill, but speak frankly."

"Well..." Bert paused. Then he led Jill away from the people in front of the warehouse to a spot near the trailers, where they had more privacy. "Felton had a way of antagonizing everyone he worked with. I'm not sure he had many friends. But he got things done and kept productions on budget. That's probably the reason for his longevity in Hollywood. He was a survivor. He'd been in the business a long time, twenty-five years or more. He got his start on Poverty Row."

Jill sat down on a bench outside one of the trailers. "What's Poverty Row? I've never heard of it."

"It's a term that means small, B-movie studios," Bert said. "Studios with low budgets, unknown actors and minimal production values. There were lots of them back in the early days. They went in and out of business with great regularity, but some of them lasted, or merged with others. Republic Pictures was created out of six Poverty Row studios, in the 1930s. Felton was on Poverty Row at the end of the silent era, when the talkies were catching fire. He went from there to RKO and Columbia."

Bert paused and took a cigarette pack from his pocket. After he'd lit up a smoke, he continued. "Felton got a job at Global Studios sometime before Pearl Harbor. That's twelve years ago, and he's been there ever since. Climbing up the ladder, so to speak. He was Peter Vesey's right-hand man. They say Vesey is moving to Paramount. That tidbit was all over the set this morning. With Vesey gone, Felton was a sure bet to take over that job."

"Antagonizing people all along the way," Jill said.

"I'm sure of it. He is...was the kind of guy who stepped on toes or ran people over on his way to the top. I'm sure he had run-ins with dozens of people over the years."

"The question is," Jill said, "did Felton have run-ins with some of the people who are here today?"

"That's a good question," Bert conceded. He puffed on his cigarette. "I understand Felton and Drake were at odds about shooting the film here in Niles instead of on a soundstage in Hollywood. Felton hated location shooting, or so I've heard. He preferred to have movies shot right there at the studio, where he could go to the set whenever he wanted. He liked to have lots of control over the whole production."

"I know he had words with the screenwriter about the script," Jill said.

"Oh, yeah. Wade hated the guy. Like most writers, he views his script as sacrosanct, not to be touched by mere philistines like studio execs. But in this business, the script changes all the time. I also heard—"

Bert stopped as Leona Alexander, dressed casually in tailored blue slacks and a rose-colored shirt, came out of the trailer that served as her dressing room. She carried a handbag and the book she had been reading when Jill talked with her a few days ago. The actress nodded to them and continued on her way, walking across Front Street in the direction of the hotel. Bert waited until she was far enough away before he began talking again.

"I also heard stories about Felton and leading ladies. Seems he sometimes had trouble keeping his hands off actresses. I don't know if that's true and I don't know if he ever made a run at Leona. But she didn't like him at all. I could tell."

Jill nodded. "So could I. At the party, she was avoiding him. And so was Neal Preston. Have you heard anything about his dealings with Felton?"

Bert shrugged. "Nothing I'm aware of. Neal's a cowboy actor. I've got a feeling he's more comfortable in the saddle. This particular role, as the detective, well, he seems to be out of his depth. It shows." He looked thoughtful. "Of the actors, I would say the only person in this cast who got along with Stu Felton was Charlie Bosworth. They've known each other a long time. I hear they are poker-playing buddies."

"Felton was planning to close down the production," Jill said.

Bert looked at her in consternation. "What? Where did that come from?"

"Let's just say I overheard something I wasn't supposed to hear."

He looked at her speculatively. "You do have a tendency to blend into the background at times. I'll bet you hear lots of things when you're working aboard the trains."

"I do. And I usually know to keep those things to myself. But in this case, with a dead studio executive, I have to wonder. Felton was the money man, the one who controlled the funds that pay all these people to make the movie. If he decided to cut off the flow of cash—" She didn't finish the sentence.

"Then a lot of people in the cast and crew would be scrambling around to pay bills," Bert said. "And our producers, like Dewitt Collier and Drake Baldwin, the ones who have invested their own money in this production, would take quite a hit. I can't believe Felton would shut down the movie. We're a couple of weeks into filming. Why would he do that?"

"To get back at someone? Or just because he could? I understand he wasn't all that fond of the project to begin with. But he was overruled by Vesey. Who is now gone..." She let the words trail off.

"I didn't know that, about Felton being against the project. That could kill it. But now? Who knows what will happen?" Bert shook his head. "I'm a character actor with no pretensions and a desire for steady work. I take the parts I'm offered, unless I have a strong objection. I just don't get tied up in the machinations of the higher-ups. My participation in this movie started when I got the script. I read it, liked, it, and told my agent I'd take the part." He looked glum as he dropped his cigarette and ground out the butt with his shoe. "Well, like Charlie Bosworth said, this is a fine kettle of fish."

"It is," Jill said. "Felton showed up to kill the production. I doubt he figured on getting killed."

"Hey, the ambulance is leaving." Bert pointed.

Jill turned to look. The ambulance, transporting Felton's body to the morgue for an autopsy, pulled out of the parking lot. It was followed by the sheriff's investigators in their sedan. As the vehicles drove off, their lights no longer flashing, the people near the warehouse began to disperse.

Jill pulled her key ring from her purse. "I'm going home. I'm really tired."

"Same here," Bert said. "I'll see you tomorrow. You're on the call sheet, right?"

She nodded. "Eight in the morning."

Chapter Fourteen ———

JILL WAS EXHAUSTED. She stifled a yawn. What a long, strange day this had been. Maybe she'd get her second wind before Tidsy came over this evening.

She started the car and turned on the radio for the ride home. Playing just then was the Ames Brothers singing, "You, You, You," all smooth voices and perfect harmony. The current number-one hit was exactly the kind of song her brother derided as sappy and sentimental.

The drive from Niles to Alameda took about forty minutes. Jill parked in the driveway of the big house on Union Street. Drew's old Mercury wasn't there and she wasn't surprised. These days, her brother was out of the house more often than he was at home.

With her parents away on vacation, the house seemed quite empty. But the elder McLeods were due home later this week. She shook her head, wondering what her father would say when he found out she'd discovered yet another body.

The mailbox on the front porch was empty. Drew must have brought in the mail before he left. Jill plucked a faded bloom from the red geranium in the pot next to the front door, then stuck her key in the lock.

Her calico cat, Sophie, bounded down the stairs, greeting her with enthusiastic meows. Jill leaned down to ruffle the cat's fur. "Well, it's nice to come home to you, even if there aren't any two-legged critters around."

The mail was on the hall table. She sifted through the collection of envelopes and magazines, seeing nothing that was addressed to her. She headed for the kitchen, where she poured herself a glass of iced tea from the pitcher in the refrigerator. Sophie circled her food bowl, purring loudly in anticipation of dinner. Jill opened a can and spooned food into the bowl. The cat put her head down and attacked dinner with relish.

Jill headed upstairs to her room. She took off the clothes she'd worn that day. Putting on pedal pushers and a floral blouse, she slipped a pair of sandals on her feet, and went back downstairs again. She might as well relax until Tidsy got here. She didn't know when her friend would arrive or whether she would have dinner with the friend she was meeting for drinks. For now, Jill needed something to eat. She rummaged in the refrigerator and took out a block of cheddar and a bowl of grapes. After slicing the cheese, she took a box of Ritz crackers from the cupboard and arranged her snack on a plate. Then she carried the plate and her tea to the living room.

Jill usually read the newspapers in the morning, but since filming started, with her early calls, she'd been reading them in the evening when she got home from the set. She kicked off the sandals and settled onto the sofa, her feet up, piling the newspapers on her lap. Then Sophie jumped up to join her, insisting that she had first priority for the lap. Jill pushed the papers to one side and stroked the cat's head. Sophie amped up her purr. Jill glanced at the headlines on the *San Francisco Chronicle*. She yawned again and settled back against the pillows, Maybe if she shut her eyes for a moment...

Jill woke up when she heard a car pull into the driveway. She dislodged Sophie from her lap and got up from the sofa, looking out the bay window. Tidsy was getting out of her bright red Dodge Coronet convertible, smoothing the skirt of her red-and-white dress. She came up the steps to the front porch, her handbag dangling from one arm.

"I hope you've got something to eat," Tidsy said when Jill opened the door. "I had drinks and hors d'oeuvres with my friend, but she had other plans for dinner. I'm hungry."

"I've got some cheese, crackers and grapes in the living room."

Tidsy breezed into the house and set her handbag on a chair. "That won't do it. I need something more substantial."

"I baked a chicken and an apple pie last night. Plenty of leftovers."

"Great. Sounds wonderful."

Jill grabbed the plate of cheese and crackers and led the way to the kitchen. She took the chicken from the refrigerator and set the dish on the oilcloth-covered table. There were still a few tomatoes in the bowl, those she'd gathered from the backyard garden yesterday afternoon. She rinsed them and grabbed a cutting board, slicing them. "Nothing like a home-grown tomato. I'm surprised there are any left. My brother has been known to devour them as he picks them."

"These look great," Tidsy said. "I love a good tomato sandwich. Some toasted bread, slathered with mayo, a little salt."

"Grab the mayo," Jill said, rinsing the knife. "It's on the top shelf of the fridge. There's bread in the box and the toaster is over there."

Tidsy opened the refrigerator door and pulled out the jar. "Bread-and-butter pickles! I'll have some of those." She stuck a couple of slices in the toaster and reached for the mayonnaise jar. Jill already had a glass of iced tea and she poured another for Tidsy. A few minutes later, both women sat at the table, plates loaded. Tidsy bit into her tomato sandwich and smiled, wiping a trickle of juice from the edge of her mouth. "Oh, yeah, these are great tomatoes."

Jill took a bite from her drumstick. "These are the last of them. There are still a few green tomatoes on the vine and maybe this warm weather we're having will ripen them."

"Nobody home but you?" Tidsy finished her sandwich and wiped her chin with a napkin. Then she reached for a chicken thigh.

"My parents are still out of town. They went to Monterey after my sister's wedding. I expect them home later this week. Wednesday, they said. Unless they're having such a good time they decide to stay longer. My brother's gone a lot these days. He plays guitar in a blues band. He was on the road for a while but he came back to town for the wedding. Now he and the other guys are playing a lot of gigs at clubs over in the Western Addition, you know, the Fillmore district."

Tidsy nodded. "The Fillmore is hopping on the weekends. I go to the clubs from time to time. Jimbo's Bop City—I saw Billie Holiday there, Louis Armstrong, too. Chet Baker and Sarah Vaughn. They have these jam sessions in the wee hours. Things start going strong at two in the morning and they're still at it when the sun comes up."

Jill remembered what Billy Dale had told her. "One of the cast members has family in the Fillmore. A few days ago, he told me that he'd heard there are plans to tear down a lot of buildings over there. Urban renewal, he called it."

"Unfortunately, the powers-that-be at City Hall have decided to call that neighborhood 'blighted.'"

"Blighted," Jill repeated. "That means damaged or deteriorated."

"I know what the word means, but the neighborhood isn't blighted." Tidsy took another bite of chicken, then wiped her mouth with a napkin. "It's actually a lively part of town, with lots of shops and clubs. But certain folks in city government have been talking about tearing things down. Urban renewal is the catch phrase for what they're proposing. My feeling is, if it ain't broke, don't fix it. Yes, a lot of those houses and apartment buildings are fairly dilapidated. Of course, you could say that about the neighborhood where I grew up, the Mission District. Now in the Western Addition, that's where a lot of the Japanese lived, up until the war, when they got hauled off to the relocation camps. Now the people who live there are Negroes."

"That's what my brother says. So does Billy Dale, the guy in the cast. He's a Negro. He used to be a song and dance man, and now he's trying to make it as an actor. He's playing a waiter in the movie. He says all this urban renewal stuff is because the city government wants to get rid of the Negroes in that part of town."

Tidsy nodded. "Could be. A lot of money to be made, first on tearing down old buildings and then on putting up new ones. You know, I remember stories I heard about the aftermath of the 1906 earthquake. The powers-that-be wanted to raze Chinatown, get rid of it entirely. But the people in Chinatown put up quite a fight and they won. Chinatown is still there. This redevelopment thing in the Western Addition, though, I don't know if the residents can fight city hall on this one. Too much money involved. And too many people in line to make a buck off the whole thing."

"That would be a shame. Billy says his family has lived there a long time and he doesn't know where they would go if they had to leave." Jill helped herself to pickles. "Your friend, the one you met for drinks, was she another government girl?" That was what Tidsy called herself, alluding to her wartime work.

Tidsy smiled and picked up a chicken wing, pulling it apart. "Yes, she was. We met in Washington in the fall of 1942. That was after my husband was killed in the Doolittle Raid and I decided on a change of scenery. I found a room in a boarding house. She was already living there. She was a widow, too. Her husband died at Pearl Harbor. So we worked together. And kept in touch after the war."

Jill wiped her hands on a napkin and looked at the food spread out on the table. "You've never told me what you did during the war."

"No, I didn't."

"I'm curious."

"Of course you are." Tidsy set the remains of the chicken wing on her plate and got up from the table, washing her hands at the sink. When she sat down again, she leaned back in the chair and crossed her shapely legs, dangling one of her spectator pumps from her big toe. She fixed Jill with a look. "This is for your ears only, I know I can trust you not to say anything. During the war, I worked for an outfit called the Office of Strategic Services, the OSS. I did things that were exciting and challenging. And dangerous."

"Did you go overseas?" Jill asked, her eyes widening.

"I did. I won't give you details. That's classified. The outfit was disbanded at the end of the war. There's a new organization that took its place. It's called the Central Intelligence Agency, the CIA. I was recruited for that, along with some of my former colleagues. But I didn't join. I had a sneaking suspicion that I'd be relegated to the typing pool." Tidsy waggled her fingers, manicured with her usual bright red nail polish. "I'm a good typist. That's how I got into the OSS in the first place. But I don't want to type and file anymore."

"What do you do?" Jill asked. "You don't have a job, that I know of, I mean."

"Oh, I have my resources. A little money inherited from my parents, and from my husband, after he was killed. I have some investments. I own real estate, in the city and the East Bay. And I do jobs now and then, on the hush-hush. Favors for friends. I get by."

Jill wondered about the nature of the jobs Tidsy did for friends. When she'd first met Tidsy, she was doing one such favor, escorting a nine-year-old girl to Denver as a favor for the child's uncle, someone she'd known during her years in Washington, D.C. As it turned out, there was another more clandestine reason for that train trip.

"That's really all I can tell you," Tidsy said. "Let's have some of that pie."

They polished off a slice of apple pie each, with ice cream. Jill set the plates in the sink. "Want me to make some coffee?"

"I'll pass."

"Me, too," Jill said, fighting down another yawn. "Might keep me awake tonight."

"Looks to me like nothing's going to keep you awake. So we'd better talk about this murder. Take it from the top and tell me what happened."

"I found the body outside the warehouse, when I was leaving for the day. There was a hobo kneeling next to the body. It was the same man I saw Friday morning, jumping out of a boxcar. On Friday, he headed into Niles, as though he had a destination in mind. Today, he was helping himself to the dead man's wallet." Jill paused for a sip of her iced tea. "He ran when he saw me. He was trying to catch a freight that was going past the depot. He didn't make it. If he had, he'd be long gone. But he fell and hurt himself. He ran back into town."

"So the cops are combing the area for him," Tidsy said.

"They won't find him. You see, I know where he is. At least where he was a couple of hours ago."

Tidsy's eyebrows went up. "How did you manage that?"

"A good guess. There's a woman named Rose who has been hanging around the warehouse. So much so that I started to wonder if she was more than just a curious Niles resident. I saw her on the street after the body was discovered and I followed her home. The hobo's name is Hal, and he's a friend of hers. He's at her house."

"A friend of hers?"

"Evidently. She didn't elaborate and neither did he, but from the way they were with each other, it's clear they have some history." Jill summarized what she'd learned from talking with Hal. "I realize he's the logical suspect, but I don't think he did it. And he won't be in town long. Rose is planning to spirit him out of Niles tonight."

"So you believe this guy Hal when he says he found the body." Tidsy looked thoughtful as she rattled the ice cubes in her glass. "I'm inclined to agree with you."

Jill gave Tidsy a quick overview of the scenario—the impending departure of Felton's boss, Peter Vesey, for Paramount, the rumors that Felton had been negative about the movie from the start, and then what she'd heard this morning, that Felton intended to shut down the production.

Tidsy took out her cigarettes and looked around for an ashtray. Jill got up and fetched one from the hall. Tidsy fired up a cigarette and inhaled. "We need to talk to those two guys who were having a smoke."

"I think I know who they are," Jill said. "One is a key grip and the other is a gaffer." She explained the terms to Tidsy. "After I left the dressing room, I saw two crew members going into the warehouse. They smelled like cigarettes. I'll bet that's who Hal saw."

"Good guess. Can you talk with them tomorrow? And the actors and other crew members. We need to find out what they were doing at the time Felton was killed." Tidsy thought for a moment. "Felton was a disagreeable specimen. I had that figured out even before he made a pass at me at the party. And I'm not the only one who feels that way. There were all sorts of emotions bouncing around that shindig."

"He was not universally loved, that's for sure," Jill said. "You should have seen the looks on the faces of the cast and crew on Thursday afternoon, when they heard that Felton was on the phone, wanting to talk with Drake. That was before we found out on Friday that Felton was going to visit the set today. And that's when Drake announced the party. He and Wade, the screenwriter, cooked that up on Thursday. I overheard them talking. And today, Bert Gallagher, the man who is playing the conductor, told me that Felton had a habit of antagonizing people, and you wouldn't want to get on his bad side."

"Vindictive." Tidsy nodded, looking thoughtful. "From what you've told me, Felton was the kind of guy who would deep-six a movie just to get back at someone, or for the hell of it."

"Sounds like it," Jill said. "And when someone like that gets murdered, there are usually a lot of people with motives to kill him. My guess is that several of them are on that movie set."

"If Felton was going to kill the production, you're probably right. That puts Dewitt right at the top of the suspect list, which explains why Addie is so anxious to clear him. Who are some of the other people with motives? Give me your best guess."

"The director, Drake Baldwin. And the screenwriter, Wade Ratliff. He was arguing with Felton this morning." Jill told Tidsy what little of the conversation she'd been able to hear, including Felton's threat to have Wade blacklisted.

"Blacklist?" Tidsy shook her head. "That's a serious threat. Careers have been ruined because of that damned blacklist. All you have to do if you're pissed off at somebody is call them a Communist, and the Red hunters will do the rest. From what I hear, the Hollywood moguls are targeting screenwriters, because of their union activities. I can see why Wade was angry. He did seem volatile at the party, all that moving around, like he had ants in his pants. I can see him having a short fuse. But did he get angry enough to kill Felton?"

"There were lots of other people at that party, and on the set, who didn't care much for Felton," Jill pointed out. "For one, Leona Alexander, the female star. She was going out of her way to avoid him at the party. She even asked me to walk her out. Which I did. A moment after she left, Felton came outside the Colliers' house, looking for her. He seemed irritated that she was gone."

"Hmm. Wonder what's going on there? Maybe he put the moves on her, like he did with me. And maybe she shut him down. I've heard stories about the casting couch. Addie worked in Hollywood during the war. She had her share of encounters with those would-be Lotharios. She was pretty good at avoiding them. I wonder if she knows anything about Felton's reputation."

"Check with her," Jill said. "As for Leona, I suspect Felton tried something with her. Tried and failed. And it seems as though she's afraid of repercussions."

"Anyone else you can think of? What about the actors? Run me through a list of those people."

"Bert Gallagher, who's playing the conductor. He's an affable sort. As far as I can tell, he gets along with everyone. I can't see him in the role of killer. Then there's Charles Bosworth, the actor playing the villain. He's pleasant enough. When Drake announced on Friday that Felton was coming to town, Bosworth seemed pleased at the news. But at the party, I saw Felton brush him off, as though he couldn't be bothered to give him the time of day. Of course, later I saw them talking at the bar. So maybe I was mistaken."

"Anyone else?"

"The male star, Neal Preston. He was also avoiding Felton at the party."

"The cowboy actor," Tidsy said. "Strong, silent type. At the party he seemed very quiet, hard to read."

"I think I know what it is," Jill said, hesitating. "When I was driving down Broadway after the party, I stopped at a light. I saw Preston on Polk Street. He was with a man. And—"

She stopped.

"Say no more," Tidsy said. "I get the picture. If Felton knew, and I'll bet he did, he had something to hold over him."

"What about the snuffbox?" Jill asked. "The one Wade Ratliff took from the cabinet at the party on Saturday. You told Addie about that?"

Tidsy nodded. "I did. She said she'd mention it to Drake. That's the last I heard, but I'll ask her about it. The plan was to have Drake lean on Wade and discreetly get it back. What did you find out from Mike?"

"Mike says Wade is a thief."

"We know that," Tidsy said with a snort. "Since he helped himself to the snuffbox."

"It's more than that. They were in the same unit during the war. Mike says on several occasions he saw Wade take things. Small things, easy to transport, that's the way Mike put it."

Tidsy considered this. "Could be the guy's a kleptomaniac, one of those people who has a compulsion to steal."

"Once he helped himself to another officer's poker winnings. And Mike saw him take something from an empty house in Germany. And that's not all. Mike thinks Wade stole something larger, something that could be a painting." She quickly outlined what Mike had told her the day before.

"Stolen art?" Tidsy looked thoughtful. "I know about the Monuments Men. In fact, I know a guy who was with that outfit. These days he's working at the Metropolitan Museum in New York City. The Nazis looted Europe from top to bottom. Some of the paintings and artworks were recovered, but plenty were never found. Like Mike said, the Soviets got a bunch of stuff. They figured they deserved it as compensation for what they went through during the war. There's a Raphael called *Portrait of a Young Man*. It was taken from a museum in Krakow during the war. It's missing to this day. And the Nazis hated what they called degenerate art. They destroyed paintings, lots of them. Just put them on a bonfire." Tidsy took out a cigarette and lit it. "This is the damnedest thing I ever heard of. How do we get from movies and a guy who writes scripts and steals little shiny things, to murder and stolen paintings?"

"We don't know for sure that Wade did steal a painting," Jill said. "It's just because Mike saw something he thought could be a painting, all wrapped up and tucked into a duffel bag."

Tidsy punctuated the air with her cigarette. "I don't know. Mike's got good instincts. But it's thin. Really thin. And what could it possibly have to do with Stuart Felton? He was a total creep and everybody hated him. Lots of suspects here."

"True enough. But there may be a connection. On Friday, when I overheard Drake, Eve and Wade talking about Felton's visit, Wade said Felton collected art, like Dewitt. They were going to convince Felton to come to the party so he could look at Dewitt's collection. And then, Wade said that he had something Felton might want. I don't have any idea what that might be."

"Leverage?" Tidsy wondered. "Information to trade? Or an item. Something small or easy to transport."

"That's not all," Jill said. "Just before I left the party, when I was coming out of the bathroom, I heard Dewitt talking in his library. He was on the phone, I think. But I'm not sure."

"Why do you say that?" Tidsy asked. "I assume that's why the maid came to get him. He excused himself and said he had to take a call."

Jill nodded. "He did. But after the call was over, he left the library. And I thought I heard someone else in the room."

"Interesting. But you didn't see anyone else?"

"No. As for the half of the conversation I heard, Dewitt said he wanted to see 'it' and he made arrangements to meet the other person on Monday, because he was going to be in the neighborhood. 'It' implies an object, don't you think? And from what I know of Dewitt's plans for Monday, he was meeting Felton at the warehouse. Which he did. He and Drake took Felton to lunch at the hotel in Niles. I didn't see Felton after that. Until I found his body."

"So who was he meeting, and what in the hell was 'it'? And if there was someone else in the room, who?" Tidsy puffed on her cigarette, then ground it out in the ashtray. "There's something else going on and we don't have enough information. Dewitt was meeting Felton in Niles this morning. But after that he went to Oakland. After you found the body, Drake called Addie looking for Dewitt. According to Addie, he was at a meeting in Oakland. Maybe she knows who he was meeting there. We'll ask her tomorrow."

"We're seeing Addie tomorrow?"

"Of course we are. I want to talk with Rose. You find out what you can during the day. Addie and I will drive down to Niles and we'll storm the ramparts at Second and G."

Chapter Fifteen

H E WAS A NASTY piece of work. I'm surprised someone didn't
kill him before now."

Tuesday morning, and Venita was in fine form, holding forth
as she applied Jill's powder and rouge. It was business as usual
on the movie set, despite the murder of the studio executive the
day before. Venita had just given her unvarnished and pungent
assessment of the dead man's character.

"You shouldn't speak ill of the dead." Nancy, her colleague,
frowned, disapproval written all over her face.

"Oh, bushwa to that," Venita retorted. "And I'll bet money I'm
not the only one saying it, or at least thinking it."

"Why do you say that?" Jill was eager to hear more. Venita's
verbal bashing of Felton might give her clues as to who actually
had bashed the executive in the head with that brick.

"Well..." The older makeup lady drew out the word as she
reached for a brush. "You've heard of the casting couch?"

"I have."

"Rumor has it that Stu Felton was one of its most frequent
practitioners." Venita flourished the brush over Jill's forehead.
"Rumor, hell. I have on several occasions heard stories from that
creep's victims."

"Gossip," Nancy said in an astringent tone. "And you shouldn't
be spreading it around. Jill will be shocked."

"I'm not easily shocked." Jill wished Nancy would shut up
and let Venita talk.

Venita didn't need much encouragement. As she wielded her

brushes, she launched into a story about a young actress who had auditioned for a part at Global Studios. "Felton cornered her in his office and well, I won't go into details, but the poor girl was traumatized. And she didn't get the part, to boot. Felton promised things and then didn't deliver."

"What happened if the young lady *didn't* deliver?" Jill asked.

"Well, a certain leggy blond actress on this particular production could tell you a tale about that."

"Leona?" Jill guessed. Though it wasn't really a guess. She'd known that it must have happened, given Leona's reaction to Felton's presence on the set and at the party.

"I know it happened because she as good as told me." Venita picked up another makeup brush and touched it to Jill's face. "She managed to escape his clutches but he said he'd get back at her. That's why he didn't want her to get the part in this movie. I hear he pitched a fit when Vesey cast her." Venita snorted in derision. "Guys like Felton, they think with their—never mind."

"They do." Jill didn't have to hear the word to know what Venita meant.

"I heard another story. About Felton." In the spirit of "If you can't beat 'em, join 'em," Nancy had given up her aversion to gossip and decided to contribute. "I don't even know if it's true. It wasn't about, well, you know, him putting the moves on some actress."

"Well, don't stop there, girl." Venita gave her partner a side-long glance filled with exasperation. "Give over. If you've got something juicy, share it."

"The way I heard it," Nancy said, "Felton collected things, paintings or sculpture or some such stuff. There was this actor who was up for a part in a movie a few years back. Felton told the actor he would give him the part if he got something in return."

That piqued Jill's interest. "The something being a piece of art?"

Nancy shrugged. "I don't know what it was or even if it's true. I mean, who would do that for some picture?"

"Blackmail," Venita declared. "Whether it's sex or some fancy painting to hang on a wall. So you can see that there were lots of people in Hollywood with reasons to want Felton dead."

"But how many of those people with reasons are in Niles right now?" Jill asked.

"Hmm." Venita set down her brush and removed the cloth drape. "That's a real good question, hon, and I don't know the answer. Well, you're done."

Jill left Makeup and headed to the dressing room to change into her costume. She kept going back to the conversation she overheard, between Drake, Eve and Wade. They had just learned that Vesey might be leaving Global Studios, with Felton taking his place in charge of the production. The two men were concerned about the studio executive's reason for making the trip. At that point, Wade said, "I have something he might want."

On Friday, Jill didn't have any idea what Wade could have that Felton would want. Now she did. Not for certain, but a theory, anyway. What if it was true, what Mike said about the package Wade put into his bag when they were leaving Germany at the end of the war? What if Wade really did have a painting, something that might interest Felton? He'd talked of having a few cards in his hand and knowing how to play them. Had he really dangled something valuable under Felton's nose, a bribe to keep the production going?

Or was this all nonsense, a farfetched supposition with no basis in reality? She was grasping at straws. She didn't really know if such a painting existed. Could be that Mike, seeing the package that Wade slipped into his luggage, had made an assumption based on his knowledge of Wade's light fingers. There was also her own knowledge, she thought, recalling the sight of Wade slipping the snuffbox into his pocket.

And what, if anything, did this have to do with the confrontation she'd seen, between Felton and Wade?

Wouldn't it be odd, Jill told herself, if the script of the movie mirrored reality? After all, *The Heist* was supposed to be about a stolen painting.

She put on her Zephyrette costume and left the dressing room, heading for the warehouse. Today's first scene was to be shot on the Pullman car set, with Jill and Neal Preston. Everyone in the warehouse—the actors as well as the crew—seemed to be on edge, Jill thought. It was business as usual, as Bert had said yesterday. The show must go on, the filming must continue. But Felton's murder was under the surface, like a splinter in a finger, one that you couldn't get out.

There was a delay while Drake and Eve discussed camera angles. Neal, who was normally contained, paced back and forth, frowning. He stumbled over one of the cables and gave it a kick. Then he apologized, to Jill, because she was closest.

"Sorry," he said. "I'm just—"

"It's all right. We'll get the scene. Don't worry."

He mustered a smile, folded his arms across his chest and resumed pacing.

Drake and Eve finished their conversation and Drake beckoned to Jill. "Okay, here's how I want the scene to play out. When you come down the corridor, you've got the reservation binder on your left arm. Stop at the roomette doorway, turn to your left and tilt your head slightly to the right. Show me. Yes, that's right. Only tilt your head just a bit more. Yes, that's it, exactly. Now do it again." Jill did the business, to Drake's satisfaction. "Perfect. Now let's do it. Places, everyone."

Neal entered the roomette and sat down, slipping into his role as Stan Gray, the detective, as easily as putting on a jacket. He looked out the window and the camera began to roll.

Holding the prop binder, Jill walked down the corridor and stopped at the doorway, just as directed. The actor looked toward her as she spoke her dialogue. "Good afternoon, Mr. Gray. I'm taking dinner reservations. Is there a particular time you'd like to eat?"

Neal gave her a crooked smile. "Has Dolores—Miss Bain—made a reservation yet?"

Jill returned his smile. "She has."

"What time?" he asked.

"I don't know if I should tell you that, Mr. Gray."

"Come on, what could it hurt?"

Jill paused, as though considering his request. Then she went on with her dialogue. "If you should decide to have dinner at seven o'clock, you might see Miss Bain."

Neal nodded. "Good. Then I'll have dinner at seven."

Jill opened the binder and handed over a white card representing a seven P.M. reservation. "I should warn you that Mr. Creswell also has a seven o'clock reservation."

"Ah," Neal said, looking thoughtful. Then he saluted her with the card. "Thanks."

Jill shut the binder and walked down the corridor.

"Cut!" Drake said. "Great. Take a break while we set up for the next scene."

By now, the cast and crew had all heard the news that Felton had been planning to shut down the production. The bit players, the extras, the supporting players like Bert Gallagher and Billy Dale were philosophical about the whole thing.

"I told you I was going into shooting on that Western in Arizona," Bert said to Jill, over a midmorning coffee at the catering trailer. "If Global closes down this production, that gives me a couple of weeks to relax at home before going back to work. My wife would like that."

"Same here." Billy Dale, who was sitting on the other side of the table, had loosened the collar of his uniform and he was firing up a cigarette. "My agent got me a gig at Columbia, starts shooting at the end of the month. Just one more part."

Ella, the bit player who had the role of a passenger, nodded in agreement. "I've got a comedy coming up. Over at MGM. Me, I'll be glad to get back to Los Angeles. This location shooting gets old."

Jill looked up and saw the two men she'd seen yesterday, coming back into the warehouse just before she'd discovered the body. Harvey and Dave, the tall, skinny key grip and his friend the gaffer, had just come outside, where they queued up at the catering trailer. Jill waited until they had their coffee and pastries and found a place to sit. Then she excused herself and picked up her own mug and the plate that held her cheese Danish. She walked over to the table where the two men sat.

"Mind if I sit down?"

"Not at all," Harvey said. He bit into a cruller, while Dave sat with both hands around his coffee mug, a bran muffin in front of him. Both men were in their forties, she guessed, and she gathered from what she'd heard on set that they had been working in the movie industry for a long time, even before the war. They were dressed casually, as usual, in comfortable slacks and lightweight shirts open at the neck.

Jill settled into her seat and took a sip of her coffee. She'd found the coffee here quite strong, but she had lightened it with a liberal splash of cream. She nibbled at the Danish. Then she smiled at the men. "May I ask you some questions?"

They looked mystified. "Fire away," Dave said.

"It's about yesterday, the murder and everything."

"Yeah, that livened things up around here," Harvey said, though his expression indicated that he didn't necessarily think that was a good thing.

"Why do you ask?" Dave took another bite of his muffin and washed it down with black coffee.

"I'm curious," Jill said. "I don't know whether it's a curse or a blessing. But I always have to know what's going on, and why."

Dave nodded. "Fair enough. What do you want to know? I mean, it's not like we know anything."

"It's possible you might." Jill toyed with her Danish. "You see, I was done for the day and just as I was leaving to walk out to my car, I saw the two of you going back into the building. That was just a few minutes before I found the body. I got the feeling you guys were out having a smoke break, which means you were on that side of the warehouse. So I just wondered. Did you see anything unusual, out of the ordinary?"

Harvey finished his cruller and wiped his hands on a napkin. "You're right, we did take a break between scenes. We went out to that oak tree to smoke."

"Did you see any people in the area while you were there?"

"You mean, suspicious characters?" Dave grinned. "We were only out there five minutes or so."

"Well, wait a minute." Harvey paused and took a sip of coffee. "There was a guy standing over there by the depot."

Dave nodded. "Yeah, you're right. I saw him. I thought he was waiting for a train, though."

"But the *California Zephyr* went right through, just about then," Harvey said. "It didn't stop. Say, I wonder if it was that hobo they're talking about."

"But he didn't look like a tramp," Dave argued. "More like a working man."

"What was he wearing?" Jill asked. "Can you describe him?"

Harvey thought about it, then nodded. "Denims and a green jacket. Dark hair."

Dave was nodding. "Yeah, that's about right."

That certainly sounded like Hal. He had been wearing blue jeans and a green jacket over his checked shirt, each time Jill had seen him.

"Couldn't be the same guy," Harvey said. "Anyway, we just caught a glimpse of him. Then we went back inside. Didn't even think of it until now."

"Did you see Felton at all?" Jill asked. "I'm asking because I found the body not long after I saw you guys going back inside the warehouse. He must have been somewhere nearby."

Dave shook his head. "Sure didn't. Earlier I heard someone say that Felton left after he had lunch with Drake and Mr. Collier."

"Yeah, that's right," Harvey added. "I was surprised to hear that his body was found outside. I thought he was long gone. Goes to show you. It's always bad news when a studio exec shows up on the set. Especially a guy like Felton. I didn't know the man, but I heard he was a pain in the ass. Excuse my language."

"Don't worry about it. Everyone seems to have a similar opinion about the man. Thanks for talking with me, I appreciate it." Jill raised her coffee to her lips.

Another man, an electrician, walked over to the table. "Hey, you guys are needed on set."

Harvey and Dave got up from the table and carried their mugs to the catering trailer. Jill watched them go, thinking about what they'd told her. They had seen Hal, as the hobo had claimed. But they hadn't seen Felton. The last she'd heard, when she eaves-dropped on the conversation on the Pullman set, was that Felton was still at the hotel where he'd had lunch with Drake and Dewitt. From that time till Jill left and found the body, it had been about two hours, she thought. What had Felton done in the interim? Where was he, until he appeared standing near his rented Cadillac, shortly before he was murdered? And who was the shadowy figure Hal had seen at the back of the building? The killer, Jill assumed. Who could it be?

What if Felton had gone back to the warehouse? But surely someone would have seen him. And why would he do that?

Jill shook her head, baffled.

She finished her coffee and took the empty mug to the catering trailer. She wasn't in the next scene, which was between Leona and Bosworth. It took place on the same Pullman set where Jill had overheard the conversation the day before. She needed to talk with Neal Preston and if he wasn't in this scene, now was a good time. But where was he?

She walked down the east side of the building to the trailer where Neal's dressing room was located. A knock on the door brought no response. Then she remembered seeing the actor a few days ago, rehearsing his lines out back on the crumbling concrete pad behind the building. The back door of the warehouse was closed, because they were shooting on the set, but she walked down the length of the building, past all the trailers, and peered around the corner. Sure enough, there was Neal, wearing his costume, script in hand as he went over his lines.

"Hello," she said.

He looked up, frowning at the interruption, then he smoothed out his face. "Hi."

"I'd like to talk with you." Jill walked toward him.

"What about?"

"Stuart Felton."

Emotions, quickly masked, played over his face. "I don't know anything about Felton. Or his murder."

"You didn't like him. Or you were afraid of him."

He held himself very still. "I don't know what you're talking about."

"Yes, you do," Jill said. "I saw you at Jack London Square on

Thursday, outside Heinhold's. And again, over in the city, after you left the party on Saturday. I stopped at a traffic light and glanced to one side. There you were, in front of a bar, with the same young man you met at Heinhold's."

"Keep your voice down," Neal growled. His face, normally composed and pleasant, changed to a grimace of anger and fear. He dropped the script and seized her by the arm, half dragging her away from the building, away from the side of the warehouse where the trailers were, and toward the other side, the parking lot where she'd found Felton's body. She stumbled but he kept going, past the parked cars, all the way to the oak tree. There was no one else there, just the two of them. He stopped and faced her.

"What the hell are you doing? Who are you working for?"

"I'm not working for anyone." Jill shook off his grasp. Her arm hurt where he'd grabbed it. She was going to have a bruise, she was sure of it. "I'm trying to find out who killed Felton."

"It wasn't me," Neal snapped, tight-lipped. "Besides, why should you care who killed him? It's nothing to you."

"I'm the one who found the body. I'd like to know what happened. I'm that way about things."

"You like to stick your nose in where it doesn't belong." The frantic look in Neal's eyes abated somewhat.

"From what I've seen, you didn't like the man very much."

He laughed, but there was no humor in it. "I hated the son of a bitch. I'm glad he's dead."

"He was threatening you. Because you're a homosexual."

"For God's sake, shut up." Neal looked around to make sure no one was close enough to hear. "You don't understand. If that gets out, my career is in the toilet. Guys who play strong rugged cowboys, or hard-boiled detectives, aren't supposed to be queer."

"I do understand." Jill rubbed her arm. "Is that what Felton was going to do? Ruin your career? When did he find out?"

Neal folded his arms over his chest and glared at her. "He's known for a while. A few months. He threatened, but he didn't actually do anything. I think he just liked to see me squirm. That son of a bitch. He enjoyed it. That's the kind of person he was. That's how he got to the top at Global Studios. He liked to dig around and find people's weak spots. And then he'd exploit them. If ever there was a guy who knew where the bodies are buried, it was Stu Felton. You just don't cross a guy like that. And being a homosexual in Hollywood, well that's as vulnerable as it gets. If it's not some rag like *Confidential* printing all sorts of rumors and threatening to expose you, it's guys like Felton using it to their advantage. He was like that with everyone. Men, women, it didn't matter just as long as he could dig up something to hold over people."

"What did he get out of it?"

Jill's question seemed to take Neal aback. "I don't know. Power, I suppose. How do you think a guy like Felton got to the top of the heap? He clawed his way up, using people as stair steps. He was always on the lookout for an advantage. A secret. Something he could use."

"Did he ever ask you for anything?"

Neal shook his head. "No. Not at first. But right before I came up here to shoot this movie, Felton approached me. He told me he wanted me to sabotage the picture, by causing delays, things like that."

"But why?"

"Hell, I don't know. Because he didn't like Peter Vesey, the exec who gave the project the green light. Because he hated the script, the idea. For all I know he hated Drake and Dewitt. Who knows what makes a man like that tick? He wanted to kill the movie, for no other reason than he could."

"Power," Jill said. "He had the power to do it, so he did."

"Something like that." Neal shook his head. "I put him off. I said, I'm a professional, I can't do things to mess up the production. But it made me so nervous I haven't been able to give the kind of performance I'd like. So when I found out he was coming to town, that he'd be on the set, well, it was like I'd been waiting for the other shoe to drop. I hadn't done what he wanted, and now that other shoe was dropping."

"You avoided him at the party."

"Yeah. I felt like it was a command performance, to help out Drake and Dewitt. So I put in an appearance, did my best to avoid

Felton, and left. It was no use. Felton called me at the hotel, on Sunday."

"He threatened to retaliate against you," Jill said.

Neal nodded. "He said he knew someone who works for that scandal sheet, *Confidential*, and he was going to make sure everyone knew about me. The queer cowboy, that's what he called me. He also waved the blacklist at me. He does that a lot. He's friends with the creep who runs that rag *Red Channels*, the one that paints people as Communists. There were lots of things Felton could do to kill my career. Now somebody's killed him. You won't get any tears from me. I'm glad he's dead. But I sure as hell didn't kill him."

"I have no intention of revealing your secret," Jill said. "But you must realize that this makes you a suspect in Felton's murder."

Neal looked at her in consternation. "I was on the set most of the day. When would I have the opportunity to kill him?"

"You could have slipped out. At any time, to go back behind the building to rehearse, the way I've seen you do. Anyone could have slipped out."

"I didn't," he insisted.

"Did you see anything, or anyone, around the time Felton was killed? It must have been around three o'clock."

"No, I didn't. I was on the set. You saw me when you came in to tell us you'd found the body. We were shooting a scene on the observation car set. Leona, Charlie Bosworth and me. That's all I can tell you. This conversation is over." He turned and took a step.

"Before you go, have you ever heard of Felton blackmailing anyone else? Anyone who's here?"

Neal's body language said he wanted to keep walking, but he stopped. "I know he tried his casting couch maneuver on Leona. And he didn't have much use for Charlie Bosworth, despite the fact Charlie thinks they were great friends."

"Thanks," Jill told him. Leona and Bosworth were next on her list.

As Neal stalked off, she pushed up the sleeve of her Zephyrette jacket. Yes, she was going to have a bruise.

Chapter Sixteen

CHARLES BOSWORTH SIMPLY wouldn't cooperate.

As she'd walked back toward the warehouse after her confrontation with Neal, Jill had wondered how best to approach Bosworth. The older actor was full of self-importance, and in most of the interactions she'd had with him, he condescended to her. Today was no exception.

She didn't have the opportunity to approach the actor until the cast and crew broke for lunch. She found him at a table near the catering trailer, with a cup of coffee and a nearby plate containing the remains of a ham sandwich. Bosworth was leafing through a copy of that morning's *San Francisco Chronicle*. She got a cup of coffee and joined him at the table. He looked annoyed when she sat down and even more annoyed when she asked questions.

"Don't worry your pretty little head about it," the actor said. "That tramp killed Felton. I'm sure the police will find the man in short order."

"They haven't yet," Jill pointed out. "I'm sure the man is long gone."

She was pretty sure she knew that for a fact.

"Besides, I'm just wondering. If the hobo didn't kill Felton, that means someone else did. Was there anyone else here who might have had a reason to kill him?"

"What?" Bosworth lowered the newspaper and looked at her with narrowed eyes, as though seeing her for the first time. "Don't be absurd. There's no one here who could possibly have done such a thing. Really, young lady. I can't imagine why you feel it necessary to meddle. What concern is it of yours?"

He didn't wait for an answer. Instead he raised the newspaper so it was between them, a clear and effective dismissal.

Jill took another sip of the coffee and got up from the table. She walked toward the catering trailer and left her mug in a bin of dirty dishes. Then she heard someone call her name. She turned. Leona Alexander stood in the doorway of the trailer that served as her dressing room. The actress waved and called again. "Jill. Come in."

Jill walked back to the trailer and climbed the steps. The trailer wasn't as large as the one for the makeup artists, but cozy and comfortably appointed, with a table, chairs, and a bed at one end. Leona sat down in one of the chairs and beckoned for Jill to join her. "I heard you asking questions. Charlie Bosworth isn't going to answer."

"I gathered that, from the way he put me off."

"He and Felton were friends. Or at least Charlie thought so." Leona paused. "I know you talked with Neal. He was upset when he came back to the warehouse."

"How well do you know Neal?"

"I know he's homosexual, if that's what you're getting at," the actress said. "It's not uncommon in Hollywood. Or anywhere for that matter. It's none of my business, or yours. Neal is a nice man. I believe in live and let live."

"So do I," Jill said. "But that's the sort of thing that would kill his career. He's vulnerable, and Felton was holding that over Neal."

Leona shook her head. "Neal wouldn't kill anyone. He's a kind, considerate man. I've known him for several years. I started out in this business about six years ago, playing bit parts and working my way up to supporting roles. In fact, I had a small part in one of his Westerns. We've been friends ever since. That's one reason I was eager to take on this role, to work with Neal again. He wasn't so sure he wanted to do this movie. He's gotten so used to riding a horse and strapping on a holster. But I told him it would be an excellent part for him. Now I'm not so sure that this movie was a good idea, for either of us. This whole thing is going sour. And now a murder. I don't know what to think."

"Felton was threatening Neal," Jill said. "A lot of people might be tempted under those circumstances."

"I'm next on your list of interviews," Leona said. "Isn't that right? That's why you're asking all these questions. You're trying to find out who killed Felton. But the police are looking for that hobo you saw yesterday."

"They think he's the most likely suspect. But I don't think he did it."

"I won't even ask you how you came to that conclusion," the actress said. "You probably talked to him. The hobo, I mean."

Jill hoped that her face didn't reveal how on-target Leona's comment was. "The police are convinced that if they find the hobo, they'll find the killer. He's a convenient suspect. They aren't looking at anyone else. But if the hobo isn't the killer, that means Felton's death wasn't random. It's someone here, on the set. Someone who knew Felton and had a reason to hate him."

"That could be just about anyone on the cast and crew," Leona said. "Which makes all of us suspects."

"Or witnesses," Jill said. "Someone in the cast or crew may have seen something. They may not know that it's important. Or that they have information that will lead to the truth."

"All right," Leona said. "If I was going to kill Felton, I would have done it a long time ago, I assure you. That should be obvious. You saw my reaction, at the party. And on the set yesterday. The man made my skin crawl."

"I have a pretty good idea why."

Leona rolled her eyes. "Venita-the-motor-mouth strikes again. She could barely contain herself while I was in Makeup."

"I know next to nothing about the movie business," Jill said. "But I can see that someone like Felton wields a lot of power."

"I'll see if I can boil it down so you can understand it. As if anyone could understand this business." Leona crossed her legs and settled back in her chair. "The studio constantly dictates how a movie is made. Or whether it gets made at all. That was certainly the case in the days of the studio system, in the Thirties and Forties. Things are unraveling there. The studio doesn't have as much control as they did. But they still have a lot of say about how it all comes together. The casting, the script, the budget. Especially the budget."

"So someone like Felton can make or break a film," Jill said.

"Yes. That's why everyone kowtows to the studio exec. Peter Vesey is a fairly decent guy, as execs go. He has good instincts about projects and what will make them succeed. He was willing to give Drake a chance to make this movie the way he wanted. But Felton's always been jealous of Vesey. This news that Vesey is leaving for Paramount was just the chance he needed to move in and put his own imprint on Global Studios. And not in a good way." Frustration colored Leona's voice. "Take all these changes in the script he's been insisting on. I expect changes, that's par for the course. But not to this degree. The script we're filming is not the same one I read when I agreed to take this role."

"How has it changed?" Jill asked.

"The character I'm playing, Dolores, as originally written, was strong and independent. She was smart. She could hold her own against Stan, the hero, the role played by Neal. And against Charles Bosworth's character, Creswell, the villain. As originally written, this movie is supposed to be a contest of wills between Dolores and Stan, since he's trying to find the painting Dolores stole. But every time Wade revises the script, Dolores's part get pushed more and more to the margins. The movie is becoming a contest between Stan and Creswell. Creswell's part—Bosworth's— is getting bigger and my part is getting smaller. And it's not just my ego talking. Neal has noticed it, too. We're getting farther away from the script that Wade initially wrote. And to hear him tell it, all the changes are coming at him from the studio. But it wasn't Vesey insisting on the rewrites. He liked the script. But Felton hated it. He's been picking away at this movie from the start."

Jill nodded, thinking of what Neal had told her earlier. Felton wanted him to sabotage the production by causing delays in filming. And he'd threatened him with exposure if he didn't do it. With Vesey leaving Global Studios, he didn't need Neal anymore.

He could cancel the production on his own, because he was now in charge.

"I've heard that Charles Bosworth is one of Felton's friends, if in fact Felton had any friends," Leona added. "Which I doubt. People like Felton have sycophants and hangers-on. He used people and people used him in turn." Leona sighed, looking suddenly weary after her outburst. "I'm sorry to go on like this. What I'm taking about must not make any sense to someone like you."

"You've explained it well," Jill said.

Leona shook her head. "I don't know where this is all going to end. I like acting and I've had a good career so far. But I'm thinking I might give it up entirely once I get married. I thought this part would give my career a boost. Now I'm about to conclude that the whole debacle will kill it entirely."

"Tell me about your day yesterday," Jill said. "Walk me through it."

"You can't think *I* had anything to do with this murder!"

"Like it or not, everyone is a suspect. And you may have seen or heard something important."

Leona frowned, her mouth a tight line. "I made it a point never to be alone with Felton, certainly not after what happened."

"What did he do?" Jill asked. Leona hesitated. "It's all right if you don't want to tell me."

The actress took a deep breath. "No. I might as well. It was about eight months ago. I got a message saying Felton wanted to see me in his office at the studio, to discuss a part. I was working on a movie at the time and it was late, early evening, by the time I went looking for him in the administration building. His secretary had left for the day. There was no one there, except Felton and me. He shut the door. And then he grabbed me. I pushed him away, and he laughed." Her voice was filled with revulsion and she shuddered. "He said if I wanted the part, I'd have to go to bed with him."

"I'm so sorry," Jill said, taking Leona's hand. "I've been grabbed, but I've never had anyone demand that."

Leona straightened, a determined look on her face. "I shoved him really hard and he fell back against his desk. He threatened me. He said I'd never have a starring role again. I got out of there, as fast as I could. From then on, I've kept out of his way, afraid he'd try it again. Or that he'd retaliate. And he has, in a way."

"How? By interfering with the production?"

"Yes," Leona said. "I didn't do what he wanted. Since then, he's been trying to wreck my career. He didn't want me for the part of Dolores, actively lobbied against me. But Vesey thought I'd be good in the role, so he overruled Felton. When I heard Felton was coming to town, that he was going to be on the set, I thought he'd figured out a way to get me fired. Especially when I found out that Vesey was going to Paramount and Felton was replacing him."

"He can't fire you from the grave," Jill said.

"Don't be too sure about that." Leona punctuated her words with a grim smile. "Dead or not, Felton could still win. He had the ear of a lot of people at the studio, people who think he's smart and astute. I suppose he was all of those things. But evil, too. A cruel man, who looked for flaws and vulnerabilities so he could exploit people. For those of us who would like to get somewhere in this business, our biggest vulnerability is our careers, our ambitions. It's easy for a man like Felton to say, you do this, and I'll see that you get the part. Or, if you don't do it, I'll wreck your career. My point is that someone Felton mentored or influenced could be the next studio executive. That means it's possible that Global can still shut down this production."

Jill considered this for a moment. "Can you tell me anything about Felton's life outside work?"

Leona shook her head. "Not really. I don't know much about him. Charlie Bosworth might be able to tell you, since they were supposedly friends. But from the brushoff he gave you, I doubt that he will. I can tell you what I've heard and seen, which makes me as big a gossip as Venita."

"Was he married, divorced?"

"Divorced, I think. I can't imagine any woman putting up with him. Rumor has it there were other actresses who gave in to his advances." Leona grimaced.

Jill decided to change direction, to find out if Leona had seen anything on Monday. "Yesterday morning, we were shooting on the dome-observation car set. It was that scene where you come down the steps from the Vista-Dome. Felton was on the set and he was making everyone nervous. We had to do several takes. Dewitt was there, too, showing Felton around, and he managed to get him away from the set. Things went smoother after that. We shot another scene, and you were in that."

"Then we took a break," Leona said. "All the baseball nuts were gathered around that TV set watching the World Series."

"Where were you after the baseball game started?"

"Here, in my dressing room. I left the set, walked outside, got a cup of coffee from catering and came in here to relax and look at the script before my next scene."

"Who did you see? Before you left the warehouse and went to your dressing room, I mean."

Leona thought for a moment before answering. "Drake and Eve were talking with the cameraman near the dome-observation set. And I saw Felton talking with Charlie Bosworth. They were standing between a couple of the sets. And Wade, the screenwriter. He was over in the corner with the rest of the crew, watching the baseball game."

That was interesting, Jill though. That was about the time she had gone for a walk, because she wasn't in the next scene. And that was when she'd witnessed the confrontation between Wade Ratliff and Stuart Felton, over near the Niles depot. She didn't mention it to Leona now, though. She wanted to find out what else the actress had seen and heard that day.

"What about Neal?"

"I didn't see Neal. I assumed he'd gone outside. He likes to go behind the warehouse to rehearse. He paces up and down and goes over his lines."

Jill nodded. "I've seen him there."

"Then I got the coffee and went into my dressing room," Leona continued. "When I came out again, I saw Dewitt and Felton walking across the street. Dewitt had said something earlier about taking him to lunch. I grabbed a light lunch for myself and after I ate that, I went to the makeup trailer for a touchup. Then I went back to the set."

"You didn't see Felton again?"

Leona shook her head. "No. Later I saw Drake and Dewitt, on the Pullman set. They were talking with Wade. And someone, I don't remember who, told me that Felton was on his way back to Hollywood. I didn't give it another thought. We had a scene to shoot on the observation car set and we did several takes. There was a break in between. Wade was there, talking with Drake. I assume it was about the script. Then Wade left and we went back to shooting the scene. That's where we were, when you came in to tell us about finding the body." She glanced at the utilitarian clock on a nearby table. "Look, I'd better get back to the set. The call sheet has us shooting another scene in ten minutes."

Jill stood up to leave. "Before you go, I understand Felton was an art collector."

Leona nodded. "Yes, I had heard that. Paintings, I think. Like Dewitt Collier. I know at the party, I heard Drake tell Dewitt to make sure that Felton saw Dewitt's collection of paintings. Presumably to get on Felton's good side, not that he had one."

"I'll tell you a story, one that was relayed to me by Nancy, Venita's assistant. She says Felton told an actor he'd get a part if he got something in return, presumably some art."

"I haven't heard that story," Leona said, frowning. "But the kind of person Felton was, I wouldn't put it past him. Look, a friend of mine, a cinematographer, collects art. I can make a phone call. Let me see what I can find out."

"Good. Let me know."

Leona tilted her head to one side. "But how could that have anything to do with Felton's murder?"

"I'm not sure," Jill said thoughtfully. "I'm just trying to pull together as many strings as I can."

Chapter Seventeen

JILL MET TIDSY and Adelaide Collier at the corner of Front and G streets later Tuesday afternoon. The two women had motored down to Niles in Tidsy's red Dodge convertible. Tidsy expertly backed the car into a space at the curb and killed the engine. Addie's hair looked a bit windblown after the drive from San Francisco. She pulled a comb and a small mirror from her handbag and smoothed a few errant strands.

Tidsy tucked her keys into her handbag, red leather that matched her shoes and her red-and-white-checked dress. Then she pointed at a small café on the nearby corner. "Let's get a cup of coffee and talk."

"Agreed," Jill said. "I have some questions for Mrs. Collier."

Addie nodded as she put her comb and mirror into her bag and got out of the car, brushing lint from the skirt of her navy blue suit. "All right. Coffee first, and then I'll answer your questions. And please, call me Addie."

They went into the café and a few minutes later were seated at a small table in the corner, coffee cups in front of them. Jill stirred cream into the strong dark brew.

"What's on your mind, Jill?" Tidsy asked. "Have you found out something new?"

"First, I want to find out about the snuffbox." Jill looked at Addie. "Did you get it back?"

"I certainly did." Addie looked annoyed as she tasted her coffee and then lightened it with a dollop of cream. "My nephew Drake spoke with him and Wade gave it back to him. He had all sorts of excuses, saying he didn't mean to take it. He was looking at it and inadvertently slipped it into his pocket." The look on her face made it clear what she thought about that.

"It didn't look like an accident to me," Jill said.

"I suspect you're right," Addie said.

Tidsy took cigarettes and lighter from her bag and lit up. "Dewitt got a phone call on Saturday during the party. He excused himself and said he'd take the call in the library. Any idea who the call was from?"

Addie took another sip of her coffee before answering. "I don't. Dewitt didn't tell me who it was from, or what it was about. That's not unusual, I might add. He has all sorts of business ventures, all over the Bay Area. I know a little bit about those, but not all the details." She looked from Tidsy to Jill. "Why? Is the call important?"

"Not sure," Jill said. "I overheard Dewitt's side of the conversation. I went to use the bathroom before I left. The library door was open, not all the way, but enough for me to hear Dewitt talking. He sounded as though he was making arrangements to look at something. On Monday, he said. Because he was going to be in the neighborhood. We know that he was here in Niles Monday, because he had lunch with Drake and Felton. Then he went to Oakland, where he was in a meeting when Drake called you, looking for him."

Addie set her coffee cup on the table. "Hmm. I knew about his plans for lunch with Drake and that man from the studio. Then he told me he was going to Oakland for another meeting, that it could take some time and he might be late."

"Who was he meeting in Oakland?" Tidsy asked.

"Someone who owns a cannery in the Fruitvale district," Addie said. "He was planning to invest. Could that have been the 'something' he was talking about? Looking at the cannery itself? Or the books, maybe?"

"It sounded like an object, a thing," Jill said.

"And because he was going to be in the neighborhood," Tidsy added, "perhaps this was in addition to the scheduled meeting."

"I really don't know. You've got me curious now. How does

this fit in with Felton's murder?" Addie paused and frowned. "I can't believe Dewitt had anything to do with it. I know how that sounds. I'm the man's wife. But he just doesn't have it in him." She sighed. "I wish he had never gotten involved in this damn movie. But Drake's my nephew and he can be really persuasive."

"Oh, hell," Tidsy said, waving her cigarette. "Dewitt's had visions of being a producer ever since he met you in Hollywood back in the Forties. I suspect Drake wanting him to invest in this movie was the thing that pushed him over the line."

"I wonder if it was a painting." Jill took another sip of coffee and shook her head when the waitress came by with a glass carafe, asking if she wanted a warm-up. "Art seems to come into play here. And Felton collected paintings."

Tidsy drummed her scarlet nails on the table. "Could be." She looked at Addie. "Has Dewitt said anything about adding to his collection?"

"He's always on the lookout," Addie said with a smile. "Especially if it's one of those Dutch paintings he's so fond of. He never tells me how much he pays for them. Nor do I tell him how much it costs when I buy a snuffbox. It's an expensive addiction. But we can afford it. And when he's buying art, he doesn't talk about it much. He thinks it will jinx the deal."

"Felton collected paintings." Tidsy finished the last of her coffee. "There's got to be a connection."

"I heard that Felton extorted a painting from an actor, in exchange for a part." Jill repeated the story told to her by Nancy, the makeup artist.

"Not the only kind of extortion, I'll bet," Tidsy said. "After that guy put his hands all over me on Saturday, I'll bet he had a reputation in Hollywood."

Jill nodded. "He certainly did. A bad one, where actresses are concerned." Jill gave them an overview of what she'd learned from Leona, about Felton's harassment and threats. She would leave Neal Preston out of the equation, for now.

"No shortage of people who'd want to kill Felton," Tidsy said. "Now, yesterday you told me you thought this woman Rose was holding something back. I think it's time we asked her just what."

They paid their tab and left the coffee shop. Jill pointed down the street. "She lives there, at the corner of G and Second. It's what they call an Essanay house, built by the Essanay Studios years ago when they were making movies here in Niles."

"Tidsy told me," Addie said.

"Rose has been hanging around the warehouse, quite a bit," Jill said. "I've seen her almost every day. I thought she was just a curious resident. We certainly got lots of those when we arrived. Then I found out she worked in Hollywood, and for Essanay. And the assistant director is her niece."

"How does she know the hobo?" Addie asked.

"His name is Hal. She didn't tell me much about him, just that he's a veteran and he had a bad war."

"We all know a few guys that description would fit," Tidsy said. "So Hal the hobo hopped off a freight on Friday, to visit Rose."

Jill nodded. "He stayed through the weekend and was planning to leave Monday, on a three o'clock freight. He knows the schedule of trains through here. He was headed for the rail yard. He told me he has a spot behind the warehouse where he can't be seen and he waits there for a freight to come through. I found him near Felton's body and he ran. Tried to catch the freight that was just coming through, but he wasn't able to get aboard. He ran into town and later I discovered that he was at Rose's house. I talked with him and that's when he told me what he heard and saw. He's probably long gone. Rose was planning to smuggle him out of Niles last night. But we can certainly talk with Rose. I'm sure she knows more about Felton than she's saying."

"Let's get to it, then." Tidsy gestured with one hand. "Lead on."

On the front porch of the corner house, Jill rang the doorbell and heard a bark from the other side. The door opened. Rose, dressed as usual in slacks and shirt, looked out. The little terrier, Bella, stood in front of the screen door, barking and wagging her tail.

"Hush, Bella." Rose frowned as she surveyed the delegation on her front porch. "Well, this is a surprise. To what do I owe the pleasure?"

Before Jill could say anything, Addie Collier stepped closer to the door, consternation in her voice. "Rose Laurent?"

A slow smile replaced the frown on Rose's face. "Addie Baldwin. After all these years."

"Jill told us your first name," Addie said. "But it didn't register until I saw your face."

"You two know each other?" Tidsy asked.

Addie turned to Jill and Tidsy. "We met during the war, when I worked at the Bureau of Motion Pictures, in the Office of War Information. Rose directed some movies for us."

Tidsy looked at Rose through the mesh of the screen door. "Rose, my name is Grace Tidsdale. My friends call me Tidsy. You've met Jill and it looks like you've known Addie for a while. So let us in. We need to talk."

Rose looked wary. "Talk about what?"

"Stuart Felton," Jill said. "As far as the police are concerned, your hobo friend Hal is still a suspect in Felton's murder."

"He didn't do it," Rose interrupted. "He told you that yesterday. He couldn't possibly have killed that man. Besides, he's long gone. I got him out of town last night. Don't even try to find him. You won't."

"I'm sure he's miles from here by now," Jill said. "There are freights going all directions, at all times of the day. Look, I told you yesterday I don't think Hal killed Felton. But the police seem to be stuck in that one line of inquiry. Which means they aren't looking elsewhere for the killer. Whatever we can find out about Felton will help. And yesterday, I felt that you didn't tell me everything you know." Jill paused and looked at the older woman. "You are holding something back, aren't you?"

Rose hesitated. "It's complicated."

"Murder usually is," Jill said. "Please, help us clear this up."

Rose reached down and took Bella by the collar before opening the screen door. Jill led the way into the house. The living room was in comfortable disarray. A threadbare blue blanket had been thrown over one end of the sofa, its frayed hem dangling onto the rug. A hardback copy of Edna Ferber's latest novel, _Giant_, a bookmark stuck between the pages, had been tossed against a pillow.

The coffee table held a plate containing pear slices, a hunk of Swiss cheese, and a pile of saltines. A half-empty glass of iced tea sat on a coaster on the end table.

"Sit down," Rose said, waving them toward the sofa and chairs. "Can I get anyone some tea?"

Jill and Tidsy shook their heads. "None for me, thanks," Addie said. She looked around the living room, at the posters and photographs from Rose's career. "This is bringing back memories of my days in Hollywood. Of course, some of these pictures are before my time there." She pointed at one, a black-and-white shot showing several people. "Is that Mabel Normand?"

"Yes. That's Mack Sennett there in the background. And me." She indicated her younger self, on the periphery of the photo. "I was doing stunts for Sennett's production company, right after Essanay closed here in Niles and I went down to Los Angeles." She smiled. "I was so young then. Weren't we all."

"I remember you saying that you grew up in the Bay Area," Addie said. "But I don't recall that you ever mentioned a town."

Rose shrugged and resumed her seat on the sofa, moving the book to the coffee table. She took a sip from the glass. Bella hopped up and snuggled in next to her. "Niles is home. My parents had a ranch up in the hills. That's where I learned to ride, when I was barely old enough to sit a horse. I wound up doing stunts for Essanay. I could do anything with horses. Rode them standing up, jumped from horses onto cars or trains. Even jumped off buildings." She pointed at a black-and-white photograph, showing a much younger Rose astride a paint pony. "I did a lot of movies with Broncho Billy. I loved that man. He was the best." She ruffled the dog's fur. "So yes, I came back here after I left Hollywood. The ranch is long gone. I sold it after Mom and Dad died. I always liked these Essanay houses. As soon as one of them went on the market, I snapped it up."

"Tell me how the two of you met," Jill said, looking from Rose to Addie.

"I was working in Washington, D.C., which is where I met Tidsy. I was at the Office of War Information and she was—" Addie stopped and looked at Tidsy. "She was working somewhere else. I got the opportunity to go to Hollywood and work at the Bureau of Motion Pictures. That was a big treat for a girl from a small town who lived at the movies on Saturday afternoons. And there I met Rose, who was directing movies for the war effort. Short documentaries, mostly."

"Producing propaganda," Rose said, her voice tart. "Me, Frank Capra and John Ford. Though they were more famous than I was."

"We didn't call it propaganda," Addie said. "We wanted to send the appropriate message and support the war effort. Movies that put the soldiers and sailors in a good light. We had a handbook. It was distributed to studio heads as well as directors, writers and producers. A lot of the studios, not all, sent us scripts to review. Anyway, you wrote and directed several documentaries for us. And they were good."

"That was a long time ago, Addie. A lot of water has gone under that bridge." Rose's tone hinted that the patriotic zeal of the war had long since dissipated.

"We went out for coffee or a drink now and then, the way coworkers do. After the war, we went our separate ways. I met Dewitt, got married, moved up here to San Francisco." She looked at Rose. "You were busy, with your career. You had all sorts of plans. You wrote scripts and you directed a couple of movies after the war. Then someone told me you were supposed to direct another picture but it fell through. That you'd given up the business and left Hollywood. What happened?"

Rose's smile held no warmth. Bitterness poured out, heating her words. "What happened? The blacklist happened. You've heard of the blacklist, I'm sure. It's a very big club, studded with nails. And the studio bosses are using it to beat the living daylights out of the people who made the business great. It's run through Hollywood like the plague. People who used to be able to find work have been tossed out with the trash, all because a bunch of politicians are falling all over themselves to show how tough they are. Well, I never was a member of the Communist Party. I'm a Roosevelt Democrat, have been ever since FDR threw his hat in the ring. Back in the Thirties, I joined the Screenwriters Guild. So many of us did. But after the war, that was a black mark. Or a red one."

"Oh, damn," Addie said. "I had no idea."

"How could you?" Rose stopped and reached for the glass, taking a sip. Then she continued. "The men who run the movie business called us screenwriters lefties and Commies, just because we were fighting to get writers their fair share of the profits. They went after us because we were unionizing. They said we were the most dangerous group in the movie industry. All because we stood up to them. But it came back to bite us in the butt in the end. With people like Dalton Trumbo and the rest of the Hollywood Ten going to jail. Writers like Mary McCall unable to work. The studio system was falling apart after the Paramount decision in 1948. So the studio executives decided to go after anyone who didn't toe the line."

She took another sip, then set the glass on the table. "There's this rag called *Red Channels*. They made a list of a bunch of TV and movie actors, writers and other people, called them Communist sympathizers. And the other magazines and newspapers take it from there." Rose quirked her mouth in a grim smile. "Myrna Loy fought back. She sued the *Hollywood Reporter*, after an article called her a Communist. She made them print a retraction. But it cost her. You notice she didn't get an Oscar nomination for *The Best Years of Our Lives*. And she should have."

Rose stopped talking and stroked her dog. Some of the heat in her words and her expression had gone away, as though something had been pricked and the steam released. Bella sighed and wagged her tail, pressing into Rose's hip.

"I'm sorry you got caught up in this crap," Tidsy said. "It's damaged a lot of people. Something specific must have happened. The movie you were set to direct, the one that fell through. Why didn't the movie get made?"

"Oh, it got made, eventually. But I didn't direct it."

"Why not?" Jill asked.

"I got fired," Rose said. "It was a picture for Global Studios. A week before we were supposed to start filming, I got called into the studio executive's office. He told me my services were no longer needed. When I asked why, I was told I was a Commie and the studio didn't need any fifth-column lefties. The person who fired me was Stuart Felton." She paused, her gaze moving from Jill to Tidsy to Addie. "So now all of you are sitting here thinking that I had a motive to kill him. I suppose I did. But think about it. Why would I wait until now? If I was going to murder the son of a bitch, I'd have done it five years ago, when I was still down in Hollywood."

"They say revenge is a dish best served cold," Jill said.

Rose ruffled her dog's ears. "I suppose it is. But it's not my style. Although I think using a Niles brick to bash in Felton's head was a supremely artistic touch. My compliments to whoever did kill him." A smile ghosted across her face. "Look, I hated the man. Hated what he and others like him are doing to the industry that I worked in for more than thirty years. Damn bean-counters. It's all about money for people like that. They wouldn't know creative if it bit them in the ass. But—" She punctuated her words with her hands. "I didn't kill Felton. Neither did my niece Eve, so don't even think that. You're barking up the wrong tree."

"Okay, I don't see you playing the role of murderer," Tidsy said. "But you knew Felton. What can you tell us about him?"

"He was a soulless, cold-hearted, gimlet-eyed son of a bitch," Rose said. "With a cash register instead of a heart. If he'd been murdered down in Hollywood, I could give you a long list of suspects. But here in Niles? That limits your cast of killers. It has to be someone in the cast or crew. Eve and I have been kicking around some theories and coming up empty."

"It can't be Drake," Addie said, looking dismayed. "He's my nephew. I just can't believe he would do such a thing. And it couldn't be Dewitt, my husband."

"Felton was going to kill the movie," Rose said. "That's what Eve told me. Cancel it, just like that. As I understand it, Drake and Dewitt have a lot of money riding on this. That gives them motives."

"I've talked with several people today—" Jill said.

"Yes, I'll bet you have. Eve told me you talked with the two men that Hal saw before he found the body."

"The key grip and the gaffer, yes. But you haven't told me what you saw."

"Me?" Rose narrowed her eyes. "What makes you think I saw anything?"

"I think you left the house the same time Hal did."

Rose didn't answer right away. Then she smiled. "You're really good at this, aren't you? Maybe you should give up being a Zephyr-ette and hang out your shingle as a detective. All right, I did leave the house the same time as Hal. I do that when he comes for a visit. He doesn't know that, by the way."

"Why?" Tidsy asked. "To make sure he gets on the train?"

"That's exactly it," Rose said. "Hal's damaged, not in body, but in his mind. I told Jill he had a bad war. He was a stunt-man in Hollywood, in the Thirties. That's when I met him. I was still doing stunts back then, late Twenties and early Thirties. We were in a movie together. For a while, we were more than friends. Even thought about marrying the guy. But it didn't happen." She sighed. "Then the war came. He joined up after Pearl Harbor. So many of them did. He was on a ship in the Pacific that got sunk. He survived. But when he came back in '45, he wasn't the same. That's when he started hoboing. Then I left Hollywood and moved back up to Niles. Somehow he found out I was here. So he stops by, every few months. I wash his clothes and make sure he gets a few good meals and a warm place to sleep. Then he goes on his way again. Until the next time. Like me, he's not getting any younger, and hoboing is hard on a guy. I keep an eye on him, yes, to make sure he catches a freight."

"What happened yesterday?" Addie asked.

"He left, and I left a minute or so later," Rose said. "I followed him to Front Street, stood there and watched him. My plan was, after he caught the freight, to go get some groceries. I saw him do what he described yesterday. He waited near the depot until those guys who were smoking near the oak tree went back into the warehouse. I saw him try to climb aboard that boxcar—and fall. I could see when he ran off that he was hurt. So I came back here, knowing he'd head for my house. Once he was safe inside, I went out again, to see if I could find out what happened. That's when you saw me, Jill. I was on the edge of the crowd, trying like hell to hear what was being said. Then Bert Gallagher saw me. I knew he'd tell you about me. I got out of there. I went to the drugstore to get some first-aid supplies for Hal. Then I came home to doctor him. And you showed up on my doorstep." She paused. "I would have told you this yesterday. But I didn't want Hal to know. About me playing watchdog, I mean."

"I appreciate your telling me now," Jill said. "What I want to know is whether you saw anything that might help us figure out who killed Felton."

Rose shook her head. "No, I didn't. It happened the way Hal described it. Felton was there at the back corner of the warehouse and then he turned, like someone had called to him. Hal didn't see that person because he heard a truck backfiring and looked away. I heard the same truck and did the same thing. I know it would be very convenient if you had an eyewitness to the murder, but I'm sorry, that's all I can tell you."

Jill thought for a moment, frustrated. "Eve told you that I'd been talking with people today, trying to get more information. And I have. Neal Preston and Leona Alexander. Charles Bosworth wouldn't cooperate."

"That doesn't surprise me," Rose said. "Charlie puts on a pleasant front but he can be as mean as a snake."

"There are things I can't share," Jill began.

"If you mean because Neal Preston is a homosexual, I already know that." Rose shrugged. "Eve told me she suspected as much. If Felton knew that, and I figure he did, he would be holding it over Neal."

"He was." Jill nodded.

"What about the other members of the cast?" Tidsy asked.

"Leona Alexander is a beauty," Rose said. "And from what I can tell, the pictures I've seen her in, she's very talented. Felton was always pressuring actresses for sex. I suspect he did the same with Leona. She's a strong woman, from what I hear, and I figure she shut him down. She doesn't strike me as the kind to give in. Felton would have done everything in his power to wreck her career. So that gives her a motive for murder, too."

"Except I can place her, Neal and Bosworth on the set, around the time the murder happened," Jill said. "Along with Drake and Eve and a lot of the crew members."

"What about the guy who's playing the conductor?" Tidsy toyed with the chunky garnet ring on her finger.

"Bert's a sweetheart," Rose said. "He wouldn't hurt a fly. And he has no motive that we know of."

"I agree." Addie shook her head. "What about the other people in the cast? The crew?"

"I don't see bit players or cameramen having any motivation to kill Felton," Rose said. "If he canceled the production, they'd find jobs elsewhere."

"There's one other person we haven't talked about," Jill said slowly. "The screenwriter, Wade Ratliff."

Rose nodded. "I don't know much about him. Neither do any of my few remaining writer friends. My niece says he's a hothead, always upset about changes in the script. As a screenwriter, I can certainly understand that."

"Yes, he complained about it a lot," Jill said, "to anyone who would listen, but mostly to Drake. I overheard something yesterday. Felton was arguing with Wade. I don't know what set it off, but Felton threatened him. With the blacklist."

"Did he indeed?" Rose narrowed her eyes.

"Yes. They were really going at it. A lot of anger. I don't know what led to it, but given what you've told us about the blacklist..." Jill's voice trailed off.

Tidsy jumped into the conversation. "We hear Felton collected art."

Addie nodded. "My husband tells me that's one reason he agreed to come to the party on Saturday, so that he could see Dewitt's art collection. He saw everything in the library as well as upstairs."

"I heard that, too," Rose said. "He liked paintings, mostly European. His place in Beverly Hills was full of them. So they tell me. I was never there. You should know, there's a story that made the rounds back in the Forties."

"What was that?" Jill asked.

"There was an actor who had a small painting Felton wanted," Rose said. "The actor wanted a part in a movie at Global Studios. Felton told the actor he could have the part—if he gave the painting to Felton. I don't know if the story is true, but I heard it from enough people to believe it might have some veracity. It sounds like something he would do."

Chapter Eighteen

THE MURDER AND ITS AFTERMATH were still the primary topics of conversation on Wednesday morning. Jill heard it everywhere, first in the makeup trailer as Venita and Nancy speculated about who was responsible. Outside near the catering trailer, where cast members were getting their morning coffee and pastries, Jill heard several theories being bandied about.

She went inside the warehouse, where the first scene was being shot in the replica of the dining car. This involved a lot of people in addition to the principal actors. Bit players and extras playing passengers filled the diner's seats, while other extras took on the roles of kitchen staff and waiters. Jill was also in the scene. As she often did in real life, she was having dinner with the passengers.

The camera began rolling and the clapperboard went down, signaling the start of the take. The people in the ersatz dining car talked, creating a background buzz of conversation as she walked through the door at the end of the car. She stopped at the counter near the kitchen and spoke to the man playing the dining car steward. With a gesture, he directed her to a nearby table, already occupied by Leona Alexander, in her role as Dolores Bain, and by Ella, the well-to-do passenger. The scene felt real enough as Jill took a seat, exchanging small talk with the two women, just as she would on the real *California Zephyr*. Then the mood changed as a fourth passenger joined them, Bosworth, playing the villain, Creswell. As he took his seat, Neal Preston made his entrance, walking past the table, with a sidelong glance at the occupants.

The script called for Ella, the passenger, to pepper the

Zephyrette with nosy, personal questions. Jill often got those while working, so the scene felt natural as Ella said her dialogue, wondering aloud if the pretty Zephyrette had a boyfriend and plans to get married. Before Jill could respond, one of the extras playing a waiter dropped a tray. Plates, glasses and cutlery crashed to the floor, with broken shards flying everywhere.

"Cut!" Drake yelled, voice full of exasperation. He ran his hands through his short blond hair as though he was ready to pull it out. "Damn it! Get the set dresser. Somebody clean that up so we can get this scene. If this is how the day is going to go—"

The actors vacated the set. Several crew members hurried over to clean up the mess. The prop master and set dresser appeared, ready to recreate the scene.

"How about a break?" Eve said. "Maybe everyone will settle down."

"Good idea," Drake said. "Okay, everyone, take ten minutes. Then be ready to get this scene done. We have a lot of scenes on the call sheet today and I need everyone at the top of their game."

The set buzzed with talk as the bit players and extras filed out, heading to the front door and the catering trailer for infusions of coffee. Neal gave Jill a wary, sidelong glance as he departed. Bosworth also gave her a look, narrowing his eyes and stroking his mustache as he always did. It make him look like a villain, Jill thought, one in a melodrama.

Leona appeared at Jill's elbow. "You're making people nervous, asking all these questions. Shall we get some coffee? I need some caffeine, even it if means I'll have to have my makeup touched up."

Jill smiled at the actress. "Yes, I could use some coffee, too."

They went out the front door and walked over to the catering trailer, getting mugs of coffee. Jill poured cream in hers and took a restorative sip.

Beside her, Leona lowered her voice. "Let's go over to the oak tree. I have something to tell you and we need some privacy."

They threaded their way through the cast and crew members gathered around the catering trailer. Others stood in front of the warehouse, talking and smoking. Jill and Leona carried their mugs past the building, walking out to the oak tree. No one was there. Leona brushed a few golden-brown leaves from the bench and they sat down.

"You have information for me?" Jill asked.

Leona took a sip of her coffee, her lipstick leaving a red mark on the rim of the mug. "I do indeed. I called my cinematographer friend last night, the one who collects art. He told me the story and swears it's true. He says he knows, because he was working on the movie in question. It happened about five years ago. An actor was going through a bad patch. He wasn't getting much work. He wanted a part in a movie that was set to start shooting at Global Studios. Not the lead, but a meaty part, a good secondary role. Another actor had already been cast. Then all of a sudden actor number one was out, and actor number two was in. My friend was curious, because he thought the first actor would have been much better in the role. So he did a little investigating of his own. He found out that Felton told actor number two that he could have the part—if the actor gave Felton a painting he'd just bought."

"But who was actor number two?" Jill asked.

Leona smiled, a conspiratory twinkle in her eyes. "It was Charlie Bosworth."

"I'm not surprised," Jill said. "Several people had heard the story, so I figured there was some truth to it. As for Bosworth, I'm not sure this gives him a motive for murder. And it looks like he was on the set at the time the murder happened."

"Depends on when Felton was killed," Leona pointed out. "And we really don't know. We just assume he hadn't been dead long when you found the body. Charlie was on the set right around that time. But not all the time. He was gone briefly between takes. I figured it was a bathroom break."

"So, gone for a little while," Jill said. "Maybe not long enough to bash Felton in the head. And why would he? Even if he didn't kill Felton, maybe he has some information that would be important."

"I don't know why Charlie might kill Felton, other than Felton was a horrible man. He and Charlie were supposed to be friends. As for Charlie having information, you'll have to corner him and talk to him. Which could be interesting," Leona added. "He's been giving you the evil eye since yesterday, when you tried to question him. And he knows you've talked to other people. So good luck with that."

"He can't avoid me any longer," Jill declared. "What you just told me gives me a way to start the conversation."

"He's in this scene, if we ever get the thing shot," Leona said. "And in the next two scenes on the call sheet. We do have a busy morning. And it's not going very well. Everyone is rattled by the murder and the talk about shutting down the production."

"I know. I looked at the call sheet this morning and it looks like he'll have a break later this morning. And definitely for lunch. I'll have to choose my moment."

They sat in silence finishing their coffee. Then they walked back to the catering trailer and dropped off their cups. Back on the set, Nancy hovered over Leona, touching up her makeup and reapplying her lipstick.

It required four more takes to get the dining car scene filmed to Drake's satisfaction. Fortunately they didn't have any more stumbles, falls, or breakages. Then they set up for a scene in one of the Pullman car sets, this one involving Bosworth.

Jill wasn't in this particular scene. Just as well. This gave her the opportunity to make a phone call. She went outside again, ignoring a wave from Bert Gallagher, who was having coffee at one of the tables. She crossed Front Street and walked to the phone booth near the drugstore. She set her change purse on the shelf inside the booth and dropped coins into the slot, then dialed Tidsy's number in San Francisco. As the phone rang, she willed Tidsy to be home. She was just about to hang up when Tidsy answered.

"Good thing you caught me. Addie and I are going to lunch. She's here."

"I'm calling to report in,"

"Great. We have something to tell you, too. Hey, Addie, it's Jill. Get on the extension in the bedroom."

A moment later, Jill heard a click. Then Addie Collier's voice came on the line. "Hi, Jill. What have you found out?"

"Leona Alexander spoke with a friend of hers in Hollywood last night," Jill said. "He's an art collector. He confirms the story about the actor who gave Felton a painting in exchange for a part. Under duress, he says. And the actor was Charles Bosworth."

"The same Charles Bosworth who has a role in this movie," Tidsy said. "Have you talked with him yet?"

"He's been avoiding me since yesterday, when I was asking questions about the murder. Now that I know about his transaction with Felton, I know why. Bosworth has been in all the scenes we've shot this morning," Jill added. "Including one that's being shot right now. As soon as he's done with that scene, I'm going to confront him and see if I can get any information out of him."

"Good. Let me know what you find out," Tidsy said.

"I hope I can find out something. What is it you want to tell me?"

Addie answered the question. "I had a chat with my husband this morning. He told me that he's been approached by someone who wants to sell a Dutch painting, but he won't say who that person is. Nor will he tell me what the asking price is. I'll bet it's a lot of money and he won't tell me because he's sure I'll fuss at him. I was quite put out with him for keeping all of this from me in the first place. I did manage to worm out the information that he was supposed to meet with the seller on Monday. But with the murder, that meeting went by the wayside. He told me he was meeting the seller in Oakland this evening."

"Not a clue as to who it could be?" Jill asked.

"Negative," Tidsy said. "Maybe it's whoever called him on Saturday, during the party."

"I've been thinking about that," Jill said. "Because I only heard one side of the conversation, Dewitt's side, I assumed it was a phone call. What if it wasn't? What if it was someone who was at the party?"

"Who at the party would have a Dutch painting to sell?" Addie asked. "Bosworth, since he's a collector? Or could it have been Felton? Maybe we're looking at this the wrong way."

Jill had a theory, one that she'd already discussed with Tidsy. "I've been thinking about Wade Ratliff, the screenwriter."

"The one who stole my snuffbox?" Addie demanded.

"The very same. Shortly after I overheard the conversation, I saw Wade standing near the display cases, right where the hallway runs into the living room. I wondered what he was doing there."

Addie huffed. "Probably looking to steal something else."

"He could have been in the library with Dewitt. I realize it's a bit of a stretch."

"No," Tidsy said. "It's worth checking out. Jill already mentioned this to me. I'll fill you in after we get off the phone."

"Good, because I have to go." Jill looked up to see a woman standing near the pay phone, waiting to use it. At least she looked a good deal more patient than the old man who had tapped on the glass the last time she was in this phone booth.

Jill walked back across Front Street, to the warehouse.

———

There was a break in filming just after noon, and the cast and crew headed out to the catering truck for lunch. Jill followed Charlie Bosworth and stood near him as he queued up with the others. Once he got a sandwich and a bottle of ginger ale, he took a seat at the end of a long table and sat down to eat. Jill, carrying a bottle of Coca-Cola, slipped into the seat opposite him.

"You and I need to have a talk," she said.

"And why would that be?" He gave her his usual condescending look as he raised the bottle to his lips.

"That would be because of a painting you gave to Stuart Felton in exchange for a role in a movie. I think the police would be interested in finding out more about your relationship with the murder victim."

Now he stared at her in consternation, hand tightening around the bottle. He set it down on the table. "Where did you hear that?"

"People talk. I heard it from several sources."

"Well, you heard it wrong." Bosworth looked around, as though hoping someone else would sit down at the table and allow him to escape Jill's questions. He picked up his roast beef sandwich and tore off a bite.

"Tell me what really happened."

"How could this possibly be any concern of yours?" he demanded.

"I'm trying to find out who killed him. After all, I found the body."

"As I told you yesterday, leave it to the police. That's their job. Surely that hobo you saw standing over the body is responsible."

Jill shrugged. "What if he isn't? What if the killer is someone working on the movie, a member of the cast or crew?"

"That's crazy," Bosworth said, wiping his mouth with a napkin. "Young lady, you have an overactive imagination." Jill didn't say anything. She just kept looking at him. He stared back in disbelief, as if he couldn't believe she could have the effrontery to accuse him of wrongdoing. "You certainly don't think that I had anything to do with Felton's death? That's absurd. I was on the set when it happened."

"I understand you left the set during a break between scenes."

"Who told you that?"

Jill shrugged. "Does it matter? Did you leave the set?"

"I went to the men's room," he snapped as he reached for the bottle. "Good God, I was gone for a minute, maybe two. I didn't leave the building. You're completely mad. I didn't kill Felton." He took a swallow of ginger ale and set the bottle down with a bang. Billy Dale, who was sitting nearby, glanced over, his attention drawn by the noise.

Probably not, Jill thought. But she wasn't going to be put off. "Tell me about the painting you gave Felton."

Bosworth sighed, as though he'd decided that answering questions about the painting was preferable to being accused of murder. "It was a gift. Felton was a friend. Not a close one, but, well, he and I are...were both in the movie business and both art lovers. He was always very supportive of my career. I gave him the painting to thank him for all his help over the years. It was just a small token, hardly worth anything at all, a landscape by an artist who wasn't very well known."

Jill wasn't sure she bought the "friends" story. "People are saying it was more like bribery. That Felton wouldn't give you a part unless you gave him the painting."

"Absolute nonsense." Bosworth pushed away his plate, as though he had no more appetite.

Jill thought she'd try another line of inquiry. "What do you know about Wade Ratliff? I understand he's an art lover, too."

"The screenwriter? Egotistical little twit." Bosworth brushed his mustache. "Why are you asking about him? Is it because you know about—" He stopped.

Jill chose her words carefully. "I've heard something else about a painting."

Bosworth didn't say anything right away. His eyes narrowed and it was almost as though she could see wheels and gears turning in his head. "I heard the same rumor. I didn't know what to make of it. There was just a whiff of a story that there was a rare painting available, for the right price. As an art collector, I was interested. A lot depending on the asking price, of course."

Jill remembered Bosworth making several attempts to speak to Felton at the party. First it looked as though the executive had brushed off the actor. Then later, the two of them had been talking, looking quite chummy. Now she realized why. "You told Felton, didn't you? You heard about the painting for sale. You heard that Dewitt Collier was thinking of buying it. So you told Felton. All the better to keep on his good side, because he was now the studio executive in charge of the picture."

The look in Bosworth's eyes told her that her speculation was on target. He started to say something, then he stopped as one of the crew members approached. "Hey, Charlie, they're looking for you on the set." Relief washed over the actor's face as he stood up and made his escape, taking his half-eaten sandwich with him.

Jill remained seated at the table. She sipped her Coke, thinking about what she'd learned: There was a painting, and Wade was selling it.

"Have you heard the latest?" Bert Gallagher sat down at the table, with a cup of coffee and a ham sandwich. "We have a new exec. Global picked one of Vesey's protégés, a guy named Lowell. So things are looking favorable."

"They're not going to shut down the production?"

"Nope. That's me, and the rest of us, breathing a sigh of relief. At least it's a bit of good news in what has been a trying day. I thought we'd never get that dining car scene done." Bert surveyed his sandwich and took a bite.

Jill and Bert chatted while he finished his lunch, then he left, going out to the oak tree to have a smoke, he said. Jill drank the last of her Coke and discarded the bottle. Then she walked to the front of the warehouse, intending to go inside. But Rose Laurent was on the sidewalk near the building, with her dog on the leash, waving at Jill. Bella greeted Jill with a bark. She leaned down to scratch the dog between her ears.

"I came looking for you," Rose said. "I remembered something I saw on Monday and I think it's important. It was about the same time I saw you find Felton's body. I saw that screenwriter, Wade. I recognized him because of his red hair. He was in front of the warehouse, over by the trailers. I saw him cross Front Street and walk to the hotel. I know it was him, because I was standing near the hotel entrance at the time. I've seen him with Eve."

Jill stood still, thinking about this. After she'd found the body, she remembered seeing Wade leave the hotel and hurry toward the murder scene.

If what Rose was telling Jill was true, Wade had been at the warehouse, not the hotel, when Felton was murdered. Rose had seen him outside. It would be a simple matter to walk along the side of the warehouse, passing by the trailers, to get to the back. Had Wade been there when Felton was killed? Had he seen something?

Or was he the killer? She kept going back to the angry scene between the executive and the screenwriter. Why was Felton threatening Wade with the blacklist?

"Thanks. Yes, it is important."

Jill turned as Rose walked away. She took a few steps and looked up as someone loomed over her. It was Billy Dale. The actor had a cigarette in his hand and a thoughtful look on his face. "I overheard a little bit of that, you putting the screws to Bosworth. And what that lady just told you. You've sure been asking a lot of questions. People are talking about you as much as that murder."

"Just naturally curious, I guess."

"Being too curious can get you in trouble. You really think old

Charlie Bosworth killed Felton?" He laughed. "The guy's no prize but I can't see him exerting himself that much."

"Probably not," Jill said. "But I figured I'd stir the pot and see what floated up."

Billy blew out smoke and pitched his cigarette to the ground. "Well, like I said, I heard what the lady with the dog said about the screenwriter. I saw him, too."

"You did?"

"Yes, indeed. Must have been about ten or fifteen minutes before you came inside to call the cops. He was walking up this side of the building." Billy pointed a thumb in the direction of the dressing room trailers that were lined up on the east side of the warehouse. "Walking this way, like he'd been all the way to the back of the building and he was coming up to the front. I thought maybe he'd gone back to the dressing rooms to talk to one of the actors. But then I realized most everyone was on the set. If he was looking for them to talk about the script, why didn't he go inside the building? He just kept walking. Went across the street and headed for the hotel."

"Why would you guess he was going to talk with someone about the script?" Jill asked.

"Well, he was carrying something," Billy said. "Couldn't see exactly what it was. I just assumed it was a copy of the script."

Something small and portable, Jill thought. And I'd certainly like to know what it was.

Chapter Nineteen

JILL'S STOMACH GROWLED, reminding her that she had not yet eaten lunch. She checked her watch. Did she have time? She was on the call sheet for two scenes this afternoon, one on the lounge car set, the other on the observation car set. Filming on those wasn't due to start for another hour. She headed for the catering trailer, where she got an iced tea and a turkey sandwich. Finding a seat at a table occupied by several of the bit players and extras, she ate her lunch and chatted with the others.

Forty minutes later she went inside the warehouse. As she approached the lounge car set, she encountered Charles Bosworth, who glared at her and walked away. Billy Dale was behind the counter and Neal Preston was in front, with several extras seated at tables. Jill waited at the edge of the set, ready to make her entrance. Everyone was in place under the bright lights as the cameras began to roll, Neal leaning on the counter, talking with the waiter as he mixed a drink.

Then Jill walked onto the set and began her dialogue with Neal. "Mr. Gray, you asked me to tell you if I saw Mr. Creswell do anything unusual. Well, I did."

Neal took her by the arm and drew her out of the lounge, into the corridor. "What was it?"

Jill glanced to one side, as though afraid of being overheard. "He was opening the linen locker, where the porter keeps the sheets. But that's supposed to be kept locked."

"He must have stolen the key from the porter." That was the

next line, but instead of "must," Neal said "mush." Then he said, "Damn it."

"Cut!" Drake called. "All right, let's try it again."

They resumed their places while the man who operated the clapperboard chalked the number 2 on the board. The camera rolled again, and Neal flubbed the line again.

Jill wondered if he was rattled because she'd confronted him earlier. Of course, since the murder, they were all under a strain. Everyone resumed their places for the third take. It went off without a hitch and she breathed a sigh of relief as she made her exit.

There was a short break as they set up for the next scene, on the observation car set. It was then that Wade Ratliff showed up at the warehouse. Wade had rewritten the scene the day before. Each time this happened, the actors had to learn new lines. Now Leona told Drake she was having trouble with the dialogue. "It's those last two lines. I just don't think Dolores would say it that way."

Drake examined the page in question. Then he turned to Wade. "I agree with Leona. Can we tweak this a bit?"

"Again?" Wade threw up his hands. "Why are you still making changes? Felton's dead. He can't dictate how the script should be anymore. Why can't you just go back to filming it the way it was originally written?"

"As it happens," Drake said, "I like the scene the way it's rewritten. I think it's better than the original scene. Just change these two lines."

Wade sputtered at him. "You can't be serious."

Drake took him by the arm and led him over to Eve's makeshift office, where they could continue their conversation.

Leona sat down in a nearby chair, rolled her eyes and smiled at Jill. "Screenwriters. They always think their words are gospel. But I'm right. I know my character and she wouldn't say it the way he wrote it."

Nancy swooped down, powder puff in hand, and did a quick touch up on Leona's makeup, then examined Jill's face and did the same. By that time Drake and Wade had evidently come to an agreement. Wade was wielding a pencil over the bottom half of the script page. He slapped the pencil down on the table and handed the page to Drake, who read it quickly and nodded. Drake walked over to where Leona sat and showed her the page.

"Yes, that's an improvement. Thank you, Wade." Leona added a pleasant smile to her words. The screenwriter glowered and stuck his hands into his pockets.

Drake looked happy that the problem was solved, at least for the moment. "Thanks, Wade, I appreciate your being flexible about this. Oh, and that other matter? Let's discuss it over dinner tonight."

Wade shook his head. "Sorry, not tonight. I'm meeting someone. Maybe I'll see you later in the bar."

Jill pricked up her ears at this. Who was Wade meeting? According to Addie, Dewitt was also meeting someone this evening, to talk about buying a painting. Dewitt hadn't told her who it was, but he had said that the meeting would take place in the East Bay. Was Wade meeting Dewitt? Was there really a painting and did Wade have it? Or was this a wild goose chase?

There was one way to find out, Jill thought. An idea began to take shape in her mind. She watched as Wade walked briskly past the nearest Pullman set where Bosworth beckoned to him. He stopped to talk with the actor.

"All right," Drake called. "Let's get on with the next scene."

The actors took their places on the observation car set as the director went over the scene, telling Leona and Neal what he wanted from them. Jill was in the scene as well, along with Bert Gallagher and several of the bit players and extras.

The camera began to roll and the clapperboard went down, signaling the start of the take. They didn't get very far before Neal flubbed his lines. "Cut," Drake yelled. "Neal, you're really off today."

"I'm sorry," Neal snapped. "Let's do it again."

For some reason, the scene wouldn't jell. On the second take, Leona stumbled on a loose bit of carpet. On the third, Drake decided the camera angle was wrong. It took four more takes and badly frayed nerves on the part of the actors and the crew before the clapperboard came down on take seven and Drake said he was satisfied with the scene. Jill heard relieved sighs all around her.

Leona looked as though she was getting a headache, if she didn't have one already. She ran her hands through her platinum blond hair, dislodging her coiffure.

"I thought we'd never get through that one," Bert Gallagher said. He removed his conductor's cap. "It's been a long day."

Jill nodded. "It has." According to the wall clock, it was after six. This was the last scene on today's call sheet. Presumably they were done. Drake confirmed this. "All right, everyone. That's it for the day. Let's shut it down. Then go back to the hotel and get some rest. See you early tomorrow morning."

The crew shut down the lights, camera and other equipment, readying them for tomorrow's filming. Jill followed the general exodus of cast members out of the warehouse to the dressing rooms. Once she had removed her costume and makeup, she dressed in her street clothes. As she left the dressing room, she saw Leona come out of her dressing room, casually dressed in slacks. Her hair was brushed back from her face, which was devoid of makeup, and she carried the Michener book she'd been reading.

"Have a good evening, Jill," the actress said. "Go home and put your feet up. That's what I'm going to do. I may have dinner in my room, instead of going down to the restaurant."

"I'll see you tomorrow." Jill waved.

Leona crossed Front Street and walked toward the hotel. Jill stood for a moment and watched as Drake and Eve left the warehouse, followed by Ralph, the head production assistant, who locked the door and put the key in his pocket. She said good evening to the three of them and headed for the Ford, parked on the west side of the building.

But she had no intention of going home, at least not yet. She drove the Ford out of the parking lot and headed west on Front Street, then she doubled back, driving east slowly as she looked for a parking space—not just any parking space. Ahead of her, a car pulled away from the curb and she quickly took the space. It was perfect, right on the corner of the intersection of Front and H Streets. From the driver's seat, she had a clear view of the hotel entrance. And as a bonus, parked on H Street, almost directly across from her, was the blue Buick Roadmaster that Wade Ratliff drove. If Wade was meeting Dewitt Collier, he would be leaving soon. Jill was going to follow him.

She could hear Mike's voice in her head, telling her that wasn't a good idea. But Tidsy would do it, she was sure of that.

Minutes ticked by on her watch, ten, then another five. Then she saw someone coming out of the hotel. Wade. And he was carrying something under his arm. He paused at the hotel entrance. But he didn't go left, which would have taken him around the corner to his car. Instead he turned right and walked east on Front Street.

This wasn't unfolding the way she thought it would. When she'd overheard Wade earlier today, she was sure he was planning to meet Dewitt. And Addie Collier had told her that Dewitt was meeting someone who wanted to sell a painting in Oakland. She'd assumed that someone was Wade. If it was, maybe their plans had changed.

Jill shoved her purse under the driver's seat, got out of the car and locked the door. She crossed H Street, following Wade. As she passed the window of the hotel restaurant, she glanced in and saw Bert Gallagher and several other cast members grouped around a table in the back corner of the restaurant, looking at menus. She looked ahead and saw Wade. He was past the drugstore now. He stepped to the curb and looked both ways, then angled across the street, heading toward the warehouse.

Had the meeting been moved to the warehouse? Jill hung back for a second, trying to decide what to do as a couple of cars went down Front Street. It was dusk now, and the cars had their lights on. She crossed the street. Wade was walking down the west side of the building, toward the place where she had found Felton's body. Then he turned the corner and disappeared behind the building.

Jill walked quickly along the same route. When she reached the corner, she hesitated. Should she? Would prudence win out, or curiosity?

Curiosity, it seemed. She peered around the corner. No one there. Where had Wade gone? To the other side of the building, where the trailers were located? No, he'd gone into the warehouse. The area in back of the warehouse, with its crumbling concrete pad, was illuminated by a nearby light from the rail yard. She could see that the back door of the building was open. She approached it, pushed the door wider and stepped inside. One light burned, the unshaded lamp on the rectangular table where the typewriter and phone sat. She didn't know if it had been left on by the production assistant, or if Wade had turned it on.

She was used to seeing the interior of the warehouse full of people, the sets lit with Klieg lights, the cameraman behind his camera, the gaffer and other electricians at their posts, the bit players and extras waiting for direction from Drake. Between takes, the buzz of conversation was ever-present. Now it was dark inside the cavernous building, that one light casting eerie shadows on the sets that resembled railcars. She stopped and listened, but she didn't hear anything. Turning slowly, she looked at the sets—the Pullmans, the lounge, the diner, the observation car—a scattered consist for a make-believe train.

The silence and the shadows spooked her. This was a bad idea, she told herself. She turned to leave, and there he was, between her and the door. The bundle was under his left arm. And in his right hand he held a gun. The light glinted off the dark gray metal. Too late she realized that she'd been lured here.

"You've been asking too many questions," Wade said.

"Have I?" Jill kept her voice even, though she didn't feel calm at all. "I'm surprised to see you here. Mrs. Collier told me her husband was planning to buy a Dutch painting and that he was meeting that person in Oakland today. I thought that was you. I was planning to follow you to that meeting."

"Instead you followed me here," he said. "Yes, I was supposed to meet Dewitt in Oakland tonight. But after seeing you nose around and question people today, I realized that might be a bad idea. So I called Dewitt and rescheduled the meeting."

Jill gestured at the wrapped bundle he held. "Is that the painting?"

"It's not just any painting. It's a Vermeer. Dewitt told me he'd do anything to get his hands on a Rembrandt or a Vermeer. So when I told him I had a Vermeer, he was practically salivating. Name my price, he said." Wade laughed. "Do you want to see it?"

"Yes, I would like to. Very much." Anything to gain a little time, she thought, and formulate a plan.

Wade set the bundle on the table, shoving the phone aside. Still holding the gun in his right hand, he used his left to untie the cord that held the fabric. Then he slowly teased away the fabric to reveal what was underneath.

She gasped, the only sound her indrawn breath. Even in the circle of illumination from the lamp, the painting glowed with a light all its own. It showed a young girl, on the cusp of woman-hood. A wisp of blond hair was visible under a pale blue headdress. Her shoulders were draped in a sky blue fabric. She stood in profile, her body facing left, but it was as though at the last minute she had turned to look at the artist. In her left hand she held a flower, raised to her chin as though she was going to inhale its fragrance. It was a rose, full blown, lush with deep pink petals that contrasted with the blue folds surrounding her shoulders.

"It's called *Girl with a Flower*," Wade said.

Jill found her voice. "It's exquisite. Where did you get it?"

"Oh, I think you know," he snapped, a sardonic twist to his mouth. "Mike probably told you all about it. He saw me put it in my duffel, right before we left Germany. I had it wrapped up in cloth, so he didn't know what it was. But he had his suspicions."

"He did." Jill tore her gaze away from the painting and focused on Wade. "It doesn't belong to you."

"It does now."

"You stole it."

"I took it off a dead Nazi," Wade said, with a cynical smile. "I'm sure he stole it from another Nazi. The Krauts were taking art right and left, all through the war. I figure the guy I got it from had helped himself to some of the spoils."

"You could have made the effort to find out who this painting belonged to," Jill said.

He laughed. "I could have, but I didn't. My guess is that it was some private collection, owned by one of those rich Jewish businessmen who got rounded up and sent to the camps. Whoever owned this painting in the past is dead."

"Like the Nazi you took it from," Jill said. "Did you kill him?"

"As a matter of fact, I did. He tried to trade it for safe passage and some walking-around money. I shot him instead." Wade gave a short, sardonic laugh. "I've held onto this little girl for a long time, waiting for the right moment and the right buyer. Enough time has gone by since the war for me to be fairly sure no one is looking for this painting. And enough time to show me that if a collector wants a painting so very badly, that he doesn't really care where it came from. Shaky provenance doesn't matter to a collector. And Dewitt's a collector who wants a Vermeer so much he can taste it, at the same time he's pulling out his checkbook."

"Then Felton came along," Jill said. "He found out you had the painting and he wanted it, as much as Dewitt. So you had two buyers. With Felton, you thought you could use that as leverage to keep him from shutting down production."

Wade nodded. "Yes. I dangled it under Felton's avaricious nose. I knew about him extorting Charlie Bosworth, Charlie's painting in exchange for a movie part. I thought I could play it right, get Felton to agree to let us continue with the production, promising to sell him the painting as soon as the movie was finished and distributed. But the son of a bitch tried to double-cross me. There are no guarantees with a louse like that. He said he was going to shut us down anyway and tell everyone I was a Commie. The blacklist. He's done it before, to dozens of people. Unless I gave him the painting, now. So I met him in back of the building. The idiot actually had the nerve to try to grab the painting away from me." Wade laughed. "I was quicker than he was. I kicked his legs out from under him. He hit his head when he fell, just enough to make him a little woozy. Then I finished him off with that brick."

"What do you intend to do now?" Jill asked. She was sure Wade's plans didn't involve letting her go. She glanced at the painting again, then at the telephone, its black bulk squatting on the table.

"I'm going to sell the painting to Dewitt," he said. "He's going to pay me a lot of money for it. But that's not all. I want a producer credit on this movie, in addition to a screenwriting credit. And a percentage of the profits. That's what I'm getting out of this deal. More than Felton was offering."

"When is this going to happen?"

"Tomorrow morning, early. That's when I'm supposed to meet him. As for you, Jill, you're a liability. You're too damn nosy. I can't let you leave here because you'll call the cops."

"Are you going to shoot me?" Jill indicated the gun he held. "Don't you think two murders in one week is excessive?"

"I'll drag your body out to the tracks. Once the next freight runs over you, it will look like an accident."

Jill gave him a deprecating look. "I should think people will wonder why I'm in the rail yard by myself at this hour. How does that fit into your scenario?"

"It fits in just fine. They won't miss you until tomorrow, when you don't show up for work. By that time I'll be gone. As soon as I get what I want from Dewitt, I'm driving back to Hollywood."

Jill hoped that someone would miss her before then, like her brother. Or Mike. Or Tidsy. She'd promised to call both of them tonight.

Wade leaned toward the table, using his left hand to cover the painting with the cloth. He tilted his right hand, the one that held the gun, in an awkward move to tie the cord.

Jill grabbed for the phone. He shoved it away from her but she had the receiver in her hand. She brought it down hard, hitting Wade on the shoulder. Then she picked up the lamp. It was connected to an electrical outlet by a long cord. She felt the cord pull free. The light went off. She used the lamp like a club to hit him on the head.

She didn't think she could make it to the back door. Wade was still between her and the exit. There was enough light from streetlights out in the rail yard that she could see his form. She pivoted and ran toward the sets grouped around the interior walls. The nearest was the Pullman ten-six sleeper.

If these were real railcars, Jill would have had all sorts of places to hide, as well as potential weapons at hand. But they weren't. Instead of the solid and comforting stainless steel of Budd railcars, the sets were made of wood and canvas. Doors opened to reveal not actual closets, but the flimsy bones behind the artifice. Still, she had resources.

Wade picked up the lamp. He plugged it in and turned on the light. Then he stood, gun glinting in his hand, his eyes darting about as he looked for her.

Jill moved as quietly as she could, from the Pullman set to the dome-observation car set. Here, in the lounge area at the end of the make-believe car, were chairs and tables with recessed tops, designed to hold glasses and ashtrays. On a real car, the tables would have been quite heavy. But these were not, all the better to move them out of the way in order to position the towering lights and the camera. Jill picked up one of the tables and tilted it over onto its side, so that the base and top served as wheels. Using all her strength, she rolled it toward Wade. He turned at the sound and dodged the table, firing the gun in the direction it came from.

As the sound of the gunshot reverberated through the warehouse, Jill darted to the dining car set. Every detail had been replicated, from the bud vases on the tables to the heavy silver serving pieces, such as menu holders and pitchers. She hid behind the small counter where the dining car steward would stand, and looked at the stack of china plates in the familiar violets-and-daisies pattern. The plates had been left on the counter where, on a real diner, the cooks would put food so that the waiter would pick up the orders. She stood for a moment and grabbed an armful of china.

Another gunshot, and she heard the bullet tear through the wall of the set. She chanced a look in Wade's direction and saw him running toward the set. She threw a plate at him, and then another. He kept coming. She lobbed plates at him until they were all gone, then she retreated, heading away from him past the tables, knocking over chairs to slow him. When he lunged over a chair, his foot caught and he stumbled, going down on his knees.

A pitcher glinted from a nearby table. Jill picked it up. It was the real thing, heavy and solid. She brought it down on Wade's head. He cried out and dropped the gun. It skittered away on the concrete floor of the warehouse.

"What the hell is going on in here?"

Neal Preston stood at the open back door.

"He killed Felton, and he's trying to kill me," Jill shouted.

Wade scrambled to his feet, reaching for the gun on the floor but Jill was quicker than he was. She kicked it out of reach and swung the pitcher again, connecting with the screenwriter's arm.

Neal grabbed Wade's other arm and put it in a hammerlock. Then he kicked the man's legs from under him,

A light went on overhead. People boiled into the warehouse through the front door. They were talking all at once, about the shots, about the spectacle of Wade on the floor, his arm bent behind him. Eve Stillman rushed to the table, picked up the phone and called the police. More people converged on the building as the sirens wailed and the flashing lights lit up the quiet small-town street.

Chapter Twenty

I'LL BE FINE," Jill said. But she was shivering and gasping, and her heart was still pounding.

"Are you sure?" Leona had her arm around Jill as the two women sat on chairs from the dining car set. Eve hovered nearby and Bert appeared with a glass of water. He held it out to Jill and she took it with a grateful nod. She took a gulp and then handed the glass back to Bert. Her breathing slowed as she willed herself to calm down.

I could have been killed, she told herself. And Mike will—I was supposed to call him tonight and he'll call the house and— My parents. It's Wednesday. My parents are due home from Monterey today. I'm not there. They'll worry. They'll call Mike and— She stopped and shook her head. She could go home soon. But she still felt too shaky to drive.

Behind them a pair of uniformed officers had handcuffed Wade Ratliff. Detectives Carlucci and Gruber had arrived a short time ago and she'd told them what happened. They wanted more details, of course. "We'd like you to come to our office tomorrow," Carlucci said. "To give a statement."

"I'll be there," Jill said.

Now they were talking with Neal, who had been first on the scene, and Drake, who was one of the people who had run in the front door. Both men were standing near the Pullman set where Jill first hid.

"I was in my dressing room," Neal explained. "It's in a trailer on the east side of the building. I find that it's quieter than the hotel. Particularly since those people down the hall from me seemed to be having a party. So after I had a quick dinner, I came over here. I was going over the script, getting ready for tomorrow. It was a nice evening, so I had the door open to get a breeze." He paused and rubbed his chin. "That's when I heard the shots. Well, the first one I wasn't sure about, so I came out of the trailer. When I heard the second one, I knew it was a gunshot, coming from inside the building. So I went to investigate."

Drake chimed in. "My key was missing. The key to this building, I mean. I discovered it after dinner. I wondered if I'd left it here at the warehouse, because Ralph—he's the production assistant—locked up. Eve and I decided to walk over here, so I could get in and find my key. Bert and Charlie were out for a walk."

"It was such a pleasant evening," Charlie Bosworth said. He sat in a chair on the observation car set, shaking his head. "Never expected to hear gunfire. Certainly never expected to see the screenwriter— Well, what a day."

"It certainly was a hell of an evening," Leona said, squeezing Jill's shoulder. "There I was, reading in my hotel room, and all of a sudden I heard sirens. I threw on my clothes and ran over."

Another half hour went by. The police took Wade away and the detectives told Jill she could go home. She got up from the chair, Leona still by her side. "I should call my family. My boyfriend."

She walked toward the table that held the phone, where Wade had pulled back the fabric wrappings to reveal the stolen Vermeer in all its glory. When she'd hit Wade with the receiver, the painting had still been there, wrapped up, the cord tied loosely to hold the fabric in place.

Jill stopped and pointed. "The painting. It's gone."

————

"Do you think I was being reckless?" Jill asked Tidsy.

A week had gone by. Once again, she was at the Grotto at Jack London Square in Oakland, seated at a window table with a view of the estuary.

Tidsy set aside her menu and reached for her Scotch on the rocks. "No. Well, maybe a little. But it was a gutsy thing to do, tailing that creep to the warehouse and confronting him." She flashed a wicked grin. "I'm proud of you. You would have made a hell of a government girl."

Jill sighed and sipped her glass of chardonnay. "My parents think I was reckless. Mike, too. Mom and Dad had just gotten home from their Monterey trip that night. Mike called, looking for me and everyone started worrying. He drove over to my house. He and Dad were leaving the house to drive to Niles, looking for me. Then I called. Mike said he was coming to get me, but as it turned out, Leona drove me and the Ford back to Alameda. Drake followed in his own car. They turned on the charm, which was good. My father was about to forbid me from going back to work on the movie. As it is, I took a couple of days off and they shot around me. That means they concentrated on filming scenes that I'm not in. I just went back to work a few days ago. We should be able to finish shooting my scenes in a couple of days."

"So *The Heist* is nearly finished. The name of the movie is certainly prophetic."

Jill nodded. "It's mostly done. They are going to shoot some exteriors in Niles Canyon and up the Feather River Canyon, as originally planned. The new studio executive signed off on that." She took another sip of wine. "I wonder what happened to that painting."

"Any theories?" Tidsy asked.

"A few," Jill said. "Things were so chaotic, with Wade taking shots at me and then getting tackled by Neal. Then everyone showed up because they heard the shots or saw the police arrive. It was crazy, people streaming in and out of the warehouse for the next couple of hours. It would have taken just a moment."

A moment, a few seconds. That's all. Someone helped himself—or herself. Someone had scooped up the small, flat bundle and tucked it under a jacket or a shirt, to transport out of the building. Or had concealed it in the building for future retrieval. Was it Charlie Bosworth? He was an art lover, too, and he'd been there inside the warehouse. In fact, she'd seen him near the table when Eve Stillman called the police. Or could it have been Eve? Bert? Any of the people who had crowded around the scene?

"All I can say is that Dewitt is in hot water with Addie, for even thinking about purchasing such a painting, one that had been stolen from its original owner." Tidsy chortled. Then she looked up. "Ah, there's my friend."

The man was tall, lean and handsome, in his late forties, with dark hair streaked with gray over a long, narrow face. He had a pair of sparkling blue eyes under thick brows and a small scar on his chin. He carried a briefcase made of warm, buttery leather, somewhat battered with use. He set the briefcase on the floor, then he leaned over and kissed Tidsy on the cheek.

"Tidsy, my sweet. I see you're already one drink ahead of me." He turned to Jill and offered his hand as well as a friendly smile. "You must be Jill. Tidsy has told me all about you. I'm Burton Phipps. I work at the Metropolitan Museum of Art in New York City. Sorry I'm late. That meeting on the Berkeley campus went on and on. You know how it is when a bunch of art historians talk shop."

Phipps took a seat at the table and picked up a menu. When the waiter appeared, he ordered a gin and tonic.

"Tidsy tells me you were with a group called the Monuments Men," Jill said.

"That's right. My group was attached to the First Army. We tracked down a lot of art, and saved it, thank goodness. But there are lots of works that are still missing." He glanced at Tidsy. "I'm glad you suggested this. I'm in the mood for seafood, and salmon fits the bill. And the Crab Louie sounds good."

The waiter returned with Phipps's drink and they ordered. Jill chose grilled sand dabs, Tidsy the sea bass, while their companion went with the salmon and the Crab Louie.

When the waiter had gone, Phipps reached for his briefcase. He pulled out a manila folder and opened it, revealing an eight-by-ten-inch photograph. He handed the photo to Jill. "I'd like you to take a look at this picture. Particularly the paintings on the wall."

Jill took the photograph. It was black-and-white, and looked as if it had been enlarged from a smaller snapshot. It showed a middle-aged man and woman, looking well-dressed and prosperous, holding hands as they sat together on a small sofa in a comfortable-looking living room. The man wore a suit, the woman an elegant dress with lace at the collar and cuffs. The style of the clothing made Jill guess that the picture had been taken in the early 1930s. She brought the photo closer to her face and looked at the three paintings on the wall behind the sofa.

Jill glanced up and met Phipps's eyes. "Yes. The one in the middle. That's the painting I saw."

"From Tidsy's description, I thought it might be." Phipps took a sip of his gin and tonic. "The painting has been called many things over the years. Most commonly *Girl with a Flower* or *Girl with a Rose*. It's a Vermeer, all right, painted around 1665, which was the same year he painted *Girl with a Pearl Earring*. Both paintings are called *tronies*. That's a seventeenth-century Dutch description of a painting of a head that wasn't supposed to be a portrait. And the poses in the paintings are similar."

Jill looked at the photo again, not at the painting on the wall, but at the people on the sofa. "These are the people who owned it?"

Phipps nodded. "Aron and Rivka Levi. They were Jewish, lived in Paris. Certainly wealthy enough to buy a Vermeer and the other two paintings on the wall. The one on the left looks like a Cézanne. I'm not sure about the one on the right. Their art was stolen some time after the Germans occupied the city. This particular painting wound up in the Jeu de Paume. We know that thanks to a woman named Rose Valland, who worked there and kept an inventory. The Jeu de Paume is a small museum in Paris that was used by the Louvre for temporary exhibits. It became a storage house for looted art. The place was crammed with furniture, decorative arts, sculpture, everything from stained glass to tapestries. And paintings. Especially paintings. High-ranking Nazis would show up and do their shopping," he added, with a twist to his mouth. "Especially Hermann Goering. He took a lot of art for Carinhall, his estate in Germany."

"There were plans to built a Führermuseum in Austria," Tidsy added, taking a sip of her Scotch.

"Yes, Hitler wanted a monument to himself." He reached for his gin and tonic, as though he wanted to wash a sour taste from his mouth. "At some point, *Girl with a Flower* disappeared from the Jeu de Paume. Mademoiselle Valland's records don't tell us where it went. Our best guess was that the painting had been taken to Germany. Or that it had been destroyed. So many paintings were, because the Nazis considered them to be what they called 'degenerate.'"

"They particularly didn't like Picasso," Tidsy said. She signaled the waiter and ordered another Scotch on the rocks.

"They burned Picassos." Phipps shook his head. He sipped his drink and looked at Jill as a boat sailed by on the estuary. "Now, this Ratliff character told you he took the painting from a Nazi officer he'd killed in Munich. But he didn't say anything about how it got there? Or how that particular German got the painting?"

Jill shook her head. "No. Nothing more than that. And he's not talking. That's what the police told me."

"Is there any way to trace the owners?" Tidsy asked.

"The Levis were rounded up and sent to the transit camp at Drancy. From there they went to Auschwitz." Phipps sighed. "They're dead. However, their niece survived the Holocaust. She lives in New York City now. She's the one who gave me this photo, when she came to the Met, looking for help in finding out what happened to her aunt and uncle's art collection. That's how I know as much as I do. From time to time, I put out feelers. When Tidsy called and told me about the painting, well, that's the biggest lead I've ever had on the Vermeer." He took the photo and tucked it in the folder, putting it in his briefcase.

"If the painting ever shows up again, maybe it can at least go back to France. But to be honest about it, a lot of these paintings are just gone. Many of them wound up in private collections, bought by people who aren't picky about where their art comes from." Phipps looked up as the waiter arrived with their food.

In the end, all Jill knew was that Vermeer's *Girl with a Flower* was gone, again, her whereabouts a mystery. She wondered if the painting would ever surface.

Chapter Twenty-One

JILL WOULD NEVER think of Niles Canyon the same way. She would always see Charlie Chaplin walking with that rocking side-to-side gait down a tree-shaded canyon path, wearing his bowler hat and his worn, baggy suit, and twirling his cane. Maybe it would be Ben Turpin with his crazy eyes, or rugged Broncho Billy in full cowboy regalia.

Even a much younger Rose Laurent astride her paint pony, ready to shoot a scene with Broncho Billy in front of the Essanay cameras.

Jill had been in the Vista-Dome of the lounge car ever since the train left Pleasanton on the last leg of its westbound journey toward the end of the run in Oakland. When the CZ went through the little town of Sunol and entered the canyon she looked around, seeing the canyon's twisting curves with different eyes. It had been carved by Alameda Creek, which rose somewhere in the rugged hills east of there. The creek had chiseled a route through the rugged coastal hills, toward the place where it would spill its waters into San Francisco Bay. The railroad tracks hugged the creek, crossing it several times on narrow bridges.

The curves became more gentle and the canyon widened as the train approached Niles, coming out of the trees into open vistas. It was the last week in October, Halloween coming up in a few days. The autumn rains had started. The East Bay hills that had been so brown earlier in the month were now changing from gold to green. In fact, it was raining as the train pulled into Niles, a fine mist, really, just enough to dampen one's clothes and put a fine spray on one's glasses. There were passengers on one of the Pullman cars who were getting off the train here. The *CZ* slowed and the familiar depot came into view.

The Heist had finished filming at the warehouse two weeks after Stuart Felton's murder. Some of the camera crew continued in Niles, shooting exteriors in the canyon and then heading up to do more filming in the Feather River Canyon.

The actors checked out of the hotel in Niles, with Leona Alexander telling Jill to call her if she had plans to come down to Los Angeles. She was taking some time off, to spend with her daughter and fiancé, before starting a romantic comedy at Global Studios. Neal Preston gave Jill a nod and took off in his Buick Skylark, heading south to his ranch in Chatsworth. Bert Gallagher had already headed to Arizona to start filming a Western. Charles Bosworth had been studiously avoiding Jill for weeks. It was as though he knew she suspected him of taking the painting. He'd gone back to Hollywood as well. She heard he was on a soundstage at Global Studios, playing another villain, the sort of role he specialized in. The bit players and extras had all gone home.

The movie itself, all those reels of film, was in the can, as they said in Tinseltown. The film was in Hollywood for editing. Drake told Jill that Global had given the movie a release date, scheduled sometime in the spring of 1954. There was some notoriety surrounding the murder of the studio executive and as far as Drake and Dewitt Collier were concerned, that might help publicize the film. Drake talked about having a grand affair in Niles, a premiere, perhaps, at the movie theater there in town.

Wade Ratliff had been arrested for the murder of Stuart Felton. As far as Jill knew, he was in jail. She hadn't heard anything else, other than his trial would be held sometime in the future, in the Alameda County Courthouse in Oakland.

Things were fine at home, after her parents and Mike had recuperated from the news of Jill's latest adventure.

Jill was back at work. A few days earlier, she'd taken an eastbound run to Chicago and now, after a layover in the Windy City, was on the return trip home. She was in the vestibule of the Pullman as it stopped and the porter opened the door and lowered the steps. She said good-bye to the man and woman who were getting off the train, and felt the misty rain on her face as they stepped down to the platform. The porter helped them with their luggage.

Yes, Jill thought. Broncho Billy, Charlie Chaplin and Rose Laurent. And Leona Alexander and Neal Preston. Her movie adventure was over, but she would have the memories. And what memories they were.

She looked back at the warehouse where the movie had been filmed, empty now, no cars or trailers parked at its side. Then she saw movement. Someone was behind the building. She recognized the clothing—the denim pants, the faded green jacket, the green cap.

It was Hal. The hobo stood there, in his favored spot behind the warehouse, watchful eyes on the freight approaching from the opposite direction.

The porter climbed back into the vestibule and closed the door. The *California Zephyr* pulled out of the Niles depot, heading home to Oakland.

AUTHOR'S NOTE

THERE WAS INDEED a film noir with a real Zephyrette playing her fictional counterpart. That movie was *Sudden Fear*, from 1952, starring Joan Crawford, Jack Palance and Gloria Grahame. The movie is lots of fun, with Oscar-nominated performances by Crawford and Palance—the former chews the scenery and the latter is appropriately sleazy, while Gloria Grahame does her femme fatale role quite well.

Also in the cast was the late Rodna Walls Taylor, who was a Zephyrette from 1949 to 1953. As the fictional Zephyrette, she has a brief scene with Crawford, when she shows up in the star's Pullman sleeper to tell Joan that it's time for her dinner reservation.

While writing the first book in the California Zephyr series, *Death Rides the Zephyr*, I interviewed both Rodna Walls Taylor, whose stint as a Zephyrette was in the time I'm writing about, and Cathy Moran Von Ibsch, who was a Zephyrette on the train's last run in 1970. Both former Zephyrettes were generous with their information and stories about riding the rails. I couldn't have written the California Zephyr books without their input.

The term film noir was coined in 1946 by French film critics do describe the dark crime dramas coming out of 1940s Hollywood. Though the term was not widely used in the United States until the 1970s, I've used it here because it is now common to describe the type of movie being made in this novel.

What I don't know about making movies would fill a book, so I read a few.

Nobody's Girl Friday: The Women Who Ran Hollywood, J. E. Smyth, Oxford University Press, 2018. Smyth describes the studio era between 1930 and 1950 as a golden age for women's employment in the film industry. The book looks at influential women and their roles in the Hollywood studio system.

Edna Ferber's Hollywood: American Fictions of Gender, Race and History, J. E. Smyth, preface by Thomas Schatz, University of Texas Press, 2009. Smyth's book looks at best-selling novelist Ferber and the landmark negotiations with Hollywood that put women's history on screen from 1924 to 1960. A good resource for seeing how Hollywood treated women on both sides of the screen.

The Silent Feminists: America's First Women Directors, Anthony Slide, The Scarecrow Press, Inc., 1996. A study of the first three decades of the film industry, when women played prominent roles in filmmaking.

Print the Legend: The Life and Times of John Ford, Scott Eyman, Simon & Schuster, 1999. A comprehensive biography of one of Hollywood's greatest directors, including a look at how he worked.

Making Movies, Sidney Lumet, Alfred A. Knopf, 1995. The noted producer, director and screenwriter talks about the craft of moviemaking.

Broncho Billy and the Essanay Film Company, David Kiehn, Farwell Books, 2003. A valuable resource for anyone interested in moviemaking during the silent era, particularly in Niles, California.

Ida Lupino, Beyond the Camera, Ida Lupino, with Mary Ann Anderson, BearManor Media, 2011. Ida Lupino acted and directed from the late 1940s on and made her mark directing B movies and in television.

Stuntwomen: The Untold Hollywood Story, Mollie Gregory, University Press of Kentucky, 2015. The progression of women doing stunts in the movies, from the silent era forward.

The Inquisition in Hollywood: Politics in the Film Community, 1930–1960, Larry Ceplair and Steven Englund, Arbor Press Doubleday, 1980. A study of the blacklist in the film community.

———

Women directors? Yes, there were lots of them, starting with Alice Guy-Blaché who was directing movies in France as early as 1896. And Lois Weber, who is considered the American film industry's first auteur, a filmmaker who was involved in all aspects of production and used the medium to convey her own ideas. Then there was Dorothy Arzner, who successfully moved from silents to talkies. To find out more about these directors, and others like them, check out the Women Film Pioneers website at Columbia University, which will enlighten readers on the role of woman making movies: https://wfpp.columbia.edu

Other websites worth checking:
https://reelrundown.com/film-industry/10-Influential-Female-Directors-from-the-Silent-Film-Era
https://www.refinery29.com/en-us/2018/04/197006/women-silent-era-hollywood-prominent-directors-writers
https://www.bustle.com/articles/92862-6-amazing-female-film-directors-from-cinema-history-that-you-should-know

The Nazis' systematic looting of art during World War II is well documented and fascinating, with many valuable works still missing and possibly destroyed. I recommend two books:

The Rape of Europa: The Fate of Europe's Treasures in the Third Reich and the Second World War, Lynn H. Nicholas, Vintage Books, a division of Random House, Inc., 1994. Well written and detailed look at the looting of Europe's art treasures and recovery efforts. Also worth watching is the 2006 documentary based on this book.

The Monuments Men: Allied Heroes, Nazi Thieves, and the Greatest Treasure Hunt in History, Robert M. Edsel, with Bret Witter, Center Street, 2009. A look at the efforts to locate and save cultural treasures looted by the Nazis.

Information on hobos comes from an article in the *San Francisco Chronicle*, "Don't call them bums: Hobos once filled the South of Market," by Gary Kamiya, July 26, 2019

———

Information on San Francisco's Western Addition/Fillmore District comes from two Internet sources:

How Urban Renewal Destroyed the Fillmore in Order to Save It, Walter Thompson, Hoodline, January 3, 2016, https://bit.ly/2PCOhqY

How "Urban Renewal" Destroyed San Francisco's Fillmore District, Carl P. Close, Independent Institute, July 21, 2008, https://bit.ly/2PdRbn9

The *California Zephyr* mysteries are the result of much research. I took train trips, I interviewed people, I read books, and I climbed around on old railroad cars. I even drove a locomotive.

When writing about a historical period or a particular subject, I strive to be accurate in conveying information. I worked hard to make this book as accurate as possible, though I may have tweaked facts from time to time for the sake of plot, characters, and a good story. Any errors are my own.

We are fortunate to have railroad museums to preserve the remaining artifacts of this country's rail era, particularly the streamliners like the *California Zephyr*. Both the California State Railroad Museum, Sacramento, California, and the Colorado Railroad Museum, Golden, Colorado, have excellent research libraries as well as railcars and locomotives. The Western Pacific Railroad Museum in Portola, California, is a treasure house of rolling stock.

The Amtrak version of the *California Zephyr* is not the same as the sleek Silver Lady of days gone by. But it's great to ride a train through most of the same route, getting an up-close look at this marvelous country. The journey may take longer, but the scenery is spectacular and the relaxation factor is 110 percent.

I hope you enjoy *Death Above the Line*. Now go ride a train! And see an old movie.

About the Author

Janet Dawson's historical mysteries, the California Zephyr series, feature protagonist Jill McLeod, a Zephyrette aboard the streamliner train. The four books are set in the early 1950s. Dawson explores another historical period by flashbacks in *Bit Player*, in the Jeri Howard PI series; it's set in the 1940s Hollywood world of movie actors. There are 12 other mysteries in that series, some of them award-nominated and -winning.

In addition, Dawson has written a suspense novel, *What You Wish For*, and a novella, *But Not Forgotten*, as well as numerous short stories. She lives in the Bay Area and welcomes visitors and email at www.janetdawson.com and on Facebook.

More Traditional Mysteries from Perseverance Press
For the New Golden Age

K.K. Beck
WORKPLACE SERIES
Tipping the Valet
ISBN 978-1-56474-563-7

Albert A. Bell, Jr.
PLINY THE YOUNGER SERIES
Death in the Ashes
ISBN 978-1-56474-532-3

The Eyes of Aurora
ISBN 978-1-56474-549-1

Fortune's Fool
ISBN 978-1-56474-587-3

The Gods Help Those
ISBN 978-1-56474-608-5

Hiding from the Past
ISBN 978-1-56474-610-8

Taffy Cannon
ROXANNE PRESCOTT SERIES
Guns and Roses
Agatha and Macavity awards nominee, Best Novel
ISBN 978-1-880284-34-6

Blood Matters
ISBN 978-1-880284-86-5

Open Season on Lawyers
ISBN 978-1-880284-51-3

Paradise Lost
ISBN 978-1-880284-80-3

Laura Crum
GAIL MCCARTHY SERIES
Moonblind
ISBN 978-1-880284-90-2

Chasing Cans
ISBN 978-1-880284-94-0

Going, Gone
ISBN 978-1-880284-98-8

Barnstorming
ISBN 978-1-56474-508-8

Jeanne M. Dams
HILDA JOHANSSON SERIES
Crimson Snow
ISBN 978-1-880284-79-7

Indigo Christmas
ISBN 978-1-880284-95-7

Murder in Burnt Orange
ISBN 978-1-56474-503-3

Janet Dawson
JERI HOWARD SERIES
Bit Player
Golden Nugget Award nominee
ISBN 978-1-56474-494-4

Cold Trail
ISBN 978-1-56474-555-2

Water Signs
ISBN 978-1-56474-586-6

The Devil Close Behind
ISBN 978-1-56474-606-1

What You Wish For
ISBN 978-1-56474-518-7

TRAIN SERIES
Death Rides the Zephyr
ISBN 978-1-56474-530-9

Death Deals a Hand
ISBN 978-1-56474-569-9

The Ghost in Roomette Four
ISBN 978-1-56474-598-9

Death above the Line
ISBN 978-1-56474-618-4

Gerald Elias
DANIEL JACOBUS MUSIC SERIES
Cloudy with a Chance of Murder
(forthcoming)
ISBN 978-1-56474-624-5

Murder at the Royal Albert
(forthcoming)
ISBN 978-1-56474-625-2

Kathy Lynn Emerson
LADY APPLETON SERIES
Face Down Below the Banqueting House
ISBN 978-1-880284-71-1

Face Down Beside St. Anne's Well
ISBN 978-1-880284-82-7

Face Down O'er the Border
ISBN 978-1-880284-91-9

Margaret Grace
MINIATURE SERIES
Mix-up in Miniature
ISBN 978-1-56474-510-1

Madness in Miniature
ISBN 978-1-56474-543-9

Manhattan in Miniature
ISBN 978-1-56474-562-0

Matrimony in Miniature
ISBN 978-1-56474-575-0

Available from your local bookstore
or from Perseverance Press/John Daniel & Company
(800) 662–8351 or www.danielpublishing.com/perseverance